SOMEONE ELSE

BY

MARY PAULA HUNTER

To Richard Meckel

Contents

CHAPTER 1

The student teacher in Home Ec told us that hobbies make people happy. "A hobby can involve work," she said, "but you don't mind the work; in fact, you love it." If only she'd permanently replace Mrs. Rancit who droned on endlessly about why margarine was better than butter or how bad it is to overbeat a cake mix.

"She's fine," Jack Jansen whispered, banging his chair into my desk as the student teacher flipped up the ends of her honey blond hair and held high a sleek green and white diary. "Hey sorry," Jack said squeaking his chair across the floor as everyone groaned, reminding me of our fourth grade gym class breaking out in laughter when he pulled up my square dancing skirt.

"Sally Tallman you should be ashamed for encouraging him," the gym teacher had scolded and now I worried the student teacher might lose her cool and reprimand the two of us, but she waited for Jack to settle down, smiling the whole time. "Thank god," I said under my breath. I'd thought about becoming her and couldn't imagine transforming myself into someone who'd taken me to task.

"Describe for future generations how important hobbies are," the student teacher said, pointing with her shimmering pink nail to the year 1968 embossed in gold above *MSU Go Spartans*.

I wasn't sure how to write about a hobby that existed in my head and that didn't involve sewing or cooking, so I called my hobby *Life Transformation* with the subtitle *The Game of Choice*. In our Hobby Folder, I wrote that my hobby was creating new games for young people. *Very different!* She'd written in loopy letters in the margin. When the bell rang, I lingered by her desk. As she packed up an array of spiral notebooks and green pens, one topped with a small helmeted Spartan head, I had a sudden urge to let her in on my secret, describe how good I was at slipping out of myself and straight into someone else. I'd never told anyone that changing into other kids was my hobby. What would they say when I described trailing someone in order to memorize every detail of that person's dress, walk, cadence, and laughter. Before launching myself as this new person I designed a world from personal tidbits I picked up eavesdropping or better, a sleepover.

"Have a great year, Sally," the student teacher said, hoisting her bag onto one shoulder. I nodded, searching for a way to divulge my secret but then Mrs. Rancit came in with a towering stack of Betty Crocker cookbooks, motioning me to move.

"Get to your next class," she said, scowling. She'd hated me ever since she caught me pilfering a spoonful of dry strawberry Jell-O from the supply cabinet. My heart sped up and for a moment as the student teacher smiled at me behind Mrs. Rancit's back, I pictured her grabbing my hand and whisking me away to her dorm room. Perhaps she lived in one of the big dorms near my house on the edge of East Lansing. Once safely inside her room, we'd dissolve into each other, sort of like the marshmallows Mrs. Rancit stirred over low heat during the lesson on no-bake desserts. I pictured the two of us giggling as we gossiped about Mrs. Rancit scorching the pan as she added a cup of Rice Krispies.

I waved goodbye to the student teacher and then pushed my way into the packed corridor. Across the wide hall a girl wearing brown moccasins and the trendy wide legged pants—

bell bottoms--slipped out of the bathroom. I wished I could hide in a stall away from the thick air and the whole school shuffling to the next class, but getting from one side of the hall to the other would be like running through the marching band at a pep rally. After a few hesitant steps, I gave up and pressed my back into a locker. A tall older girl maneuvering through the traffic elbowed me. "Sorry," she muttered, squinting at the sea of heads in front of her, a book clutched to her chest. *What's your next class?* I asked inside my brain, like she would mistake me for someone she talked to.

I tracked her path as she snaked through a bulge of students where the math and science wings crossed, her blond bubble sticking out amidst the new style of long limp hair. After she disappeared, blankness swept my brain and a numbing fatigue set in. My head fell back onto the locker and then dropped, chin to chest, before jerking up.

The sea of people moving before me blurred but above me a voice, persistent and clear, beckoned. Without thinking, I flew upwards, my feet barely missing the head of a basketball player I'd heard cheated on tests with impunity.

What's your name? Hanging from the ceiling by a thread, a skinny detective in a black suit and sunglasses raised his eyebrows. *What's your name?* He repeated the question as if I was the typical amnesiac you'd see on TV. Then he crawled across the ceiling like a spider sneering at me and at the herd of students below. *Name?* he laughed. My brain shuffled through possibilities. The bubble hair girl looked like a Pam or maybe a Sue. But I couldn't speak. Disgusted, he closed his notebook, waving it before my unblinking eyes as I fell back to the floor, cringing all the way until I made a soft landing and took a long breath.

Still deep in my brain, I stuck to the locker like a human magnet, my eyes glazing over. A boy with a red birth mark slapped across one cheek walked by. He reminded me of a stray dog I'd seen earlier that morning. The dog had been sitting on the patch of grass we called our front yard. Its face was half white and half black. The dog and I had stared at each other through my bedroom window until the dog looked away and ran into Michigan Avenue. Cars honked and swerved as he leaped onto the boulevard separating the four lanes. Stranded between racing lanes of cars and trucks, the dog lay down next to the *Welcome to East Lansing* sign, wrapping his tail tight to his legs so that no part of his body touched the city of Lansing. Smart dog I thought to keep its distance from Lansing since everyone in East Lansing thought it vile and beneath them.

My own instinct told me to clutch my Civics textbook to my chest and squint at the thinning crowd in a good imitation of the blond bubble haired girl. For a second, I thought she reappeared—an obvious sign that I must find someone like her to be, someone who knew how to move through a clogged hall as well as rat her hair to create a bubble hairdo. I'd watched a girl rat her hair during gym, half of the period given over to showering and dressing. She'd teased her curls into a halo and hurried off before smoothing it over. After she left, my locker mate whispered that hoods don't smooth their bubbles, preferring a snarly unruly hairdo. I silently prayed I wouldn't be forced to become a hood and therefore live in Tower Gardens, a poor area on the outskirts, practically in the country. Bad enough I lived on a commercial strip abutting Lansing.

Another bell sounded and I shoved off, but like a rowboat without oars, I didn't get far. Inching along between the slow flow of traffic and the lockers, I scrutinized appearances—long hair, short hair, slacks, skirts, necklaces made from beads, and boys in tee shirts next to those in nice ironed shirts—before merging into the nearest lane. The word *scrutiny* had been on last week's vocab list, and I defined it as a way of eliminating chaos through close observation, which Miss Knowles said was correct in one sense but not specific enough for the standardized test we'd take next year in sophomore English. "Start with an example," she said. While she wrote the date for our next quiz on the board I told her, without speaking, that I memorized a person's every detail in order to imperceptibly slip outside of myself and into another. She dropped the chalk like she could hear what went on in my brain and was shocked by the confession. My face flamed as she searched for the broken chalk and without raising my hand I asked if I could open a window. "Go ahead Sally," Miss Knowles said standing with a fist full of chalk and a flushed face. I hurried to the window fearing the confession still in my mouth was about to come out.

"Let's hurry or we're going to be late," a girl from Civics caught up to me in the crowd. We worked our way to an opening, slipping around people and laughing at a boy who pounded on his locker. "Memorize the combination already," the girl teased as we turned the corner. "Memorize the combination already," I repeated, and she laughed, poking me in the arm like I'd mocked her, when really I was practicing being her for a second—to keep up my skills while I searched for the right person to be. In my head I heard Miss Smith, the choir teacher, say that practicing scales made it much easier to quickly get a whole new song under your belt. "Scales are building blocks," she'd said, warning that if we didn't practice them, we'd never be excellent sight-readers. Then my mind drifted to people skirting past and how I wished I could glean one saying from each person--file their words in my hobby folder.

"Here's a pass for the library," the sub said as we closed the door to the Civics room. "If you're in Debate, go to Mr. Slater's room, otherwise work on your capitalism versus socialism report in the library. Mr. McClintock wants a rough draft bibliography by next week."

Back out in the hall, three sophomores who'd somehow missed Civics their freshman year ran ahead. "They're gonna smoke in the woods," a boy said, pointing to a kid pulling on a jacket. The rest of us separated in the empty hallway, straggling off to the library like stray dogs.

I wandered along the aisles in the new library. It had bright green carpeting, glass walls and rows of magazines and books. "Everything's weird this year," a girl in a cheerleading uniform complained to a boy with slick hair. They pressed into the bookcase as I squeezed behind them. In the next aisle, with only shelves of books separating us, I kneeled, pretending to search for a book on the bottom shelf. "My Dad said protesting Viet Nam shouldn't be allowed in a school," the boy said. The girl added that it wasn't right to go against the government. Then their voices dropped to a whisper, and I edged closer to the books, catching a word here and there until the girl spoke up.

"Don't forget, her parents will be at the country club thing by seven. Her house is next to Walker's on Woodland Pass—there's a door by the garage kind of in the woods. She's going to unlock it, just in case someone gets there early. Like before her parents are gone." I stopped breathing, straining to hear if they were talking about Patty Scott—my wild, fearless best friend who'd moved when we were young to Whitehills, a walled-off collection of sprawling houses with bedrooms and bathrooms for each person. I'd never forgotten Patty's drawings of the house the Scotts were building on Woodland

Pass. Every bathroom had a gold faucet in the shape of a bird, some with jeweled eyes.

"Tell your folks you're sleeping over somewhere."

"Cool," he said, and they laughed.

"Can you bring beer?" the girl whispered. I strained to hear their low voices, hoping to learn more about the house on Woodland Pass and maybe, if I was lucky, Patty.

Whenever I passed her old house on Kensington Road, I thought about Patty and how she disappeared from our joint life. When I'd run into her and Mrs. Scott a week ago at the gas station by our house, mother and daughter in the front seat of a shiny blue station wagon, I couldn't wait for them to drive away.

"We haven't seen you in forever!" Mrs. Scott had called to me out the window, laughing and blowing smoke into the cool air. Patty waved, a graceful one finger at a time motion. "Get the back windows, too," Mrs. Scott said to the attendant. "How are you? Getting ready for Homecoming?" She widened her eyes behind sparkly glasses and blew smoke upward. "Patty's got her dress but we're still working on shoes!" Patty said something to Mrs. Scott, who lowered her window all the way. "Patty said the two of you should get together like old times when football's over." She blew more smoke in a long stream and then signed for the gas, eager to make a fast track back to Whitehills, where there were no gas stations—just mansions. No wonder the Scotts had moved. Rich people don't want to look at gas stations and traffic. Neither had waved before pulling out of the gas station, like they'd forgotten I was still there.

As I watched the plumes of exhaust from Mrs. Scott's gleaming car hang in the air, I wondered if Patty ever missed the days when she lived nearby on Kensington Road and was my best friend, missed guiding me home from school like Anne Sullivan leading Helen Keller. I marveled at the crimes we'd gotten away with, shoving snow into mailboxes and the dry cleaners' drop box, throwing snowballs at cars, and sneaking puffs from a lit cigarette Patty found abandoned on a curb.

"Do you get the whole bibliography thing?" A boy asked out of nowhere, and I yelped, dropping *Ten Days That Shook the World.* "So, you like Russian history, I guess? Makes sense with the socialism theme." I nodded, relieved he didn't mention my obvious eavesdropping. "Here," he said handing me the book without letting go as the boy and the cheerleader rounded the end of the bookcase. They looked straight ahead, sucking in their cheeks, like they'd never seen anything as odd as two people hanging onto the same book.

"My Dad said your Dad writes a weird column, *Tallman on Track,* about horse racing?" I stared at his bent glasses, angling across his face, slipping down his greasy nose and resisted an urge to spit on the specks of dirt splattered across the lenses. "Everyone in my Dad's department at MSU says the *State Journal* stinks," he smirked, taunting me to deny that Dad worked at a lousy paper. I stepped back, pulling on *Ten Days That Shook the World* until he let go. As his grin widened, I pictured the student teacher hovering around us, advising me to defend Dad. *He's been so sick,* she whispered, and I nodded—he'd been out of work for weeks with a mysterious illness, barely able to get out of bed. *Go on,* she said.

I stared into the kid's filthy glasses as if they were the second-floor windows of our house. *You can do it,* she whispered. But instead of telling the kid off, letting him know a thing or two about reporting and how the AP picked up one of Dad's stories and some other things I could make up, I imagined Dad in bed, moaning and gulping down the water Mom brought him, cup after cup until he fell back shivering, begging for more blankets.

"He, he," I stammered, switching in my mind to Dad before the illness or whatever you call it, decked out in his long overcoat, camera strung around his neck, checking himself out in the mirror before charging off to scope out an interview without so much as a backwards glance at me. *That dance is over* was his favorite saying and finally after years of being his loyal sidekick, helping him coax a story from a reluctant guy he'd spy at a bus stop, the saying applied to me. I hoped as I lolled on the davenport that without me he'd fail, without me at his side, without his big arm circling my shoulders hugging me to his body as a signal that he meant no harm with all his leading questions—just a nice dad, after all—he'd be unable to suck in some innocent victim for a juicy interview.

The boy looked puzzled as I stared at the exit sign above his head. "No wonder people call it the *urinal*," he laughed, and I smiled, not focusing on his sneer or anything outside of my brain, where I talked to a younger version of myself, letting her know that Dad would one day leave her behind, and describing how bereft she'd be when he quit being her guide, the molder of her life. Tears rose and I quickly brushed them away.

"If you need help with the bibliography, we could like meet or something," the kid said, and I hugged the paperback to my chest as he retreated. The last thing Dad wanted in a partner, I realized as the boy bumped into a cart of books, were signs of independence—opinions or sighs—and a pimply face like this kid. I could've told my younger self this last bit of information, but I'd spent enough time with her.

The bell rang just after I plopped down on one of the new beanbag chairs near the tropical fish tank. I closed my eyes, listening to a flurry of kids leave the library and the suction of the big glass door closing again and again. Finally, I heard nothing but my heart, and in the darkness of my brain I remembered Dad interviewing a one-hundred-year-old farmer. I was too young to do anything but hold onto his coat as we raced back to the car through mud and manure so he could get a few quotes down in a notebook. Afterwards, he treated Patty Scott and me to a malt at the Rexall. "Your Dad is nice," she'd said, and now I hated them both for ditching me.

The last bell rang, and a girl rushing to class tripped on my foot. "Sorry, sorry," I said, wondering if later that night I'd apologize to Dad for not telling off the stupid boy, assuage the guilt I knew I'd feel once I turned out the light. If only the student teacher lived with us—MSU students who couldn't afford the dorms sometimes boarded with people—I'd suck her into admiring me, by telling Dad about the boy and his insults and how next time I'd tell him off. But like the glossy sterile library, I just wanted a clean slate, an empty brain to be filled by the person I'd soon become or hope to become, and the student teacher was too old and obviously not poor by the looks of her sweaters and matching skirts. She wasn't worth wasting my time on.

I heaved myself out of the beanbag chair, following the girl I'd tripped to the huge glass doors. For a second, we stood side by side, her head up to my shoulder in the mirror image. Then she pulled on the door and left me inside, staring at what had been her reflection as the librarian said everyone had to leave.

Out in the practically empty hall, I searched for the girl in the reflection, but I sensed, as her face blurred in my mind, that if I became her I'd eventually slough her off like the dead skin the Health teacher said should be toweled off after bathing. This happened last winter with a girl I thought I'd be forever, and yet one morning I woke and couldn't tolerate the idea of being her one more second.

We'd gotten into the habit of skating every Saturday and Sunday at MSU's rink, wearing matching blue pom poms tied to our skate laces. But on the fateful Saturday when I woke to the sound of her whiney voice in my brain and an image of her clunky backward crossovers, I cut the blue pom poms into bits, told Mom I was sick and couldn't skate or even talk on the phone. In a week or two the girl got the message and we began to avoid each other. It wasn't long before I couldn't remember her name as if, like others I'd absorbed so carefully, she'd disintegrated and lost the sharp edges, the simple unwavering shape and personality necessary for replication.

CHAPTER II

I dreaded the double period of Biology and was relieved to hear the P.A. system click on as I took my seat—anything to waste time. "Tigers!" a shy kid behind me screamed, and I turned fast to see if he'd lost his mind. "Tigers!" he shouted again like no one heard him the first time, and then a bunch of kids joined in. Mr. Benchley, the new teacher who never took off his green and white MSU jacket, patted the air and shushed the room. I saw a Tigers' sticker on someone's notebook and remembered that tomorrow was game seven of the 1968 World Series. If the Tigers beat St. Louis, they'd clinch it.

Yesterday in Homeroom, Mr. Novak had brought in his Little League jersey like anyone cared and then he talked about his high school batting statistics. All the school secretaries wore Tigers' caps, and Mr. Kollock, the principal, wore his glove everywhere. Hard to believe Dad wasn't hyped up about it. He covered regular sports too, not just horse racing. On the first Saturday of May, we weren't allowed to talk until the winner of the Kentucky Derby had the wreath of roses around his neck. The exception to the silence rule was Dad pacing around the house occasionally shouting out the name of a horse he'd bet on. The Tigers in the World Series was ten times bigger than the Derby, but he couldn't even get out of bed, let alone drive a hundred miles to Tiger Stadium and then call in a good story.

"Attention," Mr. Vandervelde, the vice-principal everyone called Pinky because of his red face, cleared his throat, and the P.A. crackled as he launched into a lecture about how lucky we are to be able to watch the games during school. "I doubt there are many other schools in Michigan with this privilege," he said, and the room fell silent. He coughed, rattled some papers, and reminded us that loitering for more than a minute or two in front of the TV sets the janitors had hung from the ceiling in every wing of the school would result in, firstly, never having this privilege again, even if the Tigers make it to the series next year, and it looked like they might, and, secondly, possible suspension. Then, he cleared his throat for a long time and everyone laughed. I laughed too, thinking we were all laughing because no one gets suspended from East Lansing High School. This wasn't like Lansing Eastern, where the principal had cancelled a big game Dad was going to cover because a kid brought a jackknife to school. When a kid in my English class was caught drinking vodka from a mouthwash bottle, he was banned from a pep rally and told he couldn't drive his own Jet Star 88 to school for a month.

Two boys, known to be bullies, continued to laugh, and I wondered if it was one of them who'd spray-painted Mr. Vandervelde's bike pink and strung it up the flagpole. Their sniggering sputtered to a faint "Pinky, Pinky." Mr. Benchley looked relieved when they finally quieted down, and everyone waited in silence for Mr. Vandervelde to finish up. He mumbled something and then announced in a louder than normal voice that Stephen Fedkin had killed himself, or as Mr. Vandervelde said after some more throat clearing, "taken his life," like he could give it back.

Mr. Benchley took a deep breath and other than the sound of more paper rustling through the P.A., there was no noise until Mr. Vandervelde clicked off the mc. The room was silent for so long I imagined the school year coming to an end before we got on with an experiment or whatever Mr. Benchley had planned. Someone behind me scraped a chair leg, and the grating noise turned my stomach, and I thought I might throw up. I imagined hearing the words *taken his life* coming from the P.A., and the hair on my arms stood up. Then I shivered, shaking all over, like someone had dumped a bucket of ice on my head, and at the same time, my scalp and face radiated heat. I stared at the door, wishing I could slip through the crack at the bottom like water vapor and for the rest of the day pace the hallways without being seen.

For as long as I could remember, I'd thought of killing myself, sometimes imagining in detail the reaction of classmates and teachers, and now as the class sat stunned, I worried that this was the time for me to follow through. I'd imagined my death so thoroughly that many mornings I woke convinced that I didn't really exist, and then my heart would race, and I'd dress in a flurry, fingering my clothes, clutching them in my freezing hands to convince myself that they were real and I wouldn't wander around as a naked ghost. But after I calmed down over a pop tart or some cinnamon toast, the thought that I had no right to be on earth nagged at me until visions of killing myself popped up all over again. Dad had the war to justify his life. I'd never face anything as merciless as the Japs. In fact, all that I faced each morning was the blank rush of traffic outside our house on Michigan Avenue and the perilous speed of cars, each with the goal of getting somewhere in Lansing.

But I had more to deal with than just sloughing off this obsession with suicide. Banishing Stephen Fedkin from my brain would be impossible, like begging the sun to never go down or, I guess, never come up.

My life had been intertwined with Stephen's from an impulsive moment in seventh grade English, when I stuck a wad of gum on his seat in a desperate stab at becoming cool in my own right—as myself. Whoever that was.

The girl I was at the time had moved—Jill something or other—and I'd dared myself to act on my own. Just remembering the moment when I took the purple gum from my mouth caused my heart to speed up, my brain to whirl. My skin grew so hot that I thought about asking Mr. Benchley to open a window. Stephen's face, with the gap between his front teeth and his crooked glasses and dirty brown hair appeared, filling my skull like he'd moved into my head instead of dying. My mind switched channels, and instead of Stephen, I saw myself in seventh grade; night after night waking in a sweat, uncomprehending my own meanness as the image flew about the room of Stephen crying as he struggled to remove the gum from the kind of black trousers boys wore for choir concerts. I vowed never to do anything again as myself, but the guilt attacks wouldn't go away, so I waited for him after school, hoping he'd forgive me.

"I didn't mean to do that—with the gum," I stammered.

"You did too," he said sounding almost like a normal kid. "Everyone's mean, including you—whoever you are."

"Why'd you say that about whoever I am?" I felt my face glow, and my heart pounded so hard I thought he could see it right through my sweaty white blouse. Then, when he tried to push past me, I grabbed onto his parka and pleaded for him to stay.

"Dramatics aren't going to get you anywhere," he said without even turning around to see the tears I feared weren't real but just part of a play or story I'd made up on the spot. Nothing seemed real for a moment until he turned around.

"What do you mean?" I said, wiping my cheeks and blinking like crazy, trying to bring his round face and clownish smile into focus. Before I knew it, he'd reached for my cheek, stroking it and brushing strands of hair from my face.

"Nothing, really." His voice dropped a notch, and I bent my knees, slouching to find his blue eyes. Then he leaned close, and when his lips touched mine, I kissed him back. Because my lips had never touched another's, I was unsure when to pull away. Finally, he pulled away and then quickly kissed me again. He hugged his briefcase to his chest, walking backwards as he rounded the corner at the office, smiling and staring at me like Mom did with the love she showed when I tried to draw and shade well. That always made sense to me: an obsession—in her case art—could make an unloving person loving for a second at least. Now I worried Stephen was obsessed with me, and since you can't be obsessed with no one, I felt compelled to let him in on my secret.

For a moment I wondered where he lived and how he walked home but then my heart started pounding again, like maybe I'd just tricked him into forgiving me for the gum. When he came to our house the next day, I ran to the basement pretending to want to learn about weaving with Mom, who said it was fine with her if we ignored the pounding on our front door. He came once more and Dad scared him off, saying I was busy, a quick lie. Stephen scolded me for this at our last meeting in the hall by the gym. I begged him to leave me alone. "I'm afraid of you," I said, and for once I thought something I'd said was the truth. But as he cried, I wasn't sure. I didn't know what to do so I ran to the library and pretended to read the dictionary.

Mr. Benchley cleared his throat and told us to begin the week's lab. "This lab begins with careful calculations," he said, looking blankly at the class and then, as usual, he ignored everyone but the small group of boys who were in the Science Club and sat in a clump by the long bank of windows. I wandered over to a group of desks inched together at all angles. In the middle sat Sue Miller. I'd known her since Junior High gym, when we'd made a dance routine to *Born Free* and worn black sequined leotards her mother had bought for us. She'd filled hers out while I'd looked like a pencil in mine.

"He suffocated himself with a plastic bag," Jane Noble whispered, brushing Sue Miller's desk with the charms on her silver charm bracelet. Off to the side, pretending to look for a flask amidst all the equipment stored on rows of shelves, I peeked at the silver sailboat charm hanging from Jane's bracelet and the white miniature skates with silver blades. Each small charm symbolized a bit of Jane's experience, moments she drifted through in a passive acquiescing journey that left no mark. Lucky that Jacobson's, the only department store downtown, carried an array of charms so she'd never forget what she'd done.

Gwen Peckham twisted around in her chair and I strained to hear her low voice describe how Mr. Freds, the Sophomore Guidance Counselor, had told Stephen he wouldn't be allowed to take Driver's Ed.

"No one wants an epileptic on the roads," Gwen whispered lightly, touching the eyes on Jane's swan charm. "But he'll have that on his conscience forever," she said, raising her eyebrows, and my stomach twisted like a signal that I'd have Stephen on my conscience forever too, unless, of course, I joined him. My heart raced, and my face flamed again. I squeezed my lips together, squashing a confession I felt rising in my throat. *I tortured Stephen,* I said in my brain, *and I steal lives as a hobby.*

The silent confession shut down the fiery engine in my gut. At the same time, the twinkle in the swan's eye blazed and then went dull, like these girls switching off their brains as a way to avoid attention or I guess the kind of notice that wouldn't be alluring. Stephen's face glowed in my brain, and he smiled, reassuring me, I thought, that a real confession would get me nowhere, especially to girls with airy soft hairdos—updates on the bubble still ratted underneath and smoothed lightly all over to cover the snarl, but the whole style a bit longer. *They're nothing,* he said.

But wouldn't becoming one of them erase all this turmoil? Give me someone to be and, in the process, vanquish Stephen? As someone else, even one of these followers, I'd become a person who thought nothing of Stephen, who had no history with him, who perhaps pitied him but nothing more. I was, after all, between people at the moment. Scanning the group, I realized that I'd never been someone like Jane or Sue, girls who avoided being pegged as one thing or another. They remained indefinite, I thought, prefacing every word they uttered with 'like,' not to compare different things, but as filler for so much unused time.

Stephen, still hanging out in my brain, continued to warn me against such a move. I saw him shaking his head at the mere thought of me becoming one of these girls. *You want a pattern,* he said, (like he'd infiltrated my life to such a degree that he knew Mom made her own patterns). *Someone specific, like me.* I knew he was right, and I pulled myself up to distance myself, like I was inside a straw being sucked higher and higher. The girls kept their voices low and, rather than shrink to hear them, I looked down at their faces and the group's small spontaneous movements. I envied their easy-going ways, but soon I was more and more baffled by the collective know-how and the way they fit together so that no one stood out. Not one of them provided a mold into which I could pour myself. Altogether they reminded me of a gentle sunset of melding pastel colors, like the one over Lake Michigan on the day I'd gone to the beach with Patty Scott and her mother.

"Bye Stephen, bye everybody," I whispered to myself, sinking back in time and into the soft sand that Patty poured over me as she buried me up to my neck. But then Gwen popped a bubble and chomped on her pink gum, and I remembered Dad, right before he took to his bed, screaming at me for chomping on gum. He stormed at me, fists clenched at his sides. For once, I knew the terror Beth felt, a girl from Lansing whose floozy Mom now and then dropped her at our doorstep. Dad hated Beth for slamming doors, chewing gum and just being around; he was always pissed at Mom for taking her in. As Gwen continued to chomp her gum, I knew I couldn't belong to these girls who were blatantly unaware of their impact although certain that they'd mastered the attractiveness of being bland; I guess being nothing.

Besides if all the other characters I'd been faded after a while, these girls wouldn't last a day.

Suddenly Sue turned and waved at me. I admired her effort to plump up the group, even if it meant associating with someone who'd been ditched by the ultra-cool Patty Scott and now wafted around like a ghost. Perhaps she thought she could remold me into another airy minion, and I felt bad disappointing her. It wasn't obstinance but fear of all things vague and nebulous that held me back, kept me from joining her group. I felt like whispering in her ear that soon I'd be someone. Sue locked eyes with mine for a moment but then she yawned, and I pretended to, too.

The girls laughed about something I couldn't hear, and I joined in a moment too late, so that my laugh rose above theirs, hanging in the air. I panicked for a moment fearing one of them would ask what I thought was so funny. "Do you get this lab?" Gwen turned to me, scrutinizing me from head to toe, and I knew as she frowned before turning back to the group that it had been a mistake to be out in the world as nobody, allowing people to see me, hear my voice, and decide who I am. I'd really let my guard down but finding someone to be in high school had proved hard.

"Let's go girls," Mr. Benchley said without much conviction. I wandered back to my lab partner, a nice kid who'd just moved to East Lansing and hung out with a few hoods, Towies, the way all new kids do before they find out that they shouldn't. We worked side by side without talking until he accidentally broke his pipette, cutting his finger. I jumped up, and he swore under his breath as blood dripped onto his pants. Mr. Benchley grabbed some brown paper towels and rushed over. I stood back, hugging my lab sheet to my chest, like this might be my last lab sheet. Then the bell rang, and Mr. Benchley told me to get him some more towels as everyone hurried out, some staring at the kid.

After I handed Mr. Benchley a wad of paper towels, I backed up to the door, unsure of what to do. Was this the final straw? First Stephen and now the blood dripping on the floor making it clear that I had to kill myself? "You can go," Mr. Benchley said. I nodded and stared at Mr. Benchley hunched over the boy's finger. Then the shivering began again, and my teeth rattled uncontrollably. I pressed my lips together and clenched my jaw as wild thoughts raced inside my skull. I wondered if Stephen was inside my lab partner or if he'd come back as this kid, somehow. "You've lost your mind," I whispered, remembering the day I'd heard the mailman say that the man who walked on Michigan Avenue calling people strange names and yelling at cars had lost his mind. Watching Mr. Benchley search the floor for the piece of broken pipette, I wished that Stephen could get his life back and then disappear, move to Lansing where no one would know he tied a plastic bag over his head.

My heart pounded and my brain told me to stop linking thoughts together like jigsaw pieces from different puzzles. But another voice told me it was obvious that I had to follow Stephen. I'd been given ample time to create some kind of life, and what did I have? I shut my eyes, remembering the moment Stephen realized he was stuck to the gum. He'd said something in Russian, and then his blue eyes had widened behind his glasses and he'd gasped like he'd been stabbed.

CHAPTER III

The sky swirled and clouds rushed behind the towering branches of East Lansing's dying Elm trees when I pushed through the glass doors at the front of the telescoping school. The door was cool to the touch, and I begged my mind to believe that the cold glass was real and that I hadn't already begun to disappear. Perhaps a gradual disappearance is what compelled Stephen to put the bag over his head, I worried. All things come to an end, Mom often said with a glimmer of uncharacteristic hope in her voice. Now school had come to an end, and I was freezing for real outside in the chilly air by the driving simulator the school had bought so sophomores in Driver's Ed could pretend to drive before taking to the road.

"More blood on the roads is not what we need," Mr. Vandervelde had announced one morning after describing the million-dollar simulator purchase. Why hadn't Mr. Freds allowed Stephen to pretend to drive? A little white lie couldn't hurt, something about the simulator being the first step towards the real driving he'd never experience.

Seniors dismissed early took off in their own cars with friends in the passenger seats. I'd love a ride, but not as no one, and I'd dread the look of surprise on the driver's face when I explained where I lived. As someone else, I'd live in one of the wooded neighborhoods or even in Whitehills. *That will never happen,* Stephen said in my ear as a car full of seniors careened around the parking lot. *Wait!* I yelled in my head, stopping at the edge of the school's driveway, the way I'd stopped at the water's edge as Patty ran ahead, plunging into Lake Michigan and coming up for air after a crashing wave pushed her down for what seemed like forever.

Questions flew around my head, clogging my mind petrifying my muscles so that I couldn't decide on a path away from school or move in one direction or the other. Should I kill myself just to vanquish the terror of never emerging as anyone real? Would the nameless swirling storm building in my stomach, working its way to my brain—or maybe it was the opposite, beginning in my brain and filling my body to the point I'd be forced to kill myself or risk exploding in front of everyone. Stephen nodded and laughed like he'd already been through all this wondering and debating.

When the last car of seniors peeled out of the parking lot (the driver out of control for a moment), I turned back into the crowd of freshmen through juniors that spread across the massive parking lot like molasses rolling over the counter on the day Mom, frustrated by the relentlessness of housekeeping, wacked the jar onto its side. Some kids begged rides, some hopped into their own cars. My big feet, now size ten, refused to budge. Perhaps I should kill myself in the parking lot as a tribute to Stephen. They'd find my head in a bag under an exhaust pipe, my big feet sticking out the other end like the witch's feet protruding from Dorothy's house in The Wizard of Oz. Next, I imagined Sleeping Beauty's father ordering the destruction of spinning wheels throughout the kingdom. Could plastic bags be banned, I wondered blurting out a spastic laugh. But I squashed the next laugh, fearing I'd never stop laughing until I expired in front of horrified kids. By the end of the day, I resolved to kill myself in private unless, I found someone else to be.

At the far side of the parking lot, I saw Mr. Benchley in his green and white jacket lead the boys' cross-country team into the woods. My heart pounded in my ears as I replayed Mr. Vandervelde's announcement and Mr. Benchley's pale face. The only remedy I could imagine for my pounding heart was to join the runners as they disappeared into the woods. But the space between the woods and the parking lot threatened to swallow me, and I considered returning to the safe haven of school, like I'd decided to join Debate, when a girl skirted around me, walking alone. Without thinking I followed her, but not too close, memorizing her walk and the swing of her bell-shaped wool jacket. Out on the street she slid into a car waiting at the curb. I picked up the pace, imitating her head, tilting back towards the rear window. Suddenly, she turned around and waved through the glass. Then another kid passed me waving and calling to her. "Betsy! Betsy!" he yelled.

Pretend to be her anyway, a voice inside urged, convincing me that desperation had set in: if I were to survive the suicide of Stephen Fedkin and not follow his lead, his initiative (another word on the vocab list) I had to find someone to be, definitely by the end of the day. *I get it,* I said to a voice in my brain, wondering if this girl's house was decorated and equipped with all kinds of things people needed, like stereos and portraits they had taken at Sears of kids in matching outfits. In our barren house, it was easy to recreate these interiors, easy to imagine tossing back the covers of some girl's bed, wearing her clothes, and getting in a shiny, clean car. I guess I should thank Mom for ignoring the house, concentrating instead on filling the basement, a personal fiefdom, with her paintings, clay pots, and a ton of other things she made, like her life depended on making stuff she rarely brought upstairs.

All of her art making irritated me, but as I stared at the gray sky and the branches nearly void of leaves, I wished I had talent like Mom for filling in these empty spaces. Perhaps all the pot throwing, sewing, painting, and who knew what else went on down in the basement kept Mom from erasing herself.

I ran after the girl's car as the boy climbed in, but soon it turned and disappeared.

Walk, walk, walk, I commanded myself, but my brain and body were disconnected. I stumbled forward, pushed by a rising hurricane in my stomach. "You've lost her," I said aloud and although I heard my voice, the words hung in the air and like the gray sky overhead moving under its own command, words I uttered had no relation to me but were part of a foreign landscape. More of the strange laughter rose in my throat as Stephen's goofy smile stood out in my brain, as did his crooked glasses and blue eyes.

"Can you grab that?" At the corner of Hagadorn Road and a cul de sac, Barbie Robert popped out of a silver car and pointed at a ditto flying towards me. "It's the Latin homework," she said, grabbing the sheet with purple letters before it landed in the gutter. In her other hand Barbie held a silver baton. She sat next to me in Latin and always brought a baton or two to class; I'd heard she was the best baton twirler in the school. "I'm going to the stable for my riding lesson, or I'd love to hang around," she said smiling.

"Not twirling lessons? I want to get back into baton twirling," I lied, fake smiling at the baton she tossed. "I suppose you can do the Four Finger Twirl?" Someone mentioned the trick in gym just the other day. She looked impressed, and I widened my eyes the way I 'd seen Dad mime a lie without burdening his conscience with words that might come back to haunt him. After all I hadn't said I knew what the Four Finger Twirl was or that I'd ever mastered it. Just let others fill me in with of course a little prodding on my part.

Smiling back, Barbie demonstrated an under the elbow twirl and I clapped as she laughed, and her grin widened as she repeated the move. I knew right then when her smile seemed to grow and grow that she'd never fade, and I could be this girl, Barbie, for life. Plus, a kid in the marching band had asked her to the homecoming dance--I'd heard about the invitation in Latin. He wasn't a reach. I could see us on a date. Of course, Mom would insist on making my dress, and I'm sure she'd scoff at the dress Barbie bought. I'd have to convince Mom that even a dumb boy like this guy might sense that girls weren't supposed to wear homemade dresses copied from drawings in the *Women's Wear Daily*.

"See you tomorrow in Latin," Barbie said, and then her face seemed to soften, and she looked in my eyes like she saw something in me that she needed. I turned away from her gaze and she tossed the baton. "Watch out," she said, and I caught it. We laughed, but her laugh stuttered. I knew mine wasn't real, but I needed hers to be more than real, like that of the scream in the painting the art teacher had showed us, only positive not desperate. Then I watched her run off, clutching the work sheet in one hand and her baton in the other, and I brushed off doubts that I'd never find the perfect person to be.

I followed an old dog, which looked back at me like I needed a guide or a reason to start moving. "Where do you live?" I asked, imagining Barbie petting its mangy coat. "Nice dog," I said in a new voice—an early stab at getting Barbie down. But Stephen's face appeared in my brain, shaking his head like I was wasting my time thinking about becoming a girl like Barbie. *Go away*, I shouted, but his face grew, until I considered throwing myself into traffic, just to find relief. *That's what you want*, I said to the image of Stephen's huge face, and then a car swerved and honked at a college student who dodged traffic as she crossed Michigan Avenue. I cringed, imagining me in her place suddenly paralyzed as a car slammed into me, ripping my skin, crunching my bones and then running over my fractured, bleeding skull. People I never knew would hover over me when inside, as my life seeped away, I'd beg for Dad, Mom or even Patty Scott to appear to claim me as someone they once knew.

If only I'd had a crystal ball way back, I'd have ditched Dad and Patty before they dumped me and gotten started becoming someone else—for good. Maybe I should have become Beth, the girl who stayed with us on and off. But Dad hated her too much, even though he admires people with skills--Beth could sing and stand on her head forever—that's what he loves about Mom. She can make anything, he always says, and growing up on a farm in the Depression made her strong. Growing up the son of a publisher in Port Huron made him a wimp, I guess. I'd love to tell him that I didn't care about either of their lives, just to get back at him for casting me off like a Kleenex.

I heard Dad's favorite song, *These Boots Are Made for Walkin,* coming from a car and I remembered him clutching a hand towel wrapped round his hips and me twirling in my nightgown, and then the two of us stomping during the part when the singer stomps all over someone. I loved thinking of Dad as a king stomping his enemies—all the bosses as far back as the army—to death. Whatever ailed him now, I wasn't sure, but maybe he needed another little kid to act like an anchor or perhaps a sounding board for his plans of greatness.

Mrs. Broadback grinding her tires into the curb brought me back to life, and the minute Danny rolled down his window, my head cleared. I could feel my wide smile like it was mine. I'd practiced the smile in the mirror, so I knew it was pretty and friendly. "Can you sit for an hour or two?" She put one hand on Danny's chest, pinning him to the seat. "I'm desperate to get to my sorority before our dinner tonight—I'm in charge of the flowers and I can't trust the guy from Robert The Florist to follow my directions."

I got in the front seat of the Broadbacks' wide green station wagon, hoping Mrs. Broadback would fill my head with concerns about her life in East Lansing. I hoped she tell me about Robert The Florist. Barbie had just the other day held up a Robert The Florist box while she explained one of the nine million Cicero quotes we had to memorize. "False pretensions fall as do flowers," she'd said. Everyone clapped when she took out a corsage and handed it to Mrs. Bell. After Barbie helped pin it to her sweater, Mrs. Bell said we could watch it wither over the next few weeks.

I took a deep breath when I walked into the Broadbacks.' Mom would've hated their home, decorated with pictures and nick knacks Mrs. Broadback had bought at places like Lieberman's downtown. Above the clock was a sign that read, *Leave your cares outside the door.* Tears welled as I read the sign, and for a second, I thought I could forget about Stephen Fedkin and finding someone to be if only I could stay here forever.

"Better call your mom," Mrs. Broadback said before she left. That morning, I'd told Mom I hated her and was never coming home after she practically ripped a skirt she'd basted together off my hips. I dreaded an apology. Nothing was worse than Mom begging for forgiveness for being a terrible mother or an awful person with huge defects. During these confessions she turned herself inside out with tears and a contorted face. I'd beg her to stop but rather than stop, she'd sputter out, blaming me or Dad as her face turned hard.

"I'll dial! Let me dial," Danny jumped up and knocked his head into the bottom of the phone. "Ow," he whimpered and then began to scream.

"OK, you can call, but not if you're screaming," I said, picking him up. As we listened to the ringing, I prayed Mom wouldn't answer. She wouldn't worry about me, but I could at least fantasize about her worrying. If she answered, she might remind me to clean the Broadbacks' house, since in the Depression she earned a nickel an hour for babysitting a bunch of farm kids, plus cleaning the family's silver and washing the floor. The longer the phone rang, the more my heart sped up until finally I heard her voice and fumbled with an apology I thought Mrs. Broadback would like. Right away I knew Mom was auspicious and scornful of niceties I'd learned in the outside world.

"Oh, I see," Mom answered, clearing her throat.

"Oh, I see," Danny echoed.

"Who said that?" she asked, and I hung the phone up.

"You forgot to say 'bye'," Danny said, jumping down.

"She'd take it the wrong way." I stared at a photo of the Broadbacks smiling on a beach in wherever Clearwater is.

Danny and I watched TV, as usual, and then he nagged me to play Pick Up Sticks. After I let him win two games, he fell into my lap. "I wish you lived here—you could sleep in my other bed." He touched my cheek and then rolled off like he'd made a small request that I could take or leave.

"Well, I could move in," I said. "Should we ask your Mom?" I stared at the back of his head, wondering if they could adopt me and I'd spend the rest of my life with people who needed normal things, including babysitting. Slowly I'd become a clone of Mrs. Broadback, the way white people kidnapped by Indians adapted to life in teepees and ultimately forgot about their old lives.

"When's dinner?" he asked, rolling a pick-up stick from under the davenport. I got him a snack and later fish sticks for dinner. I was about to clear his plate and wipe up the globs of ketchup on the counter when Mrs. Broadback banged through the back door. "Thanks a lot," she said, tossing her brown leather gloves dangerously close to the ketchup. "But can we settle up next time? I have to hurry and change before Dick gets here with his mother." I nodded, disappointed that I couldn't clean the kitchen and do something extra like clean out a drawer or vacuum the den, where Danny's toys were strewn.

Mrs. Broadback would never ask me to go on a vacation with them or even stay the weekend, when she and Mr. Broadback "got away" to the Holiday Inn in Detroit, if I didn't take on more responsibility. I felt my face redden, worrying that she'd never call me again. "Let her stay, let her stay! I don't want Grandma!" Mrs. Broadback laughed, and then I joined in laughing as I edged towards the door.

"You know, it's not a bad idea," Mrs. Broadback said, lighting a cigarette as Danny wrapped his arms around her slim hips. "I do need more help, and it would be so much easier to have a live-in like Jean Griswold has—I mean for weekends or school vacations." I stared at the smoke circling her auburn hair. My arms tingled for a moment as I inched towards her, picturing myself throwing my arms around her like I was her kid too. "Let's think about this—maybe next summer?" I nodded, and squeezed my lips shut so that I wouldn't suddenly blurt out the news about Stephen Fedkin and my worry that I may not be here tomorrow, let alone next summer.

"Bye Danny." I stood at the open door. "Bye," I said again, but he'd run off, and Mrs. Broadback, with her back to me, scrutinized the calendar hanging on the wall over a vase of pretty flowers. "Are the flowers from Robert The Florist?" I asked, hoping that she'd tell me more about the deal with the florist.

"I guess so, yeah," she said without turning around. "Sorry about the money—next time for sure," she called as I closed the door behind me.

Stars had begun to poke through the dull sky as I stood on the Broadbacks' welcome mat. I dragged my feet on the slate walkway sloping away from their big brick house with the white trim. Every story I'd read about someone lost or disoriented ran through my head until finally my mind was consumed with the darkening sky, the bare trees with pointy twigs and grasping branches, and the lines and angles of rooftops and chimneys. My world didn't know me, I realized, or perhaps its indifference was a sign to take my life now before the landscape flattened itself so completely that I recognized nothing. I dug my hands into my pockets and found a dollar bill—at least the moment Mrs. Broadback handed it to me stood out in my brain.

"Get some popsicles from the Good Humor man," she'd said, dropping us off at Valley Court Park.

"Oh, I love the Good Humor man," I'd told her, but when the truck didn't come around, I'd forgotten to give it back to her and had carried it around ever since like a memento or one of Jane's charms. I fingered it, imagining it still in my pocket when they lowered my body into the ground. Unlike other moms, Mrs. Broadback rarely paid me on time, but I didn't care. I 'd do anything to be Mrs. Broadback's live-in, wandering the house's wide halls, poking my head into its many bedrooms and best of all, snooping in Mr. and Mrs. Broadback's room, discovering tubes of creams in the drawer by her side of the wide bed and Playboys in the drawer on his side. If only I was older, I could easily become Mrs. Broadback.

"Bye Sally!" Danny waved to me from the front yard. "Come babysit again!" I stared at him as he showed off some awkward cartwheels and my heart raced.

"I will Danny!" *I must find someone to be, for Danny,* I thought as he tried another cartwheel. *This one's almost right.* "See you Danny!"

I left the Broadbacks' neighborhood, Glencarin, and crossed Grand River Avenue, running across the four lanes after a truck barreled past. Someone swooshing behind me honked just as I got to the curb. On Kensington Road, I lingered at the Scott's old house, staring at the doorknob I'd turned a million times. What if I lived as my former self? Forget searching for something that might not work; instead recreate the days when Patty and Dad fashioned my life like the duo Oscar and Hammerstein, the people the student teacher in music said could bring any character to life.

But right away Stephen popped up, laughing and shaking his head. *Don't be a baby,* he said. *Let go of fear and take your life. Show everyone that you can at least do that on your own. Patty drinks, has a boyfriend, and cheers for all the games. She has a life in Whitehills—the world of today. All you have are memories,* Stephen said, alluding perhaps to our kiss. I nodded, picturing me stooped over, surprised by the sound of my first kiss. I'd tried to put the whole incident out of my mind, but whenever I passed him in the hall I remembered the moment when we backed away from each other and I wiped my mouth, praying the kiss erased my cruelty. Afterwards, he had slipped notes into my locker, begging me to go to the Winter Dance. I had refused, avoiding him until he gave up, but now, on the day after his death, he was back begging me to follow him the way he had begged me to like him or at least go to a dance with him.

I continued to nod, scared out of my mind as I listened to Stephen and the traffic as I neared Michigan Avenue. *"But what about Danny?"* I said to Stephen, picturing Danny clunking to his feet after trying to walk on his hands. Stephen had nothing more to say, and I squeezed my eyes shut, praying he was gone forever. I tried to picture Danny. Could he possibly be my raison d'etre? The saying stuck in my head after the man from 4-H told freshman at orientation that we all need a raison d'etre beyond schoolwork. *But I need a person to be,* I yelled inside my head as I imagined myself jumping into the traffic on Michigan Avenue and my tall thin body ground into the cement. Could I withstand the violence? I stopped for a moment, imagining tires flattening my legs and the weight of a car puncturing my lungs and my heart sending blood out my mouth and eyes until my body blended with the cement and blood streamed everywhere.

It was dark when I finally stood in front of our house, perched above Michigan Avenue and clinging to its foundation. I walked slowly up the driveway, turning when someone screamed, "Tigers!" Then I made out a Tigers bumper sticker as it flew by on Michigan Avenue. I wondered if Barbie Robert cared about the World Series. Just then a woman walked up our driveway, stopping abruptly when she saw me. "Oh, I'm sorry! I only wanted to get a closer look at the house. I lived here when I was your age." She backed up examining the house, squinting the way Mom narrowed her eyes when she painted. "Sorry to bother you—my name's Jean Stephens. What's your name?"

"Barbie—Barbie Robert."

CHAPTER IV

"Your dad home?" A short, slender man in a black wool coat and hat appeared at the porch door, startling me as I stood by the door, trying to figure out how to open it as quietly as possible. Dad was probably still in bed, but in my brain he reminded me that a door hates being yanked. Unexpected noises always irritated him but in the weeks before his illness, his nerves had been so frayed that even the ring of the phone drove him wild.

"He's under the weather, but I could take a message." The man cocked his head and raised his eyebrows.

"Well, I saw his car," he said. "Thought I'd stop by, see if he's okay now. You know, feeling better." He flipped through the pages of a small notepad, the same kind Dad kept in his coat pocket.

"It's really old, but it tries," I said, pointing in the direction of the rusting Chevrolet. He looked at the car, and I realized I was echoing Dad's concern for the feelings of things. Instead of people, Dad took things under his wing, although he'd made an exception for me. But innocent things would never be dumped since they don't grow or change, and they'd never fight back. I wished I could go back and be as innocent as things. I'd promise to keep quiet and stare unblinkingly at nothing. As I stared at the back of the car, I thought about changing into a bumper, but then I saw Stephen's face coming out of the exhaust pipe like Jeannie from the bottle. He hovered over the trunk, locking eyes with mine.

You're not getting out of this, he said, like he was the gym aide who'd caught two girls piercing their ears in the locker room.

I know, I said silently.

It's the best option, Stephen said. *Just do it.*

I promise to become Barbie Robert, I said, cornered. Then I shut my eyes and, in the dark, watched myself put the bag over my head, gather the ends in one hand and twist like my head was a loaf of Wonder bread I wanted to keep moist and fresh.

"Your Dad's one hell of a reporter." The man raised his eyebrows as he talked like I needed convincing or was unaware of Dad's ability to write a good story. I nodded fast—up and down and up down, vanquishing the image of my head in a bag. I wished he'd go on forever but instead he stopped and took a deep breath.

"He's writing a book about horse racing—and other things of course," I said, clearing my throat. My face was so hot and my hands so cold that I rubbed my cheeks to warm my fingertips.

"I'm not surprised! Well, I'll come by again," he said, without moving. I nodded, thinking that Dad would pump up the man before getting rid of him in a flourish. "I'm one of the editors at the Journal. I remember the day you stopped by with your mother." I smiled and nodded like I remembered him.

"Tell your dad Howard stopped by—hoping he can go to the big game tomorrow. We need him."

"OK, I'm sure he will," I said in a loud voice like I'd turned into the deaf woman who sold potholders door to door, yelling the price so loud she drowned out the traffic noise. The man didn't seem to notice, and for a moment he faded as I obsessed over my tingling toes and my head radiating heat. We'd just read a Jack London story in English, and I marveled at how nature could so easily, without any pity, murder a man and his poor dog. Death by freezing would be terrifying at first until a gentle ending wiped out a life. How, I wondered, would it feel to fall asleep and never wake up? I could not feel my feet against the cold step, figuring this must be a sign that I was moving closer toward killing myself. The steps weren't that cold in October.

"Here, give this to your dad." He rushed up the stairs and handed me a sheet of paper. At the top the word *RECOVERY* was printed in big letters and underneath: *Manage Your Nerves.*

"Okay," I said, relieved to hear my normal voice resonate in the cold air.

"That might help him. I called, but your mom…." His voice trailed off, and I coughed to fill up the awkward silence. I didn't want to say that she probably thought he hated her or maybe she accused him of doubting her powers to cure Dad on her own. "I don't want to see him get fired," he mumbled. I wished I could convince him that Dad was in bed with a normal illness. I felt like bragging about Dad in the war, running the barracks as the sergeant in charge, and the books he wanted to write and definitely all the adventures Mom said they talked about when he rescued her from living with her mother for the rest of her life. Mostly, I just wanted to keep him talking— figuring out what he wanted to hear required all my concentration and his voice and sad brown eyes blotted out pictures of my head in a plastic bag. The man's hand hanging at his side caught my eye, and I thought of holding it. *The two of us could work together,* I thought.

"He hopes to get a new car," I said.

"I thought he just loved ramming around on the unicycle or that old bicycle of his," he said, smiling. I nodded, imagining us without a car—a sin in this town.

"Well, anyway. Gotta run," Howard said. "Let me give you my card. Tell him we need him, and the trip is all set up— he just has to call me."

"Thank you," I said. He nodded, and as he disappeared down the driveway, I considered running after him, begging him to take me on, like an apprentice. But then I pictured him shaking me off. Maybe Stephen lost one person after the next, too. Then Stephen nodded and widened his eyes. *There's no way,* Stephen said, frustration rising in his voice as we both stared at the end of the driveway and the cars whooshing past.

Once inside the porch, I inched the door open to the kitchen without so much as a creak and heard Mom's soft voice cloaking her constant disappointment. I felt like slashing something—maybe the curtains hanging over the kitchen window. The sound of fabric being ripped to shreds might yank her into some real distress, steer her mind towards real things that people talked about—like a nuclear war or the new disc brakes in the '67 Toronado all the people in Whitehills owned or had on order. Perhaps she'd stop dwelling on the fakeness of everyone in East Lansing—especially rich people lucky enough to have real swimming pools and new cars. Of course I wasn't sure I cared about things everyone thought were so important, but if they were necessary for being a real person, I'd worship them too. But at that moment, staring at the old faded curtains, I thought some violence on my part might stop Stephen Fedkin's face from appearing every other second. Like kicking down a door would cleanse my brain of its repository of worries—if it wasn't Stephen and the gum, another incident from the past would occupy my brain and drive me towards ending my life. I dug my nails into my palm and imagined burning the skin on my arm, a delicate but hidden place like inside the elbow, which I could hide under a blouse.

"Pin the pattern to the fabric today, and then tomorrow, we'll cut out the jacket—one step at a time," Mom proposed in the messianic tone she used when converting someone to the world of pure living through pot throwing, painting, pattern making, weaving, sewing, or baking—from scratch, of course. That's patience, I admitted as I crept through the kitchen. Or stupidity, I thought, considering she rarely convinced anyone to join her in toiling over the five thousand projects she dreamt up. On the other hand, failing to gather disciples left her mostly alone, and I think she preferred that anyway. Better to be alone than constantly confronted by the fact that no one wanted to sign up for her utopian vision of mandatory creativity.

I wasn't sure who her student was today—probably the weird neighbor who lived on Kensington or maybe the lady we'd met at the organic gardening club.

"Let's pin the interfacing first," Mom said, but still no reply. I hesitated before the door into the living room. Mom, hands on hips, stood in the middle of the dull room, wearing her typical paint splattered corduroys. A girl with shoulder length brown hair, her back to me, crouched over a large piece of blue fabric spread on the worn brown carpeting. "Rushing never gets us anywhere," Mom said, shaking her head.

"Uh-huh," the girl said, like she'd given no thought to rushing or to the painstaking work of pinning, cutting, matching fabric patterns, or any of the stages one could so easily bungle. I coughed, and she whirled around.

"Beth?" She looked plumper than before, like someone had pumped air into her cheeks. "You're back?" I said, knowing the answer to the question and wincing at the thought of her staying, once again—another episode of abandonment by her mother, who we assumed to be alcoholic, but I knew Mom hoped had more noble problems, like someone had beaten her senseless—or made her walk barefoot in the snow like *The Little Match Girl.* Finally, Mom could be the savior to someone very deserving. Dad, on the other hand, hated having Beth stay with us and tried his best not to see her. He never clapped when she sang a song or stood on her hands while I counted to ten. But sometimes he went berserk, like she was an intrusion he detested for reasons so mysterious it was easy to make one up. I decided most plausible was that since Dad worshipped those with skills and natural gifts, he probably hated Beth for making it obvious that I had none.

The three of us said nothing for what seemed like an hour, during which time Mom retied the red bandana around her thick dirty blond hair and rolled up the sleeves of an old shirt of Dad's that she wore. If only Mrs. Broadback could teach her how to dress in outfits that made sense—knee socks and loafers, navy wool skirts and matching sweaters—she'd find herself fitting into the outside world. But my stomach twisted imagining her following people like Mrs. Broadback. I'd leave, escape to the world of Mrs. Broadback, but I needed Mom to stay on her side of the world, lamenting most people's obsession with the trivial. I knew she divided the world into teams, and, as much as I hated her fixation on all the bad people on the other teams she conjured, I felt like crying at the thought of her being dragged to the other side as she surrendered, as she admitted failure. I was about to tell her the Mark Twain quote we learned in English, about how clothes make the man, when she motioned Beth away from the fabric. Beth hopped over the material, and I thought about the time Dad had grabbed her wrist and rushed her to the stairs, where the two of them stumbled over each other's feet with Dad swearing and Beth landing in a thud.

"Jesus! Can't you do anything right?" He'd screamed, spit flying. Instead of telling Beth to run to her bed, cover up, and pray for the best, I'd said nothing. Just watched her gulp air and flap her arms in a perfect imitation of our old parakeet while Dad upbraided her some more as he awkwardly straightened his tie and collar. Later, in bed, Beth told me a million times that she hadn't been taught properly—the way I'd been taught—how to close a door or eat noiselessly.

"But you're good at everything else," I said, not foreseeing that all the beauty and know-how she displayed after dropping into our lives, like Glinda floating to earth, would fade into something as nondescript as the person standing between Mom and me at this moment.

"Does everyone want a snack?" Mom blinked, breaking the spell.

"I'm good," Beth said, sighing. I sniffed.

"I'm *well*—don't you know grammar?" I rolled my eyes as I dropped my jacket on the floor. "Do you learn anything in your school?" I stared at Beth like she and possibly her whole school were responsible for the stupidity of today's youth. As soon as I said it, I felt disgusted for donning this smart girl attitude. Were everyone's impulses as bad as mine? Had Stephen Fedkin killed himself for the same reason—a sudden urge to hurt his weird Russian parents or Mr. Freds? He might still be alive if he'd become someone else—someone who had no reason to wound people or destroy their lives. "Sorry, Beth," I said, sensing how hollow and confused my voice sounded, especially since I thought that Beth had probably buried her God given talents and smarts just to go unnoticed. And yet, the longer I stared at her the more she looked like a new person, beating me at my own game, without knowing it.

"You and your father," Mom started in on what I thought would be a tirade about Dad and his long dead parents thinking they were smarter than everyone, but instead she asked why Dad and I got pleasure from sticking pins in Beth. I moved closer to Beth, hoping to see some sign of the old knowledgeable Beth, who always figured a way to make me look good. Instead, she stared out the window. Her yellow low-cut peasant blouse showed cleavage I'd never seen before, and she seemed stuffed into blue pants with faint black stripes. Long silver earrings jingled when she moved her head, like a signal that she actually had thoughts, but her face revealed nothing. I'd always loved her dimples, but she didn't smile or frown. She resembled the bust on the Latin book with her straight Roman nose and penetrating brown eyes—set back and framed by thick lashes and dark eyebrows.

"Cool bracelet, Beth," I said, pointing to a silver chain. To my relief, she smiled like she had no idea what the fuss was over. I felt like hugging her.

"I hate school," she said, plopping down in the one chair we had in the living room. I nodded, like hating school was a given when in reality, I liked translating in Latin with Mrs. Bell. I especially loved the moment when she absent mindedly got off track, and went on and on about a declension and for once a digression didn't confuse me—this wasn't Mom extrapolating with no evidence that positive thinking cures a cold and it wasn't Mom deducing that someone hid from her in the cereal aisle of Kroger's because this person hated Mom for no other reason than everyone hated Mom. I never worried that Mrs. Bell would throw the book or rip out a page. There was nothing mysteriously crazy about Mrs. Bell. She just liked declining nouns and she told me, almost whispering like no one else should hear our little secret that Latin was an inflected language. For once, I didn't nod like I understood something that I didn't, and she wrote on a note that *boys* is the inflected form of *boy* and *swam* is the inflected form of *swim*. Before she went back to the front of the room, she chuckled at herself for veering off course, and I copied her examples in my notebook.

"Why's she here?" Dad appeared on the landing in his pajamas. Beth sprang to her feet. Instead of tearing down the stairs like in the old days, Dad stared at Mom, and I stared at Dad. It was weird to see him unkempt, out of his black suit and gleaming white shirts and more like Mom—raw and disheveled.

"She's not the problem," Mom said, looking at me but pointing at Beth. I felt caught in what seemed like a series of steps leading me closer to my death, and I begged time to slow down, to drag its feet.

I'll do it, but not yet, I said without speaking. *Give me more time—at least an hour,* I reminded myself how hard it had been for me as a kid to finally get my head under water at the pool.

"Just do it; don't think about it," the swim teacher had advised until one day I held my nose and fell back into the water.

"Just do it," I said under my breath.

"I bet," Dad said, shaking his head in a vague sort of way while the tie on his robe fell apart. As he headed back upstairs, I heard a voice in my head begging him to come back and tell Beth she shouldn't be here or at least ask me to come to the basement where we'd practice ESP or go over the Racing Form. "She shouldn't be in this house!" he yelled, like he'd read my mind, but then he lost control of his voice. "Get her to where she should be," he said as he reached the second floor. I ran after him, but when I got upstairs, he'd already disappeared, and I heard him groan and the bed creak.

I stood in front of his door for a good two minutes, deciding whether to go in and smooth his forehead the way Mom always did to me when I was sick, that is before she decided I'd brought on my own illness to torment her, as proof of her evilness. When that change of heart occurred, she usually threw things or she'd demand to know why I hated her. But Dad deserved soothing; he had, after all, made an effort to get up just as I got home. Perhaps he'd heard my voice. Then I pictured the first day of high school, when Patty Scott had rushed by me in the hallway without seeing my big wave. It wasn't me Dad wanted to see. He'd gotten to his feet because Beth was in his house—like she thought she belonged there. I heard someone laughing inside my head and knew it was Stephen.

"Dad, Dad," I whispered like he'd tell me that I was actually someone. "Help me," I whispered, pressing my forehead into the door. I had to become Barbie Robert right away. But my voice inside my brain told me to stop dreading suicide and see it as foretold. It's the oracle we'd learned about in the unit on tragedy and comedy, I told myself. But still, part of me wished Dad would emerge from the bedroom dressed and ready to resume our old ways. Even if Stephen continued to nag me, I'd lean onto Dad, nod at everything he said while I changed like a lizard into Barbie. Our hair color was identical, we had blue eyes, and I could slump a little. Barbie was at least two inches shorter than me.

I knocked on his door, slouching and willing myself to shrink back to my former self. I pressed my breasts hard against the door until I almost screamed. *Tomorrow, I'll be gone,* I thought, and with me the memories of our momentary encounters on the street. "Dad, Dad," I whispered, picturing him telling me what to think about a random person he had bantered with—someone who had piqued his interest. Once he demanded of a one-eared man walking on Grand River where the other ear went. "Go right up to a crippled person and ask what the heck happened," he said to me after we left Stanley with the missing ear.

I smiled, my face hot and tight, at the thought of him and me, not far from the house, making the most of an impromptu meeting on the streets of East Lansing. Then Stephen's voice piped up, reminding me that you can't go back. *I know,* I said. *I am not stupid.* Heat spread across my scalp and neck as the past flooded my mind, torturing me as I then saw a dark emptiness ahead. *Go away,* I whispered to Stephen. When he continued to smile, I tried torturing him with images of Dad driving to the country, the two of us alone on dirt roads searching out a farm or, one time, an old raceway. It had to have been at least two years since I sat in the front seat, bouncing to the cadence of his voice, taking in the stories he made new with each telling. I hadn't seen the slow retreat to bed because even a restricted world with Dad was pretty big— at least for a kid. Without him, I grabbed onto replacements, people who'd fill me in, but no one made sense like Dad and, of course, Patty Scott—the old one who lived five minutes away.

When I heard Dad moan again, I retreated to my room, where Beth had already deposited her pink bag with the frayed monogram and the worn bear with piercing eyes that reminded me of both Dad's eyes and Beth's—blackish and impenetrable. I guess this time, since Dad was incapacitated with what Mom kept saying was a perfectly normal case of nerves, Beth would be luckier. I couldn't imagine Dad having the strength to lift a feather let alone drag Beth around.

After a minute, I fell back on my narrow bed in what now felt like a suffocating room, full of Beth's old perfume. My room felt, to me, just like the foxhole Dad hated. I thought of the guys Dad said would cry for their mothers, and I practiced forming my mouth into a huge scream like the mouth in the painting from art class. I was about to shriek, let a blood curdling sound fill the upstairs, when I heard my name. "Come on down, Sally!" Mom called in a reconciliatory tone. "Come on down!" she called again and a third time, like these were the only words she could remember.

CHAPTER V

I responded to Mom's sudden shift in mood by opening and closing my bedroom door again and again, each time with more force until I began to feel sorry for the door. With my ear to the crack, I waited for her heavy footstep on the stairs. Baiting Mom was usually pretty easy, and yet she didn't appear. Meanwhile the silence in the house expanded, pushing on the walls like the air inside a chewing gum bubble, thinning the pink gum before it burst. Desperate to interrupt the silence, I slammed the door once more, hip checking it before careening onto my bed. Splayed on my back, I plugged my ears, wondering if Mom and Beth had escaped during all the door banging.

Perhaps, I thought, my eyes glued to the door Mom is hiding in the shadows on the stairs or on the other side of the door, waiting to shove her way into my room. I flipped over, trying to squash the picture in my brain of Mom smashing the table light that sat precariously on the box between our twin beds—Beth's and mine. I pictured a shard of shattered light bulb slicing my cheek and Mom scooping up bits of glass from the floor, squeezing them in her clenched hand so that I wasn't the only one who got to bleed. Finally, as I begged my mind to scroll through the bloody scene, the image dissolved. Rather than wait for another horror story to materialize, I got up and carefully placed Beth's old teddy bear on the top of her bag.

She had balanced the same bear on her red handlebars the day, years ago, that she showed up in our backyard. After gently laying the bear next to the trike's front tire and cooing it to sleep, she surveyed the sandbox like a contractor checking on a site. "Use wet sand," she'd said, pointing at a too dry collapsing sand mold I'd hoped would serve as the base for a tower. I nodded at her rich voice—a child's alto—and stared at her thick brown hair and dark brown eyes. I wondered if she always advised people she'd only just met, or if she could tell, somehow, that I couldn't get through life without a guide—someone like Dad, who gave me his life as a blueprint.

And like Dad, Beth spewed a lot of information, although she had a sweet manner. I smashed the sand as if she'd dared me to. "Let me help," she said, lifting her palms to the sky and smiling like this was the best detour she could imagine.

Mom wafted out the backdoor on that boiling day of Beth's arrival, squinting at this part child, part adult, like she was an art project. This stranger, like others Mom welcomed into our home, wiped out, cleared her mind of all the fear and paranoia pervading a world she thought hated her, despised her; I guess wanted her gone. But unlike the average drop-in savior, like the man selling potholders who fell asleep on our front porch and had to be removed, or the woman who only wanted some water and then stole Mom's china sugar bowl, Beth was like soft wet clay she could mold. And she hadn't yet done anything illegal. A human art project had dropped in Mom's lap, and she loved Beth from the get-go. Sacrifice and art rolled into one.

I turned over in bed and the paper with *RECOVERY* written on the top crinkled in my pant pocket. I pulled it out, hoping it contained a magic spell for returning Dad and me to the old days. Or could this *RECOVERY* thing help me forget about Stephen's death and his pleading for me to follow?

If you suffer from debilitating anxiety, RECOVERY will help you live without fear and suffering. Control your thoughts and find real happiness. Release your inner person as you learn to let go of the fearful person ruling your life. You deserve a better existence! Recovery welcomes you!

Alexander Low, Founder.

I read the words over and over again, clicking at the same time through images of Stephen, his head encased in a limp plastic bag. In the first picture he was smiling but by the last one his mouth was slack and his eyes shut. Wincing, I shook my head, willing Barbie to materialize. But instead of an image of Barbie, I heard my voice listing what I'd need to become her. I rushed through an inventory like amnesia was about to strike and soon I'd forget our school colors and the design of the blue and white majorette uniform she wore at pep rallies. *Where do you get a baton?* I wondered.

I made my way to the dark hall, the Recovery sheet in hand. The darkness scared me, like after killing myself I'd wake in an abyss where I wouldn't find Stephen waiting, and worse, I couldn't see the words in my Latin text. Latin would be gone forever.

"Dad," I said pushing down a scream I felt rising from my stomach as I barged through the door. "Dad, Dad," I said, picturing him dead, a sign for me to follow his lead then and there. "The editor from your job brought you something and really wants you to go to the game tomorrow." I waved the paper over his face and his eyes fluttered. "I hope you get better, Dad," I said, collapsing onto his stomach. He propped up on his elbows and spit pooled out of the corner of his mouth.

"Get that girl out of this house," he said, ignoring the paper. Without his glasses I knew he couldn't see anything.

"It says *recovery*—the editor came to see you and remind you to go to the game tomorrow—and he wanted to make sure you got this recovery thing."

"God damn floozy!" He lay back, staring off. "They're nothing but trouble," he said gasping between coughs. I watched him close his eyes and breathe through his nose like a dying dragon. He said something about this being our house as I rested on his chest, listening to his heart and remembering Mom begging Beth to lead us to her house, like she hoped Beth was homeless. When we finally found the house over the border into Lansing, a bit of white gauzy material wafted from behind the barely cracked door before Beth's mom, Empress Martin appeared. She and Beth knocked on our door the next day, bag and bear in hand, and from that moment on, Dad hated them.

I dropped the paper by Dad's side and stood back, looking at his straight nose, deep-set closed eyes and his slack mouth. I raised my hand to touch his forehead, but I went numb all over, like I'd suddenly become a mannequin while a storm brewed through my body and brain. I missed Dad and the person I'd been at his side. *Who can I be? Who can I be?* I whispered, balancing on the edge of the bed. With my eyes shut, I saw the storm inside filling my body, swirling gray and formless—perhaps like the tornadoes we hid from each spring, crouched under tables in the basement of the school.

But no one came to mind to obliterate the scary, windy void-—not even Barbie Robert. I wanted to scream, but my tongue felt dry and big, like I'd choke on it if I tried speaking. Finally, after the longest minute, the noun we'd just learned, *vestis*—clothes—declined itself behind my closed eyes, vanquishing the flying debris and the aftermath of a destructive force. More Latin words popped up, and I declined them silently, slumping until I oozed into Dad, who stiffened and muttered something about the editor.

"He said you're a great writer, Dad," I whispered, shutting my eyes, thinking about the clothes I'd need to be Barbie. *Vestis,* I said silently, again and again.

"Uh-huh," he groaned. "Oh, I write better than any of those clowns." I stood up like I'd heard enough to realize that we were over and I must get back to becoming Barbie Robert. *Stick with a winner,* Dad always said, and I felt like crying in skewed gratitude for all the advice he no longer doled out. *Save your babysitting money,* I whispered, picturing some of the things I'd need to buy to become Barbie: a couple pair of flats, coffee colored nylons, pink nail polish.

Good luck, Stephen's voice resonated in my brain. I thought I heard him laugh. *It's so much better here,* he said, offering what I took as hope. Hope if hope ran out for becoming Barbie. I'd so easily in the past become girls at school, but it was harder to become someone in high school. People blended into their stupid groups.

I left Dad, hesitating in the darkened hallway. After a minute of imagining myself stuck in the house forever—a fixture no one noticed—I turned around, like the Greek husband—Orpheus--who looked back to make sure his wife followed him, sentencing her to Hades forever. "I won't see you again," I whispered. But I couldn't picture Dad missing me, or anyone, and I thought about Mom and then Patty Scott. They both seemed busy in my imagination, and my stomach flip-flopped. "Please someone miss me," I thought as I entered my room, saw the window and decided to crawl onto the roof, where I'd work on Barbie in the cold air if I could concentrate on that.

Once I squeezed through the small window above my bed and edged my way across to the slanted roof above the porch, I sat shivering, watching martins—non-descript black birds— squeeze through the holes in the miniature house high above the roof. In the background, the tall Horse Chestnut tree swayed in the light wind. When the breeze gave way the tree stood still—majestic like the Statue of Liberty, and I thought of Mom fitting a skirt to my shifting frame. *I'm not a tree,* I thought, picturing her yanking the material, ripping the seams she'd basted—me left in my underwear—as she screamed that I was fidgeting on purpose.

Someone behind me fiddled with the window, probably Beth. *No more looking back,* I thought as I stared ahead and observed a single chestnut abandon the other chestnuts, the broad leaves, and the comfort of the strong branches. It reminded me of one of the Wallendas separating from the others—soaring with no safety net. How much resolve did it take to leave the group, just to entertain a crowd, or in this case me perched on the asphalt roof? Stephen Fedkin's face inside the plastic bag appeared in my mind, like he was brave, too. But he'd been alone—at least at school—unlike the hundreds of chestnuts clustered in the tree, so I guess his flight to wherever wasn't quite so brave. In Stephen's case, suicide just seemed like the next step. More aloneness that was all; no wonder he begged me to follow. I wished I could jump off the roof onto the blanket of thick chestnuts. It was always such a treat in the fall to crush the thick carpet, the popping sound a small violence void of guilt.

"Are you going to stay on the roof forever?" Beth poked her head out of the window. I noticed her cheeks were a fake shade of pink, and I wondered if the color on Barbie's cheeks had been brushed on. I hoped that Barbie's flushed face was the result of a natural enthusiasm, beginning on the inside. But I couldn't be sure, and a list of times I'd been apprised of how little I knew about the ways of people flashed before my eyes, beginning with Beth explaining how to apply the lipstick we'd found in the glove compartment. I didn't think it was Mom's, and that contributed to a worry that she wouldn't want me to understand everyday things, the things that propelled other people through life.

A voice I didn't recognize warned me that I'd never be able to become someone else again. Then Dad, his voice brazen and tough like a cowboy's, interrupted with his favorite line: *That dance is over*, referring as always to people he didn't want to cross paths with, and he might as well have said it about us. But, rather than resenting his cruel indifference, I recognized it as the truth. I'd been good at becoming other people before, but as an adult, or an almost adult, I was stuck. My talents for living like a chameleon had evaporated. I couldn't tell the difference between real and fake blush for god's sake. *Perhaps I should run away and live like a shadow somewhere.*

Stay out here, jump to your death, a voice responded to my waffling—a voice of another dead person I thought Stephen might have sent like he needed back up or support.

"Should I wear blush?" I asked, my voice cracking as I stared at Beth poised outside the window, as if she was about to shake a rag. She looked like everyone else, living from moment to moment throughout each day without worrying about disappearing. The next minute she'd be inside filing her nails. She raised her eyebrows and then squinted like Mom did when she was about to draw a portrait.

"You don't need it," she said as she helped me back in the room. We held hands for a moment or two, and I thought about taking her other hand like we could gallop around the house as we used to, but then I worried that she might run into people from my school and tell them that she stayed with us from time to time. I'd seen her at a football game, and luckily, she stayed put in her team's bleachers. But I'd noticed boys from our school talking to her, and I couldn't be sure that she wouldn't brag about knowing someone from rich East Lansing, or worse, she might point to me and talk about Dad and God knows what else.

I was insignificant, but, as Barbie, I'd have a higher profile, and I needed to move into a world untarnished. No one's history was perfect, and yet a marred background was unacceptable. *Lies or cover-ups were as necessary as water*, I thought, picturing girls at school clutching books to their chests, as opposed to the boys who held their books low around their hips, uninitiated into the world of keeping secrets.

A normal person would be too embarrassed to let anyone know that Dad yanked her around, but Beth had changed from that kid who kept bad things to herself. Her cleavage alone proved she'd developed a devil-may-care attitude and wasn't the same person who'd announced in front of my fourth grade class that Mom gave her a Barbie doll and the Barbie car. After that, she told Miss Gold that both Mom and Dad talked about good nutrition and never let us drink chocolate milk. Miss Gold told me that our visitor was welcome back, and mean Susie Schilling smiled at me. Beth winked at me later like she'd made school better for me. Now, she might let our secrets out of the bag, get into truth-telling like some kind of daredevil instead of the gross fabrications meant to flatter—I couldn't be sure. She'd become a bland mystery.

"Do you still live on Cowley and go to school in Lansing?" Beth nodded, squinting under a glaring overhead light bulb.

"Don't worry," she said, "I'm moving to Texas." I looked over at Beth, noticing how even though she wore makeup, she still had the uncomplicated face of a little kid.

"Mom should paint your face—I think she'd do a good job," I said, but she ignored me. "Please," I said, "talk to me." She smiled, like my request was perfectly normal and she'd talk to me forever if I wanted. "Don't move to Texas—that's a stupid state!" I said, pushing my hair away from my face and then scratching my skin, willing my old eczema to surface. I used to pray a teacher would notice my scratching and the spots of blood on my arm or neck. "You could stay here, I mean, if you want to," I said, picturing her alone in the room.

Beth smiled. "You have good bones," she said, and I felt my cheekbones.

Your face is nothing special, the voice Stephen sent informed me.

"People have said that, but who cares about bones," I said, looking up at Beth. I stared at her as she rifled through her bag. I told myself that her supposed move to Texas was a lie, the kind we told as little kids. Although if Stephen Fedkin had told me he was about to kill himself, I probably wouldn't have believed him either. People exaggerated, edited, or, like me, made up their lives so much of the time that I rarely believed what anyone told me. But at that moment I didn't care about truth. I just hoped she'd talk forever. Her voice calmed my stomach, and I wanted more time before I killed myself.

"Have you ever thought about killing yourself?" I kept my voice even, picturing Mr. Starr doling out debate topics after the field trip to the state house in Lansing.

"Doesn't everyone?"

She handed me a comb she found in her bag and then looked at me, tilting her head. "Blush would be good, I guess," she said, pulling a comic book from her bag. I combed my hair, and with each stroke, my breathing slowed. I couldn't believe that everyone thought about suicide, but Beth seemed so sure. A copy of *The Scarlet Letter* fell out of her bag. "I wish you could read this book and tell me about it. We're reading it in English."

I could do that, I said silently. I had a knack for finding the answers to certain things everyone else puzzled over, like adjectives and nouns that didn't agree or silly mistakes in lab reports that fouled up the answer. Just thinking about a test and a quiet classroom calmed me. If only I could live in a twenty-four hour classroom, I'd gradually cleanse my brain, fill it with ideas and equations and avoid the reality of being a real person in the world or a dead one in wherever.

"At least Texas is warm," she said.

"Is that why you're moving there?"

"I have a new dad who lives there. He was a policeman, and now he's the chief of like everything," she said, placing her bear squarely on her pillow.

"You make everything sound real," I said, and I thought of Dad making up stories and how half of my brain recognized the story as a fable and the other engaged with the words like nothing in the world could be more truthful. I took a breath, drawing in air to wipe away everything inside, willing my body as I sat on the edge of my bed to take over, manufacture a fresh start—hand over a new me. But my lungs refused, shutting themselves off, and I exhaled with no sense of relief.

"When were you here last?" I swallowed the words, feeling faint, or perhaps I wished to faint like the girl who breathed into a paper bag after collapsing during the choir concert. Beth shrugged and rolled her eyes and then flipped her hair. Even her gestures made me question whether or not she was telling the truth.

"I remember. We jumped in the pool with our clothes on!" I said, forcing a laugh. "It was back in August—before freshman year started. Remember? We snuck in the new apartment building across Michigan Avenue." I laughed again, fabricating this reaction that seemed typical of girls my age— laughing for no reason.

"And a guy asked us how old we were and you, of course, wanted to run home?" Beth rolled her eyes. Then she patted my hand like she was my older sister or an older cousin tasked with helping me overcome fears about leaving childhood. I remembered grabbing her hand and pulling her away from another guy, a college student in a bathing suit with a green and white towel around his neck. Rather than acquiescing as she always had, Beth wrenched her hand free.

"Please," I whispered.

"C'mon!" she laughed, and the college student joined in, the two of them laughing as I headed towards the gate.

"I've got money," I said. "The Good Humor guy might still be around." I pulled a dollar bill from my pocket and Beth grabbed her towel off a chaise. The college student caught one end of the towel and they played mock tug-of-war before he jumped in the pool. To avoid the splash from his show-off cannonball, we ran out, Beth laughing and me quick to lock the gate

Then our next-door neighbor, Mr. Craft, pulled up, and before I knew what happened Beth hopped in the front seat. "Get in," she said as she fiddled with the radio. I wondered, sinking into the backseat, how she knew Mr. Craft so well. I remembered sensing that I was a shadow witnessing a scene from behind, and for the whole ride back to our house I worried that I knew neither Mr. Craft—our old minister as well as our neighbor—nor Beth. Had they always been different than what I remembered? My mind couldn't be trusted, and I held back tears.

"You look dazed," Beth said, switching to the present, and I panicked. I pictured her gathering her stuff and leaving. I'd never come back to our house if I was Empress or Beth, but they seemed drawn to it. "I'm fine," I said.

"I'm suspended," Beth said, articulating each syllable of the terrible word, like finally she could be her old knowledgeable self, teaching me, the one who knew nothing. "I called my Mom, and she said I should come here."

"What did you do?" I asked, propping myself up on the wall and eyeing her closely, willing her to be exactly what she'd always been. For once my mind obeyed, and she appeared as an entirely recognizable older version of her younger self. *Thank you,* I said inside my head as her unhurried style of talking, like we had a lifetime to hang out and talk about nothing important, kept Stephen's face from appearing. Even her smooth olive skin—like Mom's bread dough, rising very slowly—sent me back to the day she arrived and I thought I'd always known her. *I'll kill myself tonight, but not till later, until we stop talking,* I said silently.

"I never stole before, but of course no one believes me." I plopped back, breathing out and closing my eyes. If only she told me stories, offered life lessons like the tales Dad made up. We stayed on our beds, not talking until a bird grazed the window and Beth gasped. I sat up.

"They do that," I said, like she was Danny and I was the responsible adult. She nodded, staring at the empty window.

"So you stole, and that's why you're here? I bet that's not so unusual at a high school like yours." She nodded as she scanned the room, like this was a palace compared to what the kids had in Lansing. I immediately regretted saying anything about her living in Lansing. Stephen's face appeared and so did Beth's, even though she was lying right next to me. My stomach reknotted itself, and I wished I could give her some earrings or a necklace, anything that might get her to smile and act like nothing really mattered.

"A kid in gym said that Lansing is getting better," I said, looking at her for a hint that I hadn't wounded her in any way or done something irrevocable. "And you're lucky not to go to my school—it's modern and nice, but a lot of the kids are incredibly stuck up." My head swirled, and I realized as I turned to the wall that Beth might be the last person I'd ever talk to. Dad had warned me about clouding my mind with the dumb ideas and worries of people beneath us—those foisted on us by do-gooders. But thinking he knew everything got him nowhere. Maybe we should've listened to everyone we met instead of Dad directing people to an outcome he wanted, an outcome he approved of, an outcome he'd already created.

"You know, Mom thinks you draw really well," I said, smoothing my own forehead with my fingertips. *You're kind of desperate*, I said to myself, picturing Stephen echoing my words, realizing that I now waited for Stephen to appear and goad me to the moment when I'd suffocate myself. I hoped Mom had some plastic bags in the drawer by the sink.

"I told our principal that your Mom made me the clothes—it's just that your Mom loves sewing, and I was going to take them back before anyone found out," she said as I squirmed deeper into the mattress, my head now aching, and with no relief from the flat pillow—a pillow I'd used for possibly my whole life. I wadded it into the biggest hump possible, and this helped ease the throbbing in my temples and the pressing behind my eyes.

The day was finally over for good—the small window perfectly black with not a star or the moon to ruin the relief of checking off one more day, the last day. Beth got up to turn on the overhead light. "Do you want to read this comic?" I shook my head, fixating on the moment right before I'd be gone for good. I pictured my blazing face and my body flattened to a wall in the garage. I'd stare at the old silver garbage can, imagining its indifference to my death. I longed for it to care or at the least remember what I'd just done, as it stood, the same as always, next to my crumpled inert body.

"What kind of clothes did you steal, anyway?" I asked without changing my position, imagining my eyes bulging and my lips apart.

"Mostly stuff you wouldn't like," she said.

"How do you know?"

She smiled and looked at me with super wide eyes like she had something to teach me.

"Well, I took two really cool bras," she said, and I nodded, wondering what a really cool bra looked like before remembering that I wouldn't ever need one. "A kid I kind of know was caught by a store guard who slammed him into the wall. I got away, but our stupid gym teacher found my bag, otherwise I'd be fine—and I won't do it again because the kid who got slammed into the wall said it really hurt and he has to go to court."

Part of me hoped she would steal again—live dangerously perhaps as a reaction to my death. Maybe she'd exaggerate my paltry life when police or principals asked her why she'd become a delinquent.

"Your Mom wants you to eat something," she said and threw down the comic. I smiled—the Beth I used to know would always get me something to eat. "She made us both something," she said. As she got up, I asked if she'd bring me a plastic bag. "I've lost my shower cap," I said. "Look in the drawer by the sink."

"I wonder if you'd like me to style your hair?" Beth asked later as we finished our grilled cheese sandwiches. She reached in her pink bag and brought out a bag of curlers and then a can of hairspray. "I could help you look like that girl you said you'd maybe like to be like? The one at the skating rink."

"Oh, she moved," I said, remembering a quiet girl I'd been in junior high. "Could you help me look like someone else? Her hair is slightly flipped up at the bottom. She has bangs and on top its ratted, although I wouldn't call it a bubble because the style is longer and she tucks it behind her ears."

"Very specific," Beth said, and I wondered if she stole the word from a vocab list. "Sure," she shrugged like this was a typical look of today. "But we'd have to start by washing your hair, so you don't need the shower cap," she said, holding up the plastic bag. I stared at her straight nose and the mole near her upper lip. *Stick with life*, I said to the darkness inside my skull. *You can become Barbie. Get started.*

"Store it under my bed," I said, pointing to the floor.

"Look." She pointed at the box of Milk Duds under my bed, nearly falling off her bed as she reached for the yellow box and shoved the plastic bag under my bed.

"I'm so glad you came," I whispered as she tossed me the candy and pulled a bottle of Breck shampoo from her bag.

"I've also got this new stuff called crème rinse. I haven't used it yet, but it's supposed to make your hair really shiny and smooth."

"This girl's hair is really smooth."

"Well, she probably uses crème rinse."

"I'm so glad you came," I said again. "I had this weird kid stuck in my brain and he's gone, at least for now," I said, closing my eyes.

CHAPTER VI

The darkness had receded, and the sky was nearly white when I woke to Dad's whimpering. Even in pain, he managed to mesmerize, bleating like a stranded sheep. Mom must have urged him out of bed and into the hall where their voices slid under my bedroom door. "Please help me get the story," he whispered between sobs, like Mom could suddenly learn the ins and outs of newspaper work.

I plugged my ears, praying his sobs didn't conjure the chaos of yesterday; the turmoil seemingly neutralized by a night of rock-like sleep. Stephen popped into my mind, but not his face, just the memory of him carrying his briefcase and racing along hallways. *Please don't come back,* I whispered, waiting for his big face encased in plastic to arrive. But Mom's soothing voice, along with images of her matted hair and paint-covered outfits, filled my brain instead.

"There, there, there, this will pass." She repeated this over and over, like whatever ailed him was no more than a stalled car, waiting to be towed, only she forgot that when we broke down the guy towed our car to a junk heap.

Perhaps she could become him—fake out the newspaper. She might be able to pull it off, considering she was nearly as tall as Dad, and, although everyone said she was as beautiful as Ingrid Bergman, with a hat and Dad's coat and galoshes, she could pass for a man. She'd never be the affable, nosy reporter, though—the one who effortlessly got people talking. She would always be her unpredictable self, and Dad would never again, I thought, be the garrulous person I had chased through grade school—interviewing a guy who raised the biggest pig in Lenawee County one day and Nelson Rockefeller the next.

"This will pass," she continued to sing as I pressed my body into the thin mattress and pulled the sheet over my head, wondering where Stephen had disappeared to. "This will pass," she said for the four millionth time.

"You wish," I muttered, imagining her stuffing him into our big Chevy Bel Air with the wide fins and flying right off the earth. Somehow his dramatic pain, his inertia and what seemed like a nameless fear made sense to me. I pictured him pulled like water towards a drain from the jungles of Guadalcanal and the Philippines to projects for books and major breaking stories, until his only subjects were those he found at the bus stops of Michigan Avenue with our house as a safety net—always in view—only now he couldn't figure out where he was or, I guess, who he was.

"No one feels good all the time," she said. "You're not alone. Do you know how often I can barely get dressed and get going?"

How many people feel better just because you feel worse? I wanted to ask her. I threw off the sheet and inched my way to the door, wondering if I should protect Dad from joining her as the permanently downtrodden, awaiting the destruction of this paltry world so that in the next, she could dole out cures in the forms of positive thinking and art-making.

Her longing for the cataclysmic ending of this life led her to stack big plates on top of saucers—I swallowed hard at the memory of mixing bowls balanced on juice glasses. Worse was her hair hanging over an open burner or the way she cut herself as she sliced into an apple. *Don't trust her,* I felt like yelling— she's aching for a blow up, something big and crazy. I figured she intentionally drove him mad when she left the water on, heedlessly slammed a cupboard shut, or washed me with soap when I was little, even though he told her a million times that soap caused dysentery in the army. Sometimes I wondered if she turned her memory on and off like the radio dial. I remember crying and hugging her leg after he threw a plunger at the window over the sink because she'd clogged up the drain. To the sound of shattering glass, we ran for cover and then she smiled as we raced up the stairs.

"I can't get on that plane," he said. "I can't do it! They'll fire me for good if I can't get to St. Louis. But I can't, I can't," he said.

Yes you can, I yelled silently, picturing his receding eyes, desperate to keep contact with mine as they sunk into his skull. I squeezed my eyes shut, realizing that nothing scared me more than quicksand, and I wished I'd plugged my ears when the kid in English described an old movie his Dad showed him about a man being sucked into quicksand.

"We'll figure it out together," she said in a low voice.

Watch out! I said, again silently, like a car was about to run over Dad. *If only he still needed me*, I thought, slumping like Mom's ten-pound bag of flour. I'd forget Barbie and my life and devote myself to saving him. But part of me wanted to watch him disintegrate. I even smiled imagining the two of them pretending to board the plane and fly off together, as they sat side by side in bed all day. But I knew that at some point— perhaps after his recovery, or after Beth left—she'd go on and on about the meaninglessness of her life and the shithole Dad forced on her when he'd promised great adventure. I had encountered the entire kitchen turned upside down on occasion, and I always figured that she left a huge mess so I'd witness the outrage she harbored for landing on a highway with a man who talked a big game but failed to mention that he was on the verge of collapse. "Too bad, Dad," I whispered.

"Dad and I are leaving for St. Louis," she said, busting through my bedroom door. "For the baseball game."

From under the sheets, I peeked at her gleaming big smile, and instead of congratulating her or wishing her luck, I turned toward the wall and closed my eyes. *They won't make it,* I thought, *and I'll come home to disappointment, like the emptiness Stephen Fedkin felt when he couldn't take Driver's Ed. If only I could live with Barbie from now on.* I wasn't sure I could permanently obliterate Stephen if I lived here.

Mom called to Beth, who rolled over, tugging covers over her head. "Since Beth's suspended, she'll have to stay here." She paused. "You can stay home from school, if you want." When Mom didn't move, I opened my eyes and sat up as the room shrank and she loomed larger and larger in the doorframe.

I could hear Dad crying on the stairs, but mostly I heard my heart throb in my temples, and I looked over at Beth, completely hidden under the white sheet like Jesus wrapped in linens before being placed in the tomb. I pictured Miss Knowles nodding in approval that I'd picked up on the symbolism she said made literature so tantalizing. A girl in grade school had told me the gruesome story of Jesus dying on the cross at recess as we traded chocolate Easter eggs Everyday as we swung on side-by-side swings I grilled her on the details, especially the part about the nails piercing Jesus' flesh and the angel in the tomb. Mom stuck in the doorway could be the rock blocking the opening to the tomb and the more I thought about the ridiculousness of some angel moving the boulder-size rock, the more I felt trapped with Beth and Mom.

Move away from the door, I said silently. Mom had probably been up for hours, vacuuming or painting or doing anything that would erase the transition from night today, but I was in danger of falling into a rut between the two—no wonder Beth clung to sleep. Barbie beckoned and so did the world outside the house. *Keep moving,* a voice said.

"I'm not cut out for anything," Dad said.

"Give up those thoughts," Mom hurried back to him. I threw on a blouse and my bell bottoms and was about to run past the two of them huddled on the stairs when I heard Dad mumble that he'd try to get on the plane.

"I bet you could do it," I said, standing over them. Dad nodded. I heard Beth's bed squeak, and I wanted to leave before she had a chance to get in the mix and rile Dad up. But Dad kept nodding like I should elaborate—offer a few more encouraging words. Suddenly I wanted to stay and help Mom get him on the plane. "This could be a great day in your life, Dad," I said.

I heard Beth's bed squeak again, and I squeezed by the two of them. In the kitchen, I grabbed a Pop Tart, slipped on my jacket, and went outside, where the sun lit up the asphalt driveway, revealing the pits from my kickstand and other holes and cracks. The sky was a faint blue and the air was clammy. I wiped sweat from my forehead and hurried down Michigan Avenue to Kensington while stuffing the Pop Tart into my mouth and breathing hard—just like Dad. Part of me wanted to go back and whisper in his ear that it wasn't an option to stay home.

"This is your life, Dad," I said to the empty street. Mom would help him write everything down for a story on what would be the last game of the World Series. But secretly I knew it wasn't the writing or normal pressures that had him pleading with Mom to let him stay home. It was the uncertainty he feared even as he ordered me to shy away from nothing. He'd been the leader, introducing me to eccentrics and famous people alike, but all along he'd rather hear about a trip than live through something unforeseen. Finally, he couldn't even hear about all the vagaries and possibilities people encountered.

I pictured Patty Scott calling me when she first moved away. I'd been excited to set foot in her new mansion. But during the sleepover as she talked about her new world, sneaking a puff from her mom's cigarette and kissing boys at recess, I began to feel unsubstantial in this rich world where there seemed to be no template for being, only wild endless experience. By the third sleepover, I begged to play our old games instead of sneaking outside to meet her new friends. She got her way, and out in the moonlight, wandering among newly built mansions and telescoping ranches with circle driveways, we searched for other kids just learning about all things forbidden. Finally, when a boy appeared, I begged to go home, and Patty didn't protest. Back in my own bed, I fell into a deep sleep, waking in the middle of the night full of dread. When the light finally eked through the black sky, I curled into a tight ball, feeling as uncertain and freefalling as I'd felt in her new luxurious canopy bed. I guess Dad now felt the same, like he had no world of his own.

A gray squirrel peeked out from under one of the neighbor lady's bushes and then ran in circles around a ragged forsythia bush like it was a needle stuck on one of Mom's Chopin records. After a minute or two, the squirrel ran to the lady's doorstep and I was caught for a moment, having an urge to follow the squirrel, knock on this old biddy's door and tell her to leave Mom alone—get her free art lessons somewhere else. My heart sped up, realizing I might be turning into Mom instead of Barbie Robert. Barbie would never assume the worst about people, and she had no time with all her baton twirling to embroil her brain in a knot of mistrust and fear.

Just then, a car zipped out of a driveway, driven by a man in a gray hat and overcoat. Unlike Dad, crumpled over the steering wheel with Mom in the passenger seat, coaxing him, this guy smoked, palmed the wheel, and nodded while swinging the car towards Michigan Avenue, where he'd probably ease into the flow of traffic and head to some office in Lansing. "Yes, I see you, you perfect man," I murmured. Then I imagined Dad on his unicycle weaving in the relentless traffic, cutting this man off and taunting him with a recklessness he hoped provoked envy.

I followed the car to Michigan Avenue, where instead of turning right towards Lansing, the man zipped across the divided highway and turned left, towards downtown East Lansing. I followed, heading to the Rexall. Before I could talk myself out of an adventure—cutting school for the first time in my life—I crossed and walked along the boulevard that divided the four-lane highway.

Mom would love to be in the center of the highway, I thought, avoiding the sidewalks people were supposed to walk on. The whoosh of the traffic on either side would be her favorite part. I winced at the screaming tires, trying to squash images of one of the cars careening out of control, spinning across lanes, and finally smacking into me. The impact would send me skyward where I'd land on an electrical wire, like the motorcyclist Dad had described as a limp piece of laundry in a story he had bragged about. After he thrust the paper in my face, he asked me to read it aloud, just to make sure I read the story and registered his byline.

"Good Dad," I'd said, hoping he'd eventually run the paper and become the big shot he always claimed to be.

"Oh, I can write," he'd said, plopping onto the davenport like he should get more praise, maybe applause, for having a natural gift. "They want to box me in," he'd said staring at his byline. Maybe now he was in bed—boxed in—just to show everyone he could stay there forever if he felt like it.

By the time I saw the Rexall, I congratulated myself on this trip and skipping school, glad, too, that I had money in my pocket. I could order Dad's favorite, a Danish, and regale people at the soda fountain with big stories. "He's on his way to the World Series," I said as I looked for an opening in the traffic.

Bells on the door rang out as I headed to the soda fountain. Unlike a Sunday morning, the stools were empty except for a woman with patchy red hair sipping tea.

"No school?" She turned on her stool, and I could see that she'd forgotten to blend in her rouge.

"I have an orthodontist appointment," I said, smiling.

"I see," the woman said as the waitress brought her a powdered donut and me a Danish. "Well, doctors and dentists can't always wait for school to be out—you simply must give school the boot now and then." Her blue eyes twinkled as she bit into the donut, and powdered sugar rained onto the blue shawl around her shoulders.

"Well, I hated to consent to this appointment because I'll miss baton practice, but I have to think about my smile, and straight teeth are key to a good smile. I'm going to need perfectly straight teeth if I hope to follow my dream of being a stewardess." I covered my mouth as I ate the Danish so she wouldn't notice my already straight teeth. I also reconsidered the word *consent*. I liked the word ever since it had appeared on a vocab test, but I wondered if it was the right word in this context. Barbie wouldn't worry about that, I reminded myself.

"I'm sure you're right—kids are so much smarter today. Why don't you scoot over, and I'll treat you to a waffle with whipped cream—don't you just love waffles with whipped cream? I bet you'd like that."

I moved towards her but then reconsidered. "I'd love to, but I have to skedaddle."

She nodded at me. "I understand—what's your name?"

"Barbie," I said, and she nodded again, like she'd known all along. I left her and found the lipstick aisle. *Barbie would choose pink*, I thought, and as I fingered the tubes, the pharmacist called to me.

"Need help, Miss?"

I smiled and shook my head. He stared at me and then squinted, and I worried he suspected me of stealing. "I'm just going now," I said, hurrying to the front door.

"Good luck with the baton twirling," said the woman draped in the shawl.

"Thank you, ma'am," I said, imagining Barbie talking with a southern accent and spouting a few southern expressions. "And I do appreciate your offer—my very favorite."

She threw up her hands. "Another time," she said, smiling broadly and revealing gray, crooked teeth.

"Thank you, ma'am," I said looking straight at her, mimicking the way Barbie had never wavered during the rally where I'd first seen her twirl two batons at once. She'd tossed one behind her back as she twirled the other at her side, all while smiling and drawing us in with her eyes

Being grateful seemed like Barbie—a simple thank you, when inside I radiated success and a million fireworks went off. I'd once heard Mom call Dad a fake for bragging about his desire to parachute from an airplane. For once I didn't identify with the object of her scorn. I was living it up and refused to believe that I'd pay for it with a guilt attack; refused to believe that I'd beg her forgiveness for being a fake, like Dad.

Up ahead, I saw the twinkling sign for Robert The Florist. I froze, worrying that if Barbie's parents saw me, they might not want Barbie associating with me or having me to their house for a sleep over—something I prayed might happen soon. But I couldn't resist the chance to find out more about the family and the business. I walked to the display window, which was trimmed in twinkling lights, and admired an elaborate arrangement of birdhouses and tree branches with pots of mums balanced here and there. Then a woman who reminded me of Mrs. Broadback with a white corsage pinned to her jacket held the door open for me. "Thank you," I said with eager eyes that I imagined looked like Barbie's.

"Can I help you? If you're looking for the green and white boutonnieres, they're in the case at the back."

I nodded at a woman in a white coat and headed towards the back of the store.

"Hello, Miss—did you order one?" A slim man hurried over. "I'm getting more in this afternoon but as of now, we have not a single extra," he shook his head and pointed at a glass fridge full of square white boxes.

I stood tall like Barbie and broadened my smile. "I forgot to order one, actually—but I could come back."

"Well, that's great, let's say, three o'clock?" He looked at the clock over the register. "Yeah, I'd say that's a safe bet. The dance is at eight, right?"

"Oh yes!" I nodded. "Thank you so much—I'll be back at three!" I said in Barbie's clear voice.

"Why don't you leave your name—just in case. I don't want to accidentally sell it to someone else," he said, grabbing a pad and pen from the counter.

"Barbie," I said.

"Nice name—it's my niece's name," he said, scribbling. I smiled again and lingered, hoping he'd say more about Barbie and her family. Instead, he hurried outside.

"Can I help you with anything else?" the woman in the white coat asked.

"Oh, no, but thank you so much."

She smiled and nodded at the door. Outside, Barbie's uncle unloaded boxes from a truck with a big tulip painted on one side. "Well look, if you can't pay this time—I don't feel like delivering this load. Where's Jim?" The truck driver had one foot on the back of the truck while Barbie's uncle looked helplessly at the door as the woman emerged. "Jim's nowhere to be found and I'm sick of covering for him and, let's face it, his drinking."

"Irene!" Barbie's uncle bugged his eyes and threw his hands up. Then he turned to the driver. "Look, we'll get it for you—I'm gonna run to the bank—can you wait five minutes?" The truck driver smirked.

"Have you given me a choice? But I can tell you—this is it. I've got a delivery in Hazlett, and they pay, and I don't like to wait." Barbie's uncle ran inside and came out with a big folder with People's Bank written on the front.

"I'll be right back," he said, looking sideways at me as I hesitated for a moment, pretending to wait for a break in the traffic. But instead of taking off, he seemed to wait for me to safely cross Grand River.

"Looks good," he said, and nodded for me to cross. I smiled and waved before crossing Grand River and hurrying to an entrance to MSU.

"Thank you!" I called from the other side, but he was already running to the bank. I walked through the gate into the campus, my mind scrambling to believe that anyone related to Barbie Robert—let alone her father—could be in trouble or maybe even be a drunk.

CHAPTER VII

Through the gigantic spruces, I recognized the Student Union. Back in the old days, Dad and I went to the union every Sunday. Saturdays, we headed to his bookie in Lansing; Sundays, the dingy newsstand tucked behind the boiler in the union's basement. I knew the first floor to be warm and cozy with lounges full of big leather chairs and fireplaces. But something held me back, like I might forget Barbie if I went inside and hung out. I might sink into a past and stay there.

Up ahead, I watched a boy tug on the heavy wooden door and remembered getting whacked when I failed to scoot through after Dad yanked on it in a fury. "What's wrong? Can't keep up?" he'd say, and now the words resounded in my ears. I'd race after him along the polished floors and down the wide stairs to the filthy newsstand. Once there, I'd check out the cover of dirty magazines while pretending to help Dad scour the New York tabloids for good headlines. "Good headlines are tough to come by," he'd say, and I'd nod, only half listening but grateful that he encapsulated the truth—any truth—for me. Maybe I'd forgotten to nod at all his ideas, and that's why he dumped me.

I was about to turn away, my heart sinking as I heard in my brain the newsstand owner telling Dad how lucky he was to have a daughter like me, when a girl—at first glance, a clone of Barbie—hurried up the steps. She clutched books to her chest and wore a pink sweater around her shoulders. Without thinking I followed her, imitating her light steps and her ultra-straight backbone. Her hair shone in the light, and I examined its unusual shape, puffy on top and flipped up at the ends. A hairdo everyone recognized but this girl had somehow made it distinctive. If only Mom knew how to cut hair, I could draw this style and we could figure it out together. She'd do that for me, and for a moment my stomach twisted, picturing her hair disheveled and hanging in clumps as she brought Dad one water glass after the next, all day every day. Of course, if I mentioned anything about this weird illness, she'd let me know I knew nothing of life, and then her eyes would narrow like I blamed her for this illness and for everything wrong in our lives. I wondered if psychologists had a name for *fear of being implicated.*

This girl in the pink sweater stopped on the top step to adjust her shoulder bag and I slowly climbed the stairs, staring as she smoothed her hair and arranged her books. At school and in packs, girls like this prevented each other from staking out territory. But here against the grey stone, the girl stood out, reminding me of Mrs. Broadback although without the burden of Danny and a station wagon and of course a big house. Maybe this girl would be a stewardess for a few years before becoming a woman like Mrs. Broadback. I wished I could jump ahead many years and acquire Mrs. Broadback's life, no matter that Mom would scoff at its trivial preoccupations. Dad would think it beneath him and lacking in grandiosity, but did either of them have Stephen to deal with? Did either of them have the pressure to be someone or die?

Once inside the union I held back as the girl scanned the lounge. She chose one of the large leather chairs, and although most of the chairs scattered around the wood paneled room were empty, I sat in the chair closest to her, hoping she didn't think it weird since other students seemed to be avoiding each other—holed up reading and writing in seclusion. When she dropped a pencil, I scooped it up. "Oh, thank you," she said.

"I forgot all my things, but my friend is bringing me my books," I said, twirling the ends of my hair.

"I've got a big test that I'm totally unprepared for," she said. I nodded the way I thought Barbie would nod about how hard it was to keep up with studying. "I wish I'd never taken Bio, but my folks were totally against me taking a gut," the girl said as she tucked her hair behind her ears. She seemed in no hurry to open her books, so I nodded again, encouraging her to keep going. "And I hate the labs," she said, laughing. "They're all so early—God!"

I laughed, too, wishing that I could help her, but Barbie wouldn't offer to help with homework. "You look familiar. Don't you live in Mason?" She asked, plopping her books on the floor next to her navy-blue flats. I nodded and smiled, like she had a surprisingly good memory.

"Where do you live?" I asked, sure that Barbie would ask about details like this, and of course Dad would have. I straightened and smiled at the thought that I'd assumed Dad's position as the interviewer, inserting myself into people's lives. For a moment, I imagined Dad and Mom peering out the window of a plane as it crashed. A sign that they didn't deserve a life—only people who can function, like this girl and her parents, warranted time on earth.

She continued to smile at me, and I imagined telling her about their deaths, her taking my hand as we walked to her dorm, where I'd live with her, the two of us connected like Siamese twins. Then I pictured Stephen searching for a bigger than normal plastic bag in his kitchen. *Find it, find it,* I said like I hovered somewhere in the kitchen, and then my face heated up and my heart pumped like crazy. Barbie would never want a plane to crash or a kid like Stephen to kill himself. She'd ask polite questions because she has good manners, not because she has an ulterior motive. The word *subterfuge* had been on the vocab test and I had left it blank, even though I knew the definition and couldn't get the word out of my head. Once I became Barbie, I'd ask questions just to be sweet and polite.

"I got Brody—it's not great, so I'm looking off campus for next year, but my folks are dead set against it. They're the protective types."

Wonderful, I thought, staring at her nails—identical to the student teacher's pink curved fingernails. Everything about her, including her parents, made sense, I thought.

"So are mine," I said, rolling my eyes as I tucked my nails up under my cuff. She shook her head and smiled, like we were lucky to have parents who loved us so much, even if they were annoying. I noticed that my breathing was now barely noticeable, and I eased myself into the big chair, letting it swallow me up as I wondered if I was actually seeping into this girl's body instead of Barbie's—sort of a practice run.

"Well, I have to go to class and find out where my friend is with my books." I laughed, and she laughed too. I imagined myself laughing in the mirror, practicing different happy faces.

Sometimes when Dad was out of the house and Mom in the basement, I stood in front of the mirror in the upstairs bathroom and painted my lips with a tube of lipstick Kathy Scott's sister had given me. A couple times, I tried rearranging my hair—wadding the long thin strands into something resembling a top knot or a bun, but everything about me looked idiosyncratic, as if I'd never fit into one of the patterns, the models of viable people I saw every day. I'd stare at my face in the mirror, entering a trance, and like a word said again and again metamorphosizing into a meaningless chunk of sound, my face blurred so that I wasn't sure it was mine. Quickly panicking at the thought of wandering the earth alone and unidentifiable, I yanked on the nest of tangles and washed off the lipstick.

"Hope we catch up again—I have a good friend from Eight Mile Road who lives in Mason. We're on the new synchronized swim team, so you might have seen her at dinner with wet hair," she laughed. "We have a meet next week—try to come." I nodded and waved, just like I was sure Barbie would. For a moment as I pushed on the heavy oak door, I had an overwhelming urge to run back and hug this girl. Thank her for talking to me and for letting me practice being someone so much like Barbie. Emotions must've gotten the best of me because as I stood on the wide granite step outside the Union, I felt happier than the day it was announced that I scored in the top five percent of a nation-wide science test. Faces rushed past me: Patty Scott, Dad, Mom—people who'd never recognize me again.

I wished I had some books to hug and a sweater to tie around my shoulders. Outside, students streamed towards me—girls with long blond hair and boys holding books on their narrow hips. It was as if the dorms had been turned upside down. I wove in between guys and girls, some alone and some in small groups, and while I laced my way deeper into the lush green campus, I could feel Barbie fading and some version of me welling up. I kept my eyes down, avoiding all the bright eyes and smiles of students, who would expect the truth—no one wants a fake unless the fake is so perfect it seems real, and I knew I could ultimately conjure a perfect new me and one I bet they'd like, but I needed more time. Time to make so complete a transformation--slough off the taint of a former life--so that no one could expose me as a fraud. I had to make everyone believe that I was now a simple, single version of someone else. I walked fast towards a bench ahead, nestled in a trio of spruce trees where I could disappear. But when I finally got to the bench, I was terrified that I'd never get the real me back if I needed her or, I guess, missed her. I calmed down once I sat on the cold stone and began to concentrate on Barbie and the stream of baby Box Elder bugs with their bright red backs parading near my feet. Transfixed by the bugs, I decided to stay put until I couldn't, until something in my brain told me why I was skipping school and watching a line of bugs. I wondered if I should learn something from them about who I am as a person and who they are and if Stephen, like them, had no choice in killing himself, the same way their destiny was obviously to get around my feet because the tree they now circled was on the other side of my feet and they had no choice but to circle it.

A gardener dug a hole near the bugs, and I worried he might ask me to move. "Thank you," I said for no reason, standing and crushing a bug that had been separated from the group. Ducking under a low branch, I entered a garden that stretched along one side of the road. I imagined the gardener yelling at me as I stepped over a bed of flowers and ripped up some ivy. But like following the car along Michigan Avenue instead of walking to school, I was unsure what I was doing or why.

Deeper into the woodsy area to my left, I saw denim bell bottoms grazing the top of brown moccasins that were decorated in tiny blue beads. Then I heard a voice and without thinking pulled back a branch of an old shaggy spruce tree. A girl with a halo of curly brown hair spoke urgently to a boy who sat cross-legged on the ground smoking. He smiled and waved at me. The girl smiled, encouraging me to join them, while she talked about something they were organizing.

"You know historically America's been opposed to Colonialism," the boy said.

"We could definitely talk about that at the rally," the girl scribbled in a notebook.

"This reminds me so much of everything Professor Graf's talking about. We're becoming the next Roman Empire—consuming cultures and assuming that a colonial power knows best. Let's put that on the poster!"

The girl smiled and pointed her pen at me. "Are you Karen's friend? The one who makes posters?"

I shook my head, forcing out the truth instead of a lie just to keep the conversation going.

She squinted at me. "Well hi anyway," she said. The boy lit another cigarette and then reached one up to her. "Do you want to smoke?"

She shook her head and then he offered the cigarette to me. I took it, and he jumped up striking a match against his boot. After wasting two matches he chuckled.

"You have to inhale," he said, striking his last match. I nodded, breathing hard and then spastically coughed as the hot smoke filled my lungs. The boy raised his eyebrows. "You OK?"

I nodded, suppressing another cough, and we smoked together—me mainly faking it as I imitated his slow draws. "You've got to read this," the boy said waving a thick paperback above his head. "*Catch-22* by Joseph Heller. The guy says it so perfectly about the absurdity of war."

The girl nodded, her gold hoop earrings glowing in the sunlight that streamed through the tall trees before gathering itself into a small circle where the three of us stood on a thick mat of brown pine needles. She ran her fingers through her mass of curls as she studied something she'd written in her notebook. I thought about giving up on Barbie and joining these two who seemed consumed with ideas they'd learned in classes and books.

"Let's get some food. I'm starved," the boy said, throwing the cigarette onto the ground. I wasn't sure if I should throw mine, too.

"Paul! At least put it out," the girl said as she grabbed her purse, and we headed out to the street through the rows of plants and ivy.

"You can get rid of yours—just stamp it out."

I worried she'd caught on that I didn't smoke as I tried stamping it out, and when it wouldn't stop burning, I ground it out with my heel. *Wait,* I said in my head as she hurried to the Union. I caught up with her, and the two of us followed Paul to the basement cafeteria where she ordered large fries, three cokes, and some garlic bread. Paul paid for everything after she reminded him that she'd paid for their donuts and coffee. We sat together at a long table, and between sips of coke, she wrote slogans in large letters, one on each page of her notebook. My favorite, *Hell No We Won't Go,* reminded me of something Dad would chant in the bathtub, even though I knew he thought the U.S. should bomb Viet Nam into smithereens and get it over with. But he'd love the rhyme and the power of words. I watched the girl concentrate on each slogan while Paul underlined parts of *Catch 22.* I wanted to ask Paul more about the book, but I didn't want to blow my cover by asking something stupid; something any college student would know.

Then, in a flash, I remembered sixth period. It was unrealistic to try to become this girl or a female version of Paul, and I could definitely see Barbie if I left now. I wasn't sure what to say. I scanned their faces as they sipped cokes through straws and devoured the fries—she had a mole above her lip, just like

Patty Scott. When she smiled at me with her mouth full, I remembered Patty and I stuffing our cheeks with marshmallows. We had finished the whole bag and then lit the bag with her Dad's lighter in the backyard. This girl pushed the plate of fries toward me.

"I have a class in an hour—can we meet after that?" I nodded, wondering who she thought I was. Paul said he had to work. Then she pointed at a cut on my thumb. You need a Band-Aid," she said, looking around like there might be a first aid kit somewhere in the big bright cafeteria. For a moment she reminded me of Patty Scott, always acting like my private nurse, and her profile, with the straight nose and upturned chin, was perfectly sculpted like Patty's. As I stared at her while Paul crunched on the garlic bread, I remembered telling Patty one night before we fell asleep that I wished I didn't have to go home in the morning, and she'd looked at me puzzled, but then she told me to roll over and she'd rub my back. The next thing I knew it was morning and she'd made breakfast and brought it to me on a tray.

I knew that I should leave, but a voice inside told me to get the girl's phone number or at least her name. But then she called to a girl whose bell bottoms dragged along the floor and whose long brown hair reached her waist. The friend carried a book with *German* written across the front in black letters, and I remembered that next year I could take German and Latin. For a moment, I imagined the three of us walking together, but I couldn't figure out who I'd be, and I wondered what the friend's name was and what the girl's name was and how they knew each other. The friend said something to the girl from her place in line as she shifted her books, and I realized that I couldn't imagine ever knowing anyone again the way I'd known Patty—except for Barbie, of course, and that would essentially mean knowing myself. The vision came back of the three of us walking, holding books, and I thought that I'd never find a group because everyone else in the group would be the person they'd always been, and they'd feel betrayed and angry if it leaked out that I was a replica of another person. Perhaps as part of this trio I could be the person who looked like me and had been me. The problem was that since I'd been so many other people I'd never been me for long enough to make a real impression.

"Oh my God," I whispered. "There's my science teacher!" I slipped under the table, hitting my head hard. "Can I have my coke?" I said to the girl's knees. She snuck it under the table along with a couple of French fries. "Thanks," I said, balancing on my toes and trying not to topple over.

"Are you in high school?" the girl whispered, her face upside down under the table. I nodded. "How cool that you want to get involved—good luck! What's your name, anyway?"

"Sally," I whispered, listening to the sound of that name and wondering how long it would be before someone saw me hiding under a table. I could see Mr. Benchley's back in his green and white MSU jacket and decided to make a dash for one of the doors.

"Come to the rally, if you can," the girl called after me, and I nodded, turning around for a moment and smiling at Paul, who looked up from *Catch 22* with a blank look on his face like he had no idea where we'd met or who I was.

CHAPTER VIII

No one noticed when I pushed through the school's big glass doors even though I was out of breath and my hair tangled from running. The front hall was packed with boys talking and looking up at a blank TV like the game could start any minute. I heard talk of yesterday's blow-out, the Tigers winning 13–1. "If the Cardinals lose the seventh game, it will be the first time in their whole history that they've lost Game 7," some boy said to a big cheer. "We better hurry," a kid from English said to a boy I sat next to, and I followed them to the English wing.

I slid into my desk just as Mr. Vandervelde announced over the PA that since the game started at 2:07, he'd keep the school open for the whole game—at least till six o'clock—so that no one missed the final innings while driving home. "Those with jobs must leave, unfortunately," he said. "Boys, there will be no sports practice today, and girls, we will have Yearbook and the Typing Club," He finished by reminding everyone about the Pep Rally on Friday.

"I heard you and Steve Gardener in the library yesterday, and I just want to say that my dad is against horse racing. He thinks using an animal for gambling is cruel." A girl, named Anne, looked back at me with hate in her eyes. Once, in fourth grade, she brought her pet rabbit to school. I remembered petting the rabbit pretending to love its soft coat, when in reality the animal's red-rimmed eyes made me uneasy. As I lowered the rabbit into its cage, its sharp claws scratched my skin. "Come to my house after school. You can hold my other rabbits and my guinea pig." I hid my hand behind my back so she couldn't see the pricks of blood and smiled hard, trying not to cry out in pain.

"Sure--okay," I said and hurried to my desk. But then at dismissal I came up with some excuse, and she acted like she'd known all along I wouldn't come and that I didn't like animals. Perhaps now she'd gathered enough evidence to know that I erased myself and stole other people's lives. Normally, I'd freak out at being discovered, but I guess the adventure at MSU erased the worry and anxiety at least for the length of this conversation. Whatever, my brain felt like it had been shot with that numbing stuff—Novocain—the dentist used, and I wondered when it would wear off. She started to turn away but stopped and raised her eyebrows. I laughed.

"What's so funny?" she asked.

I shook my head, picturing her eavesdropping on Steve Gardener and me while I was eavesdropping on the two cool kids. "Nothing. Did you pierce your ears?" I said, speaking without thinking, without weighing any possibility for an *error*—a word I heard Mr. Novak say with mild disgust when talking to Bill Greene about the Tigers' loss in game one. She smoothed her long thin hair behind her ears to show me her reddened earlobes and silver drop earrings.

"I skipped school this morning and met some cool kids at MSU." I waited for her response, excited to hear myself announce that I'd done something she probably thought unlike me.

"Let's hope you don't get in trouble," she said. "What were they like?"

"Cool," I said as everyone around us talked about Kaline, Northrup, and Mickey Lolich. "I can't wait for college. You can be anyone—no one cares. It's a place where you can start over and be anyone," I said. "I mean, be yourself," I said, wishing I hadn't hinted at being other people.

"Don't get your hopes up. We've joined the Quakers because my parents were sick of being herded like sheep at the other churches. My dad always says that most people don't want to think for themselves," she said, staring at me like I should describe my own conformist ways, giving her an opportunity to correct them.

"I met a girl I bet you'd like," I said, half listening to a boy talk about Denny McLain—a player I remember Dad calling a big jerk. My mind flipped from Paul's girlfriend to the synchronized swimming girl, picturing her neat posture and crossed ankles as she sat engulfed in the Union's leather chairs. I worried that I was the first person who'd lied to her—violated her trust. Was I responsible for changing her, destroying her innocence forever? Had I killed some part of her? The Novocain in my brain was beginning to wear off. Before I became consumed with guilt, my mind like a viewfinder switched to a picture of Barbie's uncle as he shook his head, incredulous that Barbie's dad would threaten the business. And then as someone behind me snickered at what I wasn't sure, the idea of living together on the same planet seemed impossible.

Baseball talk filled the classroom, and I begged my brain to absorb it all, perhaps becoming a repository for the game and its vocabulary. I wished I'd never talked to this girl named Anne, someone else who hated my dad (or the Journal) and who continued to stare at me. *Stick to becoming Barbie*, a voice said, and I squeezed shut my eyes praying the voice wasn't Stephen's. He'd see my confusion as an opportunity to get inside my brain again. But instead of waiting for him to pop up, I pictured him dead, and then I pictured myself by him, also dead. *Avoid girls like Anne and everyone except for Barbie and the first girl at the Union if you care about living; if you care at all about having a life in the long run.* "Long run," I whispered under my breath, and laughed at an image of me running for my whole life as if Dad had been right all along to keep moving. Anne smirked at me, and I laughed again just to annoy her.

In English, Miss Knowles stood by the board where she'd written all the lyrics to Jefferson Airplane's *White Rabbit.* She'd brought her own record player and the forty-five. After she played the song, she pointed to lyrics like *sloppy dead* and *Remember what the Dormouse said. Feed your head. Feed your head.* "Surrealism is an important movement in twentieth century art," she said, rewriting some of the words she'd smeared with the side of her hand. She called on a boy I assumed was repeating freshman English because he had sideburns and I'd heard he was actually the father of a baby a girl. He and his girlfriend had flown to Colorado to have the baby and then they gave her up for adoption. "It's two-oh-four now, so by the time we get to the game it will have started, so can we leave like Pinky said?" The boy was half out of his seat, like he was heading to the game whether or not Miss Knowles granted permission. I caught Miss Knowles' eye, raised my eyebrows to complement hers and nodded, impulsively matching my head bob to hers like we'd cast spells on each other, perhaps to exchange lives. Finally, she smiled and pointed to the door.

"Thank you, Miss Knowles. That's one of my favorite songs," I lied as I ran my hand along her desk as most of the class filed out in front of me. She smiled, and her blue eyes deepened. Perhaps she should marry Mr. Novak, I thought, picturing the three of us eating in the new Little Caesar's Pizza while we signed papers for my adoption. Once I grew up, we could talk about history and English all the time. I pictured a triangle, each of us at a point in a strong construction. There was no order to Mom, Dad, and me, just a messy entanglement.

"Maybe you should write some poetry?" Miss Knowles asked like this was just one type of writing I should consider and if I declined she might advise me to write an essay or a play.

I nodded as if I'd considered writing poetry. "I love the sonnet we read," I said, placing my hand on her copy of *Shakespeare's Sonnets for Young Readers.* The boy with the sideburns slid by. I wished I could've asked him if it was true what people said, that the two of them flew to Colorado together to have the baby. Mostly I wanted to know if after the baby was born had he and the girl signed adoption papers alongside a real couple. I pictured the real couple pushing an empty stroller into one of these new restaurants that our econ teacher said was transforming the economy.

"I've written some poetry," I lied, but her eyes registered neither approval nor disapproval, and I retracted the lie, stumbling over my words. "I mean, I did in my head—I wrote some in my head," I said, reducing the lie to something that didn't seem to violate the unwavering beauty of learning.

I hesitated at the language wing, like it was the most important moment in my life so far—the day I'd slip into Barbie. I pictured the girl in the Union and composed myself, smoothing my hair and straightening my collar. But I knew that I looked nothing like Barbie or the girl. My hair clung to my head, and I sensed that my cheekbones, like Mom's, were too high, and my eyes, like Dad's, too far back in my head. Worse was the thought that I'd never figure out Barbie's clothes, and Mom might scoff at the prescriptions for clothes when she wanted everything to spring from her imagination or at least from the images in magazines she got in the mail. The first line of the sonnet, "Shall I compare thee to a summer's day," popped into my head, and for the first time, I thought about memorizing the sonnets—for no reason—except that without knowing it I'd memorized all the theorems in Advanced Geometry and my brain, perhaps my whole body, seemed to love being full of solutions, or, in the case of the sonnets, word puzzles.

"Well, at least someone's here!" Mrs. Bell smiled, and I stopped the minute I realized the classroom was empty except for Mrs. Bell. "Come on in—we can do some translating," she said, waving me to take any seat. "Your choice!" She continued to smile and enthuse, like this was the best day of her teaching career.

"Maybe others will come," I said, not really caring if anyone except Barbie showed up. I looked around at the empty desks, relieved by the certainty that I liked the patterns in Latin and the unscrambling of words into meaning. I waited for my brain to refute this easy truth, scramble my thoughts and conjure some worry that I'd fabricated a love of learning. Before the fear that I couldn't possibly believe in anything, let alone the world of rational thought, blossomed into a full-blown storm of worry and fear, I conjugated a verb I saw on a worksheet, and my heart slowed down.

"Cicero might be too easy for you!" Mrs. Bell laughed as she opened a book, and I laughed too. After we translated some Cicero, Mrs. Bell waved her hand toward the door and pushed her wide body to standing. "Go join the others—this isn't fair to you."

"I almost wish I lived back then," I said. Mrs. Bell looked surprised. "I guess building the society allowed people like

Cicero to, I don't know, believe in who he actually was or what he thought was right."

"But let's not forget he lost his head for denouncing tyranny." She raised her eyebrows, and I thought of Stephen Fedkin's head encased in plastic and Cicero's rolling around.

"I know, but he wasn't afraid of his own life. He didn't want to just give it away," I said as she stared at the blackboard.

"True, he had convictions," she said and then looked at me. "Do you Sally?"

The room began to move slowly, like a ride at the carnival but in slow motion. Even the blackboard seemed to slide by. I put my head down as dizziness consumed me. "I hope I don't throw up," I murmured.

"Oh, c'mon now! It's an important question but don't fret," she said, rubbing my back. I hoped she'd let her hand drop, and when she didn't, I straightened, and the room was still. "Just something to think about," she said as we quickly translated a sentence before she said we were done for the day.

The new commons, with the bright green carpeting and a few benches for, as Pinky said, *appropriate* congregating, was full of kids by the time I arrived. Mr. Hiddema, the tall, slim basketball coach and Driver's Ed. teacher, roamed the wide-open area, motioning those sitting on the carpet to push back to the walls, and telling a senior to stop lounging on her boyfriend's lap.

The game had started, and except for a few boys with long hair and bandannas and some girls with wire rimmed glasses and bell bottoms who talked amongst themselves, everyone stared at the televisions. Someone said it was a scoreless game. I took in their vocabulary, echoing words I liked or that made sense to me. I felt an arm touch my arm before a spindly boy unconsciously moved further away, like my arm was a tree branch he'd bumped into. When the seventh inning got under way, my knees locked, and I took a deep breath. The clock said almost five.

A scoreless game drained the room of energy, and for a moment I hoped something cataclysmic would happen, even a loss. I looked for an empty bench, but the boys surrounding me moved closer to the middle, pushing our group towards the TV. Finally, one boy shouted, "Yes!" Along with everyone in the room, I watched a ball sail far and high. There wasn't a sound, and I shut my eyes for a moment, fearing that if I watched any longer, the ball would fall into someone's mitt, and we'd be back to a scoreless game. As the moment before the ball landed stretched on and on, I closed my eyes again and pictured an empty world, possibly the day after someone accidentally pushed the nuclear button we'd learned about in some assembly. Balls of weeds and trash rolled down Michigan Avenue instead of cars, and our house had collapsed. But the crowd, screaming, brought me back to the game, and I opened my eyes and began to yell with everyone else. I screamed louder than I thought possible because, I realized, we were all still here, the school was intact, and the Tigers were on base. I smiled at the boy next to me and then turned completely around, relieved to see that no one had left. The entire school, it seemed, would stay, especially now that it looked like we might win.

"Tigers, Tigers!" A few kids I thought were probably in the choir sang in harmony, and I wished I could sing like these girls and Beth. But most of all, I wished I'd see Barbie.

"A triple!" A boy with red cheeks turned to me. "Can you believe it? Flood blew it!" I stared into his eyes, wondering if he saw me, but then he put his hand on my shoulder, and I knew that he was talking to me.

"Incredible!" I shouted. "Incredible!" I said it a bunch of times as two runs came in. Then I saw Mr. Vandervelde with his arms folded over his wide chest. Next to him were the secretaries and Mr. Freds, all of them cheering. Even a girl with a peace sign on her shirt and a sign on her notebook that said *STOP THE WAR NOW* was jumping and hooting. I'd heard her in the cafeteria tell a table of kids, who also wore the new hippie clothes and dangly necklaces made from beads, that she'd never watch baseball as long as we were still in Viet Nam. Someone in front of me screamed something about Mickey Lolich, and the new Commons shook with cheers.

Once the seventh inning ended—after Freehan hit a double and Northrup scored—the Commons quieted down. "Flood slipped," a boy on the edge of our group said as he faked running forward with a mitt in the air and then backwards, slipping to the carpet. "My dad hates Curt Flood," I heard a boy from art say, and then the TV was full of Curt Flood's dispassionate face, and I looked around for the one black boy in the school, hoping he didn't think he was our own Curt Flood. If only, I wished, Curt Flood could redo the play and not goof up—not slip or misjudge the ball, not humiliate himself, but somehow, we could still score the two runs off Northrup's big hit. I knew if I mentioned this impossibility to the boy next to me, he'd scoff. I wondered what Barbie would think. I worried she might not care about Curt Flood, and her dad might hate him too. Could I convincingly become Barbie if she didn't notice the black kid wandering the halls alone? Then I wondered if Dad had gotten on the plane.

I stared at the black and white diamond and at the Detroit players in the dugout smacking Jim Northrup on the back. For the first time, I thought the game more than a boring endurance test. The clean lines on each side of the diamond and the flurry of motion preceded by a foreboding tension drew me in, and I wished I could comment on the game's beauty. The diamond reminded me of a painting the art teacher had shown us as an example of abstract art. "Almost over," I said, racking my brain for something to add to the off-hand remarks circulating the Commons as we waited for the whole thing to end.

"Yeah," the boy who'd touched my shoulder said, talking to the screen. "Yeah," he said again, his voice trailing off like the evaporating innings and the series itself.

I had a huge desire to confide to this boy that I wished we could live indefinitely in the Commons, surrounded by the flickering light of the TV sets and the announcer's voice giving us a blow by blow. This little world could be the end for us— East Lansing obliterated—but he and I and perhaps others living for games and this man's wonderful knowing voice and an enclosed world in which my brain took flight.

The boy's hand dangled near mine and sweat dripped down the sides of my ribcage as I imagined impulsively grabbing it and begging him to stay put and start a commune with me, but not like the one we'd read about in *Animal Farm*. Watching the game in a crowd, at school, reminded me of the day Mrs. Scott drove us to Lake Michigan and how much I didn't want the day to end, and how good I'd gotten at creating brand new worlds for myself out of a single experience. After the trip home, when we came to the sign saying: *Welcome to East Lansing Home of the Spartans*, I'd wanted to go back to the endless lake, and the waves, and Patty and I bouncing on our rafts, and at the very least, I wanted the trip to keep going, with Patty snoring and me and Mrs. Scott talking about building their new house in Whitehills and the trouble she was having finding fixtures she liked.

It was late, the light fading as big groups streamed from the school in a quiet daze, like we didn't yet fully believe that it was 1968 and we'd destroyed the champion Cardinals and their star pitcher Bill Gibbons. Everyone flew from the parking lot in waiting cars as I wove between the plumes of exhaust, wishing that I had somewhere to go before I learned if Dad made it to the game. I'd like to sit in the big chair in the Student Union and relive the day, cutting out the scene at Robert The Florist. I'd worked my whole life to become someone else, and I wouldn't let Barbie's dad spoil what I couldn't let go of. I'd become Barbie hell or high water, as Mom said. Then, feeling confident, I brushed Barbie aside and her nice uncle to relive the Cicero translation and the geometry of baseball and the words of the girl at MSU who talked about ancient Rome.

CHAPTER IX

"Thank heavens I found you!" Mrs. Broadback called out the driver's window. "When it rains it pours, I swear." She lifted her hands off the steering wheel and widened her eyes like she'd run out of patience with the world's idiocies or at least those she confronted in East Lansing. "Get in, get in—that is if you're free?" I nodded, and she let out a big sigh before chuckling. I copied her, giggling and sighing as I ran around the car, pleading with the clouds, the trees, even the cement and curb to admit that I belonged to Mrs. Broadback and her car.

Danny made a face at me through his window, and I made the same face back. He toppled over in hysterics as I slid into the front seat. Mrs. Broadback smiled, tilting her head my way as Danny draped himself over the front seat and twirled my hair around his fingers. Desperate to move closer to Mrs. Broadback, the way I'd nestle into Dad back in the old days, I quickly leaned against the door and pinned my arms to my sides. I pictured Mrs. Broadback's surprised face as I tossed my arms around her and squeezed, the way people on TV hug and sometimes kiss.

"Dick has no idea how crazy some of his ideas are. He called to tell me we're going out with a big wig from the Detroit office—a post-World Series party, and of course he doesn't think about the details—like what am I wearing?" I nodded as Danny yelled out the window at two older kids teetering on a curb. "Danny—cut it out," Mrs. Broadback said, checking on him in the mirror.

A truck cut her off on Grand River squeezing us into the turning lane. "What else can happen?" She honked and shook her head. I shook mine, copying her over and over until Danny asked why I was shaking my head. Mrs. Broadback raised an eyebrow like she wanted to know too. I could hardly breath. My shoulders rose and my heart pounded in my ears while I waited for her to accuse me of tricking her into believing I was actually the Sally she knew or thought she knew.

But then she rolled her eyes. "Men are just such dopes," she whispered.

"That's exactly what my mom says," I lied, immediately wishing I hadn't mentioned Mom, not wanting Mrs. Broadback to think that my allegiance to Mom was greater than my attachment to her. Luckily, she didn't seem to hear as she repeated that men could be very dumb. *Please adopt me*, I said silently, picturing the two of us as a team—like Dad and me in the old days.

Then Stephen's face popped up over the windshield, and I knew that he thought I was moving on, forgetting him or at least trying to get out of killing myself. *She's just a mom. Besides, we'll be partners,* he said in my ear.

"I just have to get to this hair appointment—she's sneaking me in. I don't even have time to go home first. Can you and Danny play at Valley Court Park?" Before she dropped us at the park, she remembered a bag of clothes. "I didn't know if you'd like these things, but Dick says they're all too young for me."

I widened my eyes and smiled at the bag while inside I pictured it stashed in the basement, waiting for Barbie to marry one day and move to a brick house in Glencarin. "Thanks so much! I can stay tonight," I said as Danny hopped at my side like a pogo stick.

"Thanks, but Dick got his mother—at least he thought of that," she said, lighting a cigarette. "I'll be back in, oh, I don't know—here, take this in case the ice cream truck shows up."

Danny ran off, and I hurried after him, gripping the dollar bill in one hand and the bag of clothes in the other. A kid on a bike whizzed by, and I dropped the bag of clothes. The last thing I wanted was someone from school to see me at Valley Court with a bag of Mrs. Broadback's clothes. *Why do you care? Everyone's oblivious.* Stephen's voice piped up, and his crazy grin flashed across the blue sky as I watched Danny fly down a slide at one end of the park and then throw a handful of sand over his head. *But I'm preparing to be Barbie.* I said, looking for Stephen's face obscured at times by the clouds skirting across the sky.

You better hurry, he laughed.

"Be careful, Danny!" I screamed as he climbed up the slide backwards. Standing at the top, he waved a stick above his head, and I imagined Barbie and I each hoisting a baton above our heads, walking through the crowded hallways with kids parting to let us pass. She was after all, somewhat famous, at least during football season. "Watch me!" Danny yelled as he slid down feet first on his stomach, still clutching the stick.

For a moment I worried about all the details. Without a lot of thought and preparation I'd never get Barbie down; never transform myself into the *ideal* we learned about during a kid's report on Plato in Civics. I picked up the bag, scanning the park for a place to stash it. The bag's handles dug into my palm, and my arm ached like Mrs. Broadback had filled the white bag with bricks. I pictured dumping out the clothes and filling it with everything I needed to become Barbie—getting her down in a split second. In the back of my mind I knew not to rush, having ruined my chances of becoming this girl who rode horses out in the country by cutting out two right legs from the fabric Mom bought specially to match her riding pants. I'd been frantic to be her right away—almost as if I knew she would fall off her horse and be home in bed for the rest of the year with a fractured skull.

Mom pardoned me like she always did when I ruined something I attempted to make from scratch. Even so, I wouldn't make the mistake again. I'd get Mom to make Barbie's whole wardrobe. Plus, I considered taking a baton twirling lesson—somehow. Then, as I pictured myself tossing a baton, watching it sail, I sensed a hollowness starting in my stomach, urging me on, filling me with a sense of urgency as if suicide was chasing me, and I nodded at the sky where Stephen's face used to be.

"Danny!" I yelled, taking off for the far end of the park, the bag bouncing off my legs. "Danny!" I got to him, panting. "Do you want to get a donut or something at the Rexall?"

"Nah," he said, throwing sand at my knees.

"What about candy?" He nodded, and I hid the bag of clothes under the Merry Go Round.

"Those are from my mom," Danny said, his voice low.

"They're cool, but they don't allow big bags in stores," I said, squeezing his hand as we ran across the street and through the parking lot.

We smelled flowers the minute we stepped inside.

"What about candy?" Danny complained.

"We'll get it—I promise—after I get something."

"That's not what you said," Danny pouted. I hushed him so that I could hear whispering coming from the cash register.

"We have a reputation to maintain, and I don't want to be one of the rats—you know they're the last to leave a sinking ship," the woman from the morning kept her voice low.

"Deliveries have to be paid," Barbie's uncle said with a note of disbelief in his voice, and the woman reminded him that two deliveries were coming in the next morning. "Dad never would've put up with this," he said. "But damn it, he didn't have a drunk on his hands." The woman pressed her finger to her lips, pointing to Danny and me, and I wondered if this was what they talked about all day long. "Well look who's back! And boy oh boy, do we have Boutonnieres," he said, wiping sweat from his upper lip.

"Sorry I'm a bit late picking it up." I handed the woman the dollar Mrs. Broadback gave me as I took the box from Barbie's uncle.

"You need a quarter, Miss," she said, looking over my head at Barbie's uncle.

"That's all I have."

"And she's buying me candy," Danny smiled.

The woman pulled two lollipops from the pocket in her apron. Would this do?"

"Bring the quarter another day," Barbie's uncle said, waving a hand.

"Thanks so much. My uncle owns a florist shop in Detroit. It's tough for him dealing with my other uncle who well—has problems." I blurted the lie as fast as I could, picturing Dad, pad in hand, getting the inside scoop through little white lies he said were the trick of the trade. Barbie's uncle's face reddened, and I backed up still holding Danny's hand.

"Do you need anything else?" The woman turned sharply and stared at me behind her sparkly glasses. I shook my head, imagining Dad's big smile and a pat on my shoulder.

Back at Valley Court, I hid in the shadows, staring at the dyed green and white carnation while I imagined being at the dance with the girl from the Union and our dates. But my mind drifted to Barbie's father and her life or, really, my future life that seemed to sink before my eyes like the deep creases in her uncle's face. My heart sped up, and against the cool air my cheeks flamed, and my tongue felt big and dry. Stephen's warning, that time was running out and I'd join him, tortured me, and I refused to look at the sky, keeping my eyes on the dirt and sand. I suddenly couldn't imagine starting over with a new girl and a new family if Barbie's was on the verge of collapse. *He's right,* I said to myself. Time was running out the way it had for Stephen. I needed Barbie to be perfect. Maybe another uncle drank too much. Not her father but someone Barbie hardly knew. I looked up at a ball arcing above my head like an arrow without a target. Luckily a kid caught the ball, and my heart stopped pounding as I told myself that I needed to get to Barbie's house right away.

Everything got a lot worse when Danny crawled around the Merry Go Around and announced that the bag of clothes was gone.

"It will show up," I lied as I brushed sand off his shirt.

"Where's the bag?" Mrs. Broadback said when she arrived looking puzzled. My face heated up.

"Someone stole it from under the Merry Go Round," Danny said.

"I'm so sorry—I was about to search for it." She squinted at the white box in my hand. "You don't have to pay me for at least a year," I said, wishing I'd hid the Boutonniere.

"Don't be silly! It's just that there were some nice things, but I don't know if you'd wear the stuff anyway." She smiled and shrugged as if nothing had happened and I'd never hear about it again.

The car pulled away with Danny waving out the back window. I waved back as I silently begged them not to leave before I'd persuaded her that I hadn't deliberately lost the bag.

I felt like running after the car and begging her to believe some story I'd make up. She might harbor anger like Mom. In fact, I thought, she might be writing me off at this very moment. *She is writing you off,* Stephen said, and I looked at him in the sky, but like Mrs. Broadback and Danny he disappeared.

I couldn't wait to get home and hide under my covers, where I'd watch Mrs. Broadback smile and shrug for what I hoped would be the rest of my life. Could it be possible, I wondered, to lead a life full of moments that connect to nothing but each other or nothing at all, like the leaf wafting lower and lower before my eyes. I frantically tried to grab it, but instead the red and brown leaf slipped through my hands. I stared at its jagged edges resting on the flow of gray cement reminding me of the sharp edges of broken glass in a stream of milk rolling across the kitchen table. This had been the usual, Mom connecting the disconnected. *You're just like everyone in this hateful town spiting me.* And that was just after we'd cleaned up spilled milk like friends, but when I handed her the sponge after carefully wringing out milk in a silver bowl she grabbed it, cocked her arm back, and threw it as if she was an outfielder. It went nowhere, floating before our eyes like a failed attempt to reach home plate. In a rage she whisked the metal bowl of milk to the floor. I ground the leaf and winced as the clanging bowl resonated deep in my brain.

I found myself at the gas station near our house on Michigan Avenue, not remembering how I got there. Gasoline fumes cleared my head as did a roaring car limping before collapsing in front of a mechanic who signaled the driver to turn off the engine. Inside the small office I scanned the rows of candy. "That's a nickel," the gas station owner said, pushing a box of Dots across the greasy counter. I grazed his dirty fingernails, praying the contact proved I hadn't begun to slip away. "You're Louis' girl—where's the old man been? Monday night poker hasn't been the same without him," he said, smiling as he raised his thick black eyebrows. I searched for an answer, staring at the silver cap on his front tooth. Finally, as I pictured Dad in bed, moaning and tossing fitfully in a weird sleep, and Mom, hovered over him, calling his condition a normal fit of nerves; I told the guy that Dad was away on an assignment having to do with his column on horse racing. "He is, is he? Well, here, take another box of candy on us—your Dad always said you loved a box of Milk Duds. Sometimes he took a box or two as a payoff!"

"Thank you," I whispered, pretending to be shy like the girl in homeroom who could barely speak above a whisper. Back outside, the cool air hit my cheeks and above the noise of the traffic I could hear Dad in my head effortlessly making up a story about the Milk Duds and his demure daughter's preference for the hard candies. Lying for Dad was normal, and he was much better than me at convincing people of any version of the truth he made up. Maybe this had to do with a thing called the learning curve a girl told the Psychology teacher about. "My Dad's a psychology professor," she'd said, and I wished I could go home with her and learn all about whatever he knew—the objective truths she said he lectured about over dinner.

I chewed noisily because I knew it would aggravate Dad and for once I didn't have to worry about what would and wouldn't drive him crazy. If Beth was still around, I'd give her the Milk Duds; she's the one who loves Milk Duds. Across the wide highway, I noticed two students holding hands. The girl's dark brown hair curled under in a pageboy, and her straight blunt cut bangs reminded me of Beth. If only Beth were gone, I could envision my room void of any memory. Maybe Beth had been whisked away—this happened sometimes. Even though Mom had reported with certainty that Beth would be with us for just a few days, like the on again, off again completely unpredictable situation she'd gotten our family into had naturally straightened itself out. But I knew better. You couldn't trust her mom, Empress Martin, with a loaf of bread, let alone a kid. "Just a few days," Mom said, beaming like now that some kind of order had supposedly been established she could revel in her impression that Empress had been sent to her from heaven—the heaven of people who needed her.

Mom and Dad should've discussed their versions of heaven before they got married, I thought as I stashed the Boutonnière in a garbage can by the side of the gas station. But the only picture I'd seen of their wedding day showed the two of them a foot apart in their best clothes, squinting in the sun. I'd hid the picture under a cushion when I' realized Mom had a crush on our neighbor, Mr. Craft. Once she began to hate Mr. Craft, I brought it out again.

I pushed the door to the back porch and saw that everything was the same—even the dustballs in the corner were stuck. But I'd been to MSU alone, the Rexall, and Robert The Florist—part of me had already left, and no one knew about the creation of my new life. I'd step into it and never look back. For a moment, I wished that Danny was at my side—he'd notice the tiles hanging here and there from the ceiling. I wished that someone like the girl at the Union could open the door to the kitchen and lead the way, verify that everything about this place was off kilter—perhaps uninhabitable. Then it dawned on me, as I inched my way across the porch, that I should consider running away. Hadn't Beth found a new family by taking off on her trike, turning onto our driveway like it was a cul-de-sac off an old beat up highway? It was her bad luck to wind up with our family, but I'd do better, maybe team up with the skinny teenager in a black suit who went door-to-door advertising bomb shelters and talking about the evil ruler

Khrushchev. Running away might vanquish Stephen forever. *This is the last time you'll turn this knob,* I said silently, loving the way tears immediately pressed against my closed eyelids.

CHAPTER X

Inside the kitchen, Mom said something I couldn't hear, and Dad sat at the kitchen table, staring straight ahead in his pajamas, saying nothing. Then she tried a tactic of enthusiasm. "I don't care that the game is over! Get dressed and let's go somewhere. Anywhere!"

"You didn't go?" I said. "You missed the game?"

"And here you are, Sally—Miss Know It All," Mom said switching. "I'm stuck here. Do you realize that?" Dad's chin fell. He wanted to go to bed. I bet Mom forced him downstairs, hoping against hope that she could get him in the car. There were pots and pans scattered on the floor like she'd spent the day cleaning the cupboard and hadn't gotten around to putting everything back, but I knew she'd thrown them in a rage.

"Why don't you just go wherever it would be better for you?" I said, thinking hard for something that might go straight to her heart. "You obviously hate us, and we don't need you, either," I said, twisting the ends of my hair. I hesitated, afraid I'd said something irrevocable—like what Mr. Freds had said to Stephen Fedkin. We stared at each other as I backed up, and Dad put his hand on Mom's arm like he didn't want her wasting her energy on me when he needed help getting back upstairs.

"Have a piece of bread," she said, giving up. I took a thick yeasty slice she'd cut. She stared past me clutching a bread knife with the blade pointed to the ceiling. The mystery of when and why the world turned on her haunted me. For as long as I could remember, I'd imagine Mom as I flew to the sky on the swing at recess, emerging from a cloud sometimes as a spear carrying warrior, streaked in war paint and other times dead by her own hand, drowning in our tub. No note, of course; she was elusive to the end

"Thanks," I said, heading to the backyard, where I sat on the rope swing and tossed wads of bread to the Martins that I sometimes fed. Soon two of the black birds landed near my feet, piercing the bread with their pointed beaks. They looked like the black birds tearing at some strange animal's flesh in the painting Miss Silver brought into art. *"The Garden of the Earthly Delights* influenced the Surrealists," she said, and the more she pointed at and lingered over all the horrid images, the more I saw Mom everywhere in the panels, saying surreal things—confusing things—and her vivid words had no trouble penetrating my brain, where I knew they'd die a fake-out death, turning my mind into a graveyard of her weird thoughts and stupid ideas that somehow morphed into terrifying nightmares as if she had the power to turn my head into a haunted house, which, unfortunately, she did.

Mrs. Broadback keeps her mind on the day at hand, I thought, fearing that if she read my mind she'd never ask me to babysit again if only because she'd find Mom's terrifying associations and, I guess, mine too, inscrutable or at least unrecognizable. As Barbie, I'd eventually become Mrs. Broadback or practically her twin, and part of me wished I could skip over Barbie and transform straight into Mrs. Broadback. If only I could move into one of her guest rooms with the soft bedspreads and the big pillows.

"She loves you, yeah, yeah, yeah," I sang as a brain blotting method. Then, ignoring the raindrops landing on my nose and bare arms, I hummed the melody while I tried to forget that Dad had just missed the most important event I could possibly think of, aside from the assassination of President Kennedy. That was back in fourth grade. The World Series was now.

The birds flew away with bits of bread hanging from their beaks, and I crab-walked the old swing through dirt and ant holes, my brain conjuring a picture of Khrushchev shaking his fist at America, and I shuddered—my whole body suddenly heating up, remembering the day I saw his contorting face on TV. "Help, Help," I whispered, realizing that I might have no one to turn to once this evil Russian began burying people like me alive. *Help, Help,* I yelled, without moving my lips. Luckily and thankfully, my brain filled itself with the letters H-E-L-P, wiping out the Russian leader with his bald bullet head, and Mom, and Kennedy, and Oswald recoiling the moment he was shot by the other man I had seen on TV one day as I searched the three channels for cartoons.

I heard the back door bang a few times like gun fire, and I seized up, dreading Mom's arrival at the swing, standing tall above me, offering a present she'd made with her own two hands. "And you know you should be glad," I sang, hoping she'd think me oblivious to her crazy outbursts or at least unable to produce a knee jerk response, unlike the snarling dog on Cowley someone told me had been kicked and beaten by a former owner. Singing would surely trick her into seeing me as a light-hearted spirit on a swing—a type of newborn fairy— arrived from the blue sky.

"Is everything okay?" Mr. Craft stuck his head out the door of the only other house on Michigan Avenue occupied by regular people. "We heard a door banging, and Bev heard a lot of ruckus earlier." Across our shared driveway, I stared at his blue eyes, searching for the answer. "Then she found Beth holed up on our back porch for we don't know how long," he said blankly and then frowned and furrowed his white eyebrows.

"Will you move soon?" I asked Mr. Craft as I ran across the driveway. "Soon, soon," he said, leading me into their back porch—identical to ours but with wicker furniture and a carpet. Beth was curled up in the white wicker chair on which I'd often placed pies or loaves of banana bread Mom whipped up for the meetings Mr. Craft held on Sundays. Although it seemed like forever, it was only a few years ago that followers of Mr. Craft's new religion jammed cars into our joint driveway and then learned how to enter a higher kingdom by allowing bad and harmful thoughts to float away like the bubbles he drew on a big pad of paper that rested on an easel Mom had given him.

Before Mom threw the chair at Mrs. Craft for questioning her proposal to have some kind of joint art school as well as a center for religion, she couldn't believe our luck when they moved into the long empty house. Her face glowed when she heard he'd been kicked out of the regular church downtown by people she said were just socialites and not the least attuned to transcending the current mania for buying ready-made things, and certainly not to questioning the dogma of Christianity. "They're like sheep, worshipping money and afraid to think for themselves—no man, not even Jesus, should lay down rules like he's got some special link to God," she said, narrowing her eyes like a wolf. I wanted to scream something that would make sense of her hatred of the only world we had and the one person everyone said was above it all.

"I'm not sure Jesus would appreciate being scorned," I'd said, smirking. Before I could run, she slapped my face, yelling that I was like everyone else. I stared at her florid face, deciding never to forgive her for lumping me with everyone else when I knew no one at school would agree with that. *Wishful thinking,* I thought, imagining me outside the groups on the playground, picking out people to be. Of course, I'd never admit that I loved the heat my stinging cheek produced, vanquishing the grayness of our life, while she was left with nothing but guilt. But at least for the few moments, before the guilt and torment set in, she was all of a piece—a firebrand for reform of nothing less than the whole world, a person with queen-like cheekbones who saw herself ruling even Jesus and assuming everyone who didn't get with the program and worship her ideas hated her.

Beth tilted a bag of Fritos towards me. I took a few, and we both crunched on the chips as the three of us stared at each other. "Oh!" Beth pointed at blood suddenly flowing from Mr. Craft's nose.

"Dang," he said, rushing into the kitchen.

"Why did you come over here?" I asked Beth, who offered me more chips as she stuffed a handful in her mouth. I scooped out the rest of the chips and motioned Beth to follow me home. "Do you smoke?" I said fanning the air.

"Not very often, but I snuck one in your basement, and I saw this drawing of a man hanging in a noose and a girl standing by his feet. Did you do that?"

I rolled my eyes, realizing that Mom would love the *Garden of Earthly Delight.* "Obviously no," I said hating that Beth knew anything about our house and Mom's bizarre mind. "Whatever, I don't care," I said worrying that I'd be drawn to it and, along with Stephen Fedkin, the image might stick in my mind.

"It's okay if she'd like to stay with us." Mr. Craft had reappeared, pressing a wad of Kleenex to his nose. "She said her mother's coming in just a few days," he checked the

Kleenex, showing us a circle of blood. Beth made a face, and I thought about taking her hand, pulling her across the driveway, but then I considered staying here, erasing the past or starting over—maybe Beth and I could move to wherever the Crafts were moving. I hadn't given up on the idea of running away, although I kept it on the back burner like the teakettle Dad insisted keeping on a low whistle. I guess we both saw hope in the steam, as if one day it might flow out the door, leading us to the people we'd like to be.

"Will your church move, too? I mean, will you start it up again?"

He shook his head, staring at me the way he did in the Sunday meetings, and I wished I could run home, wash my hair, braid it, and let him see me the way I looked when he'd fallen in love with me.

I'd tricked him into loving me by nodding at everything he said, but so did Mom. The two of us, nodding at the ideas he repeated each week about giving up bad thoughts and rising gradually to the Kingdom of Heaven. It was obvious that I'd grown too tall and too thin, but I still had long blond hair and I could still fake believing in his system if it meant that he'd see, once again, something inside me that was mine alone.

He'd never even liked Beth. I remembered him scowling when she raised her hand during a Sunday meeting, announcing that Jesus died for our sins. Mr. Craft shook his head, as did a woman in front of me. "That is not what we believe," he'd said, motioning to the easel and pad of paper where he'd drawn the stages of getting into the highest kingdom. He pointed to the Mineral Kingdom at the bottom of the chart, written in his broad strokes with a squeaky black marker. Above was the Animal Kingdom and then, the Kingdom of Man—a place where negative thoughts flourished and were at the root of all problems. "Purifying our thoughts will save us, Beth —not dwelling on fake sainthood." He'd looked at me for approval, and I immediately scribbled THOUGHT CONTROL on the little pad he gave out to each person who belonged to his church (though he called it a *foundation*). He nodded approvingly and then we locked eyes for so long, I looked down.

Later, Beth told me that at a church in Texas, a real minister said many times that Jesus had died for our sins. "You'll never get into the Kingdom of Heaven thinking that," I scolded.

More blood flowed from Mr. Craft's nose and he backed up into the kitchen, closing the door and leaving Beth and me alone. "Having a church in your house is weird," I said. "Besides, does he know about the shoplifting and your suspension—or whatever they call it?" Beth buttoned her jacket and unbuttoned it. "I skipped school today," I said, suddenly imitating Beth's coy and quiet tone.

"You?" she said. "Why? You're the perfect student and all." She dropped her chin in disappointment. "I can't believe it," she said, picking lint off her pants. "Why?" She looked at me squarely, her eyes begging me to undo the news.

"I'm not sure," I said wishing I'd remembered to divide myself —responsible with Beth and alluring with Mr. Craft. "I'm never going to do it again," I said quickly. "It's just that I wasn't quite ready for a test, and I just hid outside the school and studied. No one even knows," I lied, and to my relief, Beth smiled.

"Oh hello." Mrs. Craft came in, gripping the handles of a white shopping bag from Sears. "Well, I can see he's had visitors." She blinked, frowning as she looked from Beth to me and finally back to Beth. I stared at Mrs. Craft, worried that she thought we had no business lounging in their porch.

"Don't you girls have something to do?" She asked as she untied her scarf. Then she looked hard at Beth, who didn't flinch.

"We're going," I said, but Beth didn't budge.

"C'mon," I whispered, but Beth glared at the wall and Mrs. Craft sniffed and went inside. Beth looked up at me, and for a moment I thought it was my destiny to be confused by all conversation. Mrs. Craft seemed irritated at Beth and me for talking to Mr. Craft—perhaps taking up his time when he could be writing sermons for some future church? Beth rolled her eyes as Mrs. Craft passed by, and I backed up, tripping on a pot of geraniums. I grabbed the wide pot before it crashed, screaming impulsively the way Mrs. Craft had on that boiling day when Mom had thrown a chair at her, even though the chair landed far from her feet." Then Mom had screamed like they were inventing a new language.

Mr. Craft appeared with a red stain on his upper lip. "Giving up your bad feelings, or at least replacing your negative thoughts with positive ones, will help you reach the kingdom of heaven," he said, waving his hand at the light coming through a window. I'd heard that line many times in the years we'd trooped across the driveway to his weekly lessons, as he called them. I'd memorized all the lines—there weren't many—and even told kids at school about giving up their bad thoughts with the idea that the teacher might like me more than the other kids and maybe this would get back to Mr. Craft. It worked. Mrs. Brown called Mr. Craft to let him know that his teachings had a most positive effect on me. "You're helping others understand the higher power," he'd said, and Mom glared at me.

I guess that was the beginning of our competition. *Mom has a boyfriend*, I scribbled in black ink on the wall near my bed. Then, with a red crayon, I wrote Mr. Craft's initials and mine with small red lips between the letters, but the wax wouldn't stick to the bumpy plaster. I didn't care because I knew Mr. Craft stared at me and only liked Mom for her cakes and loaves of bread. Every time I saw him, I smoothed my hair, loved the way he looked approvingly at my smile and now and then mentioned how nice I looked and how pretty my legs had become.

"You could be a Ballet dancer," he'd said one day when I ran outside in tights and a short shift. I immediately scoured the Yellow Pages for Ballet studios—not that I cared about Ballet, but I thought maybe he'd admire a Ballet dancer even more than a girl next door. Unfortunately, all the Ballet studios were in Lansing and I couldn't imagine how I'd get there.

Then one day, Mr. Craft stopped his sermon on the dangers of holding onto bad thoughts to announce that I was practically a missionary for his foundation. I looked around as he said that I'd told kids at school to give up their bad thoughts. Mom stared stony-faced, and by the next day she'd painted an ugly green streak over the black ink next to my bed, and from then on we began to sleep in on Sundays.

About that time someone mistook our door for the Craft's and Mom told an unsuspecting man that Mr. Craft hated the three of us, and I felt like pushing her against the wall the way the gym teacher had shoved David Beeman against the gym wall for missing the ball at home plate. But now we've forgotten about competing for his love. Neither of us cares about him anymore, although I bet she could be lured back by his blue eyes. I'd never resort to that kind of crush again—Barbie Robert would never love a man with white hair and especially a married man. Most girls, I guessed, didn't know the thrill of an older man like Mr. Craft. Boys at school noticed me, now and then, but not with such laser focus.

I pushed out the Craft's door, dreading the moment when I'd wade through the pots and pans in our kitchen, but also relieved to go. "What was I thinking? Live with the Crafts?" I said, remembering the boring meetings and Mom's pandering with all the baked goods. Moving with the Crafts or Beth would be better than spending my days with Mom and Dad, but barely. I had to get to my room and go over my adventure, how easily I snuck back into school, the winning game, and the boy who touched my shoulder, and after all that, I'd think about what to say to Barbie Robert tomorrow. Maybe the trip to MSU was my first solo attempt at meeting people the way Dad had taught me way back when we were a team—me silent and observing his great technique. I smiled as I ran across the driveway, thinking that maybe I'd brag to Beth later.

"Where's Beth?" Mom sat at the kitchen table. I stopped in the middle of the kitchen, envisioning the bag of clothes from Mrs. Broadback and Mrs. Craft carrying a shopping bag. Why couldn't Mom rush about the town, carrying bags and attending to special dinners like everyone else? *The mystery of Mom,* I chuckled inwardly, priding myself on my complete lack of empathy. It dawned on me that my internal meanness rarely surfaced because I feared the real me emerging like some Godzilla style moth poisoning the world. And yet my own heartlessness gave me a thrill now and then.

"Too bad you didn't get to St. Louis," I taunted while staring at the glass of milk she'd poured for me—a typical gift of natural goodness. I stared at the milk, willing it to tip over so she'd go nuts and despair. How about buying some normal accouterments like the HOME SWEET HOME welcome mat Mrs. Broadback just ordered? "Nestles Quick," I said, and she jumped to get the yellow and brown box of my favorite cocoa mix. I dumped about ten spoonfuls into my glass, stirring as Mom stared at me. "Stop staring at me!" I grabbed the glass and hurried to my room, eager to slam the door—shut everyone out. But as I hurried through the living room, Dad was at the top of the stairs, holding his hand like he'd slammed it into a wall. Both hands shook, and his moaning was no more than vague muttering I couldn't understand. He retreated to bed, and I followed him. Once back under the covers, he pointed a thick index finger at the door and then his hand fell onto the cream colored bedspread embroidered in French Knots, and I leaned over his face, hoping he'd tell me exactly what ailed him and what he needed.

"Dad," I whispered, sensing that only a cruel person would run from his side even though his breath was hot and the room stifling.

"Mom," he whispered, turning his head.

"Mom!" I called. Instead of moving closer, I backed away like he was an animal who'd attack me if we lost eye contact.

"Let's not think about this day," she said, passing me as I inched backwards towards my room. "I'll go to the Journal tomorrow and they'll understand. I hate planes anyway. You can't trust them." I listened, wondering how much yelling Beth had endured before escaping to the Crafts.

I fell into bed, kicking off my shoes and sinking as far as I could into the flat mattress and pillow. The day had proved exciting—actually thrilling. I hoped the girl at the Union would look for me at the Mixer. I closed my eyes, and the Commons appeared with the bright green carpeting, the TVs on each wall and the floor to ceiling windows, where just a few weeks back I'd looked out at the courtyard—also newly established for appropriate congregating—at kids marching in circles and one boy, whose acne had turned my stomach, holding a sign about Viet Nam.

I closed my eyes as Mom slipped into my room and wedged her thick body on to the edge of my bed. Before I could flip over, she began to stroke my back. "We need to be kind to Beth," she said. "Dad," she hesitated, "is going to be in bed for a while, and I don't want you to worry. Don't think about it." She continued to rub my back.

"What exactly is wrong?"

"We don't know everything, and the sooner we understand that, the sooner we'll accept things like this and not fight what is natural fear—fear of living and going on," she said. "I told Dad that feeling like a failure is not unusual."

I stared into my pillow, thinking that Patty Scott and her mother would think that failing is very unusual, and so would Barbie and Mrs. Broadback.

"Did you know Stephen Fedkin killed himself?" I said. She stopped rubbing my back, and I could feel her stomach breathing in and out. I turned over, hoping we might hug or just look into each other's eyes.

"Put that on a back burner—we don't want you thinking about that. "For a moment, she reminded me of Mrs. Scott, mentioning the clothes for Homecoming—like certain things were unquestionable. "Never dwell on that," Mom said, now sounding more like the teachers warning us not to get into a stranger's car. Stephen's face appeared on the ceiling, deflated and defeated, like he assumed I'd obey Mom.

"Dwell on what?" I asked, wondering what Mom would say if I told her that Stephen was on the ceiling. She might talk to him about giving up his bad thoughts as if he'd return—call our hoax—after some good positive thinking.

"I hope that Beth isn't at the Crafts for good," I muttered, wishing I didn't get such joy out of torturing Mom. She looked out the window over my bed and I stared at the hard bones in her face and her thick hair, combed for the trip to St. Louis. "How much did she steal, anyway?" We both looked to the door because Dad called again to Mom. "I think the Crafts want her for themselves or something," I said.

"They would," Mom said, back to whispering as she smoothed my forehead. I had an urge to tell her about Stephen, ask for her forgiveness or absolution. "We must offer up our negatives thoughts. Stop all the fakery," she said, her gray eyes absorbing the light coming in from the window above my bed. I heard Stephen scoff, and I wanted to laugh, but my throat felt stuck. I hated her for conjuring a vague world perhaps with no end but with no beginning either. No wonder Stephen rushed to my side with a definite solution. No wonder he begged me to follow him. "I'll never forget all the bread you slaved over for Mr. Craft," I sniffed.

"I have no idea what you're talking about," she said narrowing her eyes like she struggled to see me and make out my features. Then she turned to leave, and my heart raced. I pictured myself grabbing onto her knees while she easily walked out of my tight grasp.

CHAPTER XI

"Do you know the poem, *The Road Not Taken?*" Beth asked, lying on her side and sniffling quietly.

"What are you talking about?" I said, pulling my covers to my chin. Beth rolled over, pulling her sheet to her chin like today we'd begin our lives as twins.

"I just had a dream about that poem—our English teacher puts a different poem on the board every week, and I guess I liked that one."

"I think Dad loves that poem," I said, throwing off the covers. Beth gripped her stomach and moaned.

"Seems like you're always sick." I slipped on a white shirt Mom had made. I'd begged for money to buy one that I'd seen on a mannequin at Jacobson's. I'd never admit to her that she'd produced a good imitation of what looked like a man's shirt, with little white buttons up the front and a neat buttoned-down collar. I pulled on a pair of red bellbottoms she'd also made, but then changed into a skirt since I'd never seen Barbie Robert in bellbottoms.

"I'll be right back," I said, flipping my hair. Beth nodded, taking a deep breath.

I snuck into Mom and Dad's room. Mom's side of the bed was empty, but Dad hung over the edge on his side. "Sock drawer," he whispered.

"Thanks, Dad," I said, gathering coins scattered among the balls of black socks and hoping he'd utter some advice, old or new, on rising to the top. But he couldn't talk. He could barely breathe. I crawled over the bed to him, keeping my flats off the sheets. His deep set eyes were closed, sinking further into his skull, and his straight Roman nose, beginning halfway up his forehead, puffed out and collapsed with each breath. I wanted to touch his purplish lips. Finally, like he knew I wanted to hold him somehow, he shook his head, and the dark brown curls he usually slicked down trembled.

"I'm going to join the Debate club," I lied, reminding myself that dad's file of lies about me needed replenishing. He nodded, but never opened his eyes, making it a good possibility that in this state he registered nothing. I wished I could tell him about Barbie and her baton twirling. He turned onto his side, curling up, gasping, and moaning. I thought of hugging him the way I'd watched Timmy cuddle Lassie but instead pictured a teacher scolding me for going along with Dad's lies, someone wagging her finger in my face who didn't admire as I did the composite approach—taking this and that from various people—to making me up. We'd learned the word in English, and as a definition I wrote that it was a technique or an alternate to finding other people who were finished or complete personalities.

I rolled off the bed and decided to search for more money. Sometimes he stashed bills in a cufflink box from his days in college. Inside the black box, I felt what I hoped was a dollar bill beneath the shiny silk lining. I gently peeled back the lining, but to my disappointment there was no dollar bill, only a photo with crinkly white edges. At first, I thought it was a picture of Mom in a bathing suit. I'd never seen Mom in a bathing suit; even at Devil's Lake she wore her old painting clothes. The woman in the picture had light hair that was carefully curled in a pageboy with razor sharp bangs. In the light pooling by the window I stared at the picture, finally realizing that the lady in the bathing suit was Empress Martin. Why would Dad hide a picture of Empress? He'd told me about his fraternity at Duke and all the boys he'd met there before going to war. He'd said he'd never even had a girlfriend because he was waiting for Mom—the only woman he'd ever loved. I felt tears well. I missed his stories that I knew were crafted to teach me something about life. Where was the man who never hesitated to turn the smallest of moments into a life lesson? I stared at the picture, and my tears became hot and angry. This woman continued to invade our lives, I thought, tearing one edge of the photo until I stopped and hid it in my pocket. Poor Dad, I thought as I looked at him before leaving. She probably gave him the picture hoping he'd fall in love with her or who knows what? Give her money? I slid the box under a handkerchief and closed the drawer. "Bye Dad," I whispered as I left the door open a crack and ran downstairs.

"Dad looks like a mummy—should we get some help?" I said, grabbing a pop tart and ignoring the blob of oatmeal floating in disgusting warm milk and glistening in a shroud of melted butter.

"No one can do it for us," Mom said as she pulled on a coat she'd made out of green corduroy. "Whose life isn't full of pain? Accepting it is our job.

"Why are you dressed?" I asked, searching for Beth's pop in the fridge. "Can you take this to Beth?" I shook the big bottle of cherry pop, checking for fizz.]

"We've got to try to help her," Mom said, and all I could think of was 'why'? Didn't we have enough to worry about with Dad not working? But I guessed that Beth was Mom's best chance for some kind of redemption—from what I wasn't sure. The drawing Beth had discovered on the basement wall popped into my head like a clue that had been under my nose all the time. I'd look at it later. Then I felt the photo in my pocket and wished Empress and Beth would disappear for good.

"You go ahead and help her all you want," I sniffed. She stared at me, her high cheekbones expanding and as she sucked in her cheeks, I realized that we might as well be cats, hissing and spitting at each other but never accomplishing anything.

"You know nothing," she whispered. I laughed, but my face felt hot and my heart sped up. Between the drawing Beth told me about in the basement, Stephen Fedkin, and the photo of Empress, I knew a lot. The problem was I could make no sense of what I knew. It all seemed jumbled, nonsensical and confusing, and also sort of frightening. I might know a lot when I wished I could rid my brain of anything but Mrs. Broadback, explaining how to work her new machine for washing dishes. I backed away, grabbing the bottle of pop.

Beth snored. "You sleep a lot," I whispered, but she didn't stir. I paused for a moment and considered waking her to give her a chance to become me or at least form a team with me against Mom. There was no doubt that Dad and I were no longer a team—he was, after all, fading into what looked like a permanent limbo, which seemed much worse than actual death and reminded me of how frustrating it was to play on the teeter totter with someone whose weight matched yours. I continued to stare at Beth and then at my rumpled bed—it looked inviting. Skipping school had been easy, and no one seemed to notice. I could, so easily, drift into a life at home— daydreaming in bed and when up, embroiled in fights that went nowhere. I set the bottle of pop on the floor between our beds and took off, focusing on Barbie Robert twirling and smiling. In the bright morning light,

Mom brushed horse chestnuts off the windshield with a glove. I focused on the traffic noise along Michigan Avenue. "Why are you leaving?" I blurted, examining the soft coat hanging off her wide shoulders. She adjusted the outside mirror, manipulating it with care. "I think that coat is too hot," I said, hoping she didn't think I was toying with her. "I could get you a sweater," I tilted my head like a nurse helping a patient—praying I could persuade her to start over at this very moment. Odd, but nothing seemed more important than our sticking together and getting along. Her gray eyes met mine and then went past me as I strained to keep contact, but the more I tried the more she avoided my gaze and her face reddened like I was trying to strangle her with a fake and unwanted togetherness. She'd left me so many times I learned to forget the scenes in train stations and buses, but now and then a word would pop into my head or an image like the conductor handing me a swirly lollipop, and I'd feel the terror all over again of being in the huge Chicago Train station alone at five or the hospital with a cracked skull after falling into a fire hydrant while flying a kite.

The doctor had told her she could stay with me as he stitched my skull, but when he left to wash his hands, she said that I'd have a huge scar, on the back of my head, a constant reminder that our little world was marred and essentially ruined. I screamed when she fled the hospital. After the doctor finished, the nurse gave me Ginger Ale and told me all about her cottage on a lake so murky everyone called it Dirt Lake and then she dabbed some ointment on the stitches so they wouldn't itch and pull on my scalp. I calmed down as she patted the long snake-like row of stitches, but at the last second as she turned to leave, I grabbed her sleeve and ripped the cuff. She said she thought I was a nice girl and shook her head as she held up the dangling cuff. After she yanked the curtain closed, I screamed for Mom until the hospital called our house and begged her to come get me. We drove home in silence, me holding my throbbing head as I imagined her driving past our house and then out into the country where she'd consent to be my mother if we'd lived the rest of our lives in the woods and never talked about the hospital and the stitches.

Please say you need me, I said under my breath as she peered at the clouds. I was about to wrap my arms around her thick waist when I yanked myself back and silently told her that I'd never need her again since a person could only be ditched so many times. In my imagination, tears rolled down her cheeks as if this news was new to her. Then I pictured her raging at me for pointing this out like it was my obligation to erase the past. I heard Dad's voice somewhere deep in my brain--*that dance is over* he muttered like he had plenty of practice tossing someone aside. I looked at her, thinking about this standard of Dad's--a saying he doled out back in the old days about every other day--hoping to see an innocent, a person like the Holly Golightly character in the movie Dad took me to. This Holly lady couldn't figure out life, couldn't systemize a day, an hour, or even a minute. At that moment, as she scanned the sky and the trees, I imagined her needing my protection. But she backed away, scrutinizing the car or the driveway or something inanimate, and all my feelings died.

"Dad can't go to work right now. I need to ask the publisher for a little more vacation time for him—that's all." I nudged closer, but then my brain came up with practical questions she'd detest.

"How will we have any money?" Her gray eyes narrowed, and behind her I saw Mr. Craft on his porch. I ran down the driveway from the two of them, towards Michigan Avenue with a vision of hurtling myself before one of the trucks that sped towards Lansing. I slowed down, wishing I had the guts to climb one of the dying elm trees in the boulevard, dangle from a branch hanging over our side of Michigan Avenue and then splat onto the pavement, in the middle of traffic, like the kid in co-ed gym whose hands had slipped off the rings. Mom and Mr. Craft could fall into each other's arms as blood pooled around my blond hair, matting it into a red and yellow halo like the paintings of Jesus in Mom's medieval art book. Maybe Dad would stop hating Beth, and the two of them could sleep all day.

I turned sharply on to Kensington, staring at my feet, too embarrassed by all my weird visions to look straight ahead until I heard barking and recognized the mean black dog zigzagging across Kensington Road. I imagined his teeth sinking deep into my calf. I screamed and walked quickly backwards towards Michigan Avenue, where I hoped swerving cars would miss me by an inch but kill or stun the dog—perhaps for good.

"Do you want a ride?" Mom called from the car. I ran back to the driveway still panting and wincing at the picture of the dog's teeth piercing my calves. "You could come to the Journal with me if you want. I'll get you to school a little late, but..." she said, and I thought for a moment that she was afraid to go alone.

Dad's empty desk was in a grid of desks, each with a big black typewriter. Men pounded on keys and a few nodded at us as we waited outside the Managing Editor's door. Mom stood tall, breathing hard and fingering the car keys.

"C'mon in." A white-haired man poked his head out of an office with lots of windows. Mom and I crept inside, and he hurried back to answer the phone. "Okay, this won't take long," he said and hung up. Before we sat down, he told Mom that she should take Dad to a special home near Detroit. "They'll know what to do, Mrs. Tallman," he said from behind his cluttered desk. Birds flew past the windows and behind him lights shone in the offices of a tall building.

"He's getting better every day," she lied. "And soon I hope to begin substitute teaching. But for now, can we continue with our arrangement if I guarantee he'll be back? You know he's one of your best reporters, Mr. Palmer. I think we both know that," she said with authority. Mr. Palmer stared at Mom and nodded before glancing out a window. I heard a quiet knock on Mr. Palmer's door and turned around. A man holding a file waited for Mr. Palmer to answer or perhaps beckon him inside. I thought of Dad, like one of the birds skirting the big windows not suited to being inside on the eleventh floor waiting patiently for anything.

"You actually think he'll recover from this? I have a cousin who still is not right. I don't mean to be pessimistic, and you're right, Louis is a first rate reporter but," he stopped. "Could've been the war, could've been who knows what." His phone rang, and he told someone that he'd be another moment. "Guadalcanal was tough, and some came back rattled, and you know there have been times we couldn't find Louis. He would be off on his own trail, which could be good, but could've been a sign that he can't handle the work." He stopped and squared some papers. "Terrible to see that much combat and all," he pinched his lips and then looked at us like we were both Dad's children, learning the truth about our father.

"He's stronger today than he was yesterday, and those homes are not for us, I

have to be honest." I looked at Mom like she'd slipped out of her body and straight

into one of my elementary teachers--stalwart and levelheaded like she might pull a used Kleenex from her sweater cuff. I nodded when she said that Dad would be ready to return in a week or two. Mr. Palmer hesitated for what seemed like forever.

"Well, all right," he said, like he was suddenly too busy to think about this anymore and then handed Mom an envelope he pulled from a side drawer.

As we walked to the car, I smiled, following her and imitating the swing of her long arms. The sun caressed my head, and I imagined myself holding Mom's hand. The cool air felt almost like water, lifting my step as I floated along, oblivious to the grime and boarded windows near the gleaming Journal building. Could it be possible that I didn't need to become Barbie Robert? At the thought of living as myself with Mom, my stomach jumped—in a scary way, like I was about to get a test back.

She looked both ways at the traffic before gently guiding me, her hand on my back, towards the parking lot. At her touch I felt warmth, and then guilt washed over me as I thought that I'd wanted to abandon Mom in favor of Barbie Robert's family—a family maybe about to fall apart. When she expertly turned the car key and slid into the zooming traffic in Michigan Avenue, I moved closer to her on the wide bench seat. She zipped along like she didn't want me to be late for school, like she knew how to operate in our world as a parent.

"Everyone thinks they know best for you," she said, squinting and sucking in her lips. "Mr. Palmer sure hates me," she said as we passed our house. The words pushed me back to the passenger door, where I fingered the door handle. Surely, I'd die if I opened the door and rolled out at this speed. I breathed hard, and a kind of hateful relief swept over me. The meeting with Mr. Palmer was a momentary blip, I told myself, and I need to get back on track to becoming Barbie. "I can walk from here, Mom. I said I'd meet someone. "The minute the car pulled away I saw the scary black dog. Ignoring the warnings never to show a dog fear, I took off, hoping that I didn't sweat through my shirt. Barbie Robert would never wear a shirt she'd sweat through.

When I got to the corner of Grand River, I realized I was late and began to run. For a block or two, I pictured Mom, tall and confident with clear eyes in the face of the managing editor. I caught my breath and tried to remember the exact words of her calm persuasive speech. Then the crossing guard yelled, "C'mon!" and I picked up the pace, wondering if I could ask Barbie Robert to let me come to her house after school. But Mom's ranting about horrible people and Barbie's possible troubles swirled in my head as anger and fear clouded my vision. I tried to shut out any thoughts of my own persecution. I remember the day *persecution* had appeared on our SAT prep list, and my stomach twisted as I wondered if I was destined to turn into Mom. She'd alluded to her happy youth on the farm—perhaps one day she woke with strange feelings of being persecuted. If only I could change into Barbie like Samantha twitching her nose in *Bewitched. Today, I must get to her house,* I said, clenching my fists.

Yet, by the time the crossing guard at Harrison shooed me to the other side of Grand River, I relaxed. I'd do my best to become Barbie—as I'd discovered, it was harder to quickly become someone else in high school when everyone traveled in groups with only a few people, like Barbie, on a different path. Once I got inside her house, I'd forget about Mom and, best of all, I'd stop worrying that I'd find her dead. If all else failed, I'd kill myself. At least, after committing suicide, I'd be the talk of the town for a day or two, and that's a bit of free entertainment for anyone who got wind of it. My choice— clear and free. I smiled at a girl to my side, and when she smiled back, I grinned. I fingered the coins in my pocket and thought about getting to work changing into Barbie. I bet she'd like my hair—I'd parted it on the side and smoothed both sides behind my ears--and my outfit. There was always such a simple clarity to her outfits, and I smiled at the thought of her hurrying around the hallways with an armful of books and a few batons—no hangers-on diluting Barbie and her goals.

CHAPTER XII

In the school parking lot, I squeezed past a car with a huge blue bow stuck to the antenna and a *Happy Sixteen Bill!* sign taped to the back bumper. "I can't be late again," a girl in front of me picked up the pace.

"Me either," I said, hurrying not because I worried about being late but just to keep a conversation going—to fill in the void before I reached the front door. Meanwhile I searched the parking lot for the boy who'd touched my shoulder yesterday.

The lobby was choked with kids. I wondered if all sixteen hundred of us were jammed together. When the drum major ran through, lifting his knees high, I remembered that this was the first of our early morning Pep Rallies. Cheerleaders cleared the center, pushing us into a ring of spectators as they clapped and went through some cheers we'd learned in gym.

Patty Scott, an underclass cheerleader, wore a long hairpiece called a fall. The only other girls I'd seen wearing falls sat behind me in homeroom, and when they weren't talking about having sex, they combed and fussed over each other's fall. I wanted to ask the girls standing next to me where you'd buy a fall, but they never stopped whispering long enough for me to break in, so I gave up and stood apart, staring at Patty. Like the other cheerleaders, she smiled and waved at the crowd, before twirling and chanting *Trojans, Trojans.*

As Patty pivoted, her skirt swirled and flared up dangerously, showing hints of her underwear. Although a freshman, she stood out with her deep brown eyes and her smile bigger than any of the other ten cheerleaders. The pep rally rested on her shoulders, and I imagined that she loved the responsibility. As she set one of the cheers in motion with a resounding *GO TROJANS!* I pictured the two of us walking to school arm in arm, singing songs from music class. When cars speeding along Michigan Avenue splashed us, she'd yell at the driver, especially if I was the one who stood dripping and cold. One morning a truck driver honked at us and I worried he might be a kidnapper. "I can't breathe and my heart is pouncing," I blubbered. She listened to my chest and said I might have a heart murmur. The next morning she pulled her Dad's stethoscope from her gym back. "Let me take a listen," she said. I smiled at the memory of her pronouncing me okay— "for now," she'd said, like she'd need to check on me periodically.

Suddenly, Patty's fake hair flew up and swished around her face, blinding her for a moment. Then she slipped and fell hard to her knees. There was a hush as she scrambled to her feet, her knees and face bright red. She adjusted the fall, but I backed out of the crowd, hoping, since I'd barely attended the pep rally, that I could forget her embarrassed stare and red cheeks. If only she could help someone at that moment, everyone would see that she was a nurse at heart and that she'd loved me like a mother. No one knew about that, and they never would. Sometimes I wish I could forget about Patty and her hand squeezing mine, but deep down I didn't want to forget.

"She's probably drunk," an older girl whispered to a boy, and they both rolled their eyes. My stomached tightened and my skin prickled in embarrassment for Patty. Hearing them laugh and snicker made me realize how awful it would be to live forever with your own life history—even if you hadn't done anything terribly wrong. The girl in the Union knew nothing about me, or Patty, or anyone I shared my life with. She only knew a made up me, and that would never be humiliating. The truth about the past is always different from what everyone thinks it is until they finally learn the real, unfiltered truth and they're shocked and revolted.

The trick will be getting all of Barbie's memories to wipe out my own. But as I stared at the bricks and the plaques lining the wall, I feared slamming the door shut on everyone like Mom and Dad and Patty and even Beth. Would I actually be too scared to become Barbie and wipe out the past for good? What if I heard someone call to me—like Mom? She'd never change, but she might miss me for a moment, and I'd be unable to find any of them again once I'd signed on with Barbie, once I got her life inside mine.

As I followed kids obviously not interested in learning the cheer towards our lockers and homeroom, I wondered if Patty had gathered herself. I'd never go back to witness, just in case she fell again. In fact, I wanted to sit somewhere and devise a scheme for erasing people from my brain. Stephen's face popped up. *It will only get worse,* he said, and I wished I could run through the woods until I lost Stephen forever. *Okay, okay,* I said, but his face wouldn't go away until I got closer to my locker and saw two senior boys leaning on the lockers next to mine. I recognized one of them—a boy with greasy blond hair and thin sideburns; Dad had asked him to pump up his unicycle tire not so long ago at the gas station. The other boy had on a navy-blue Barracuda jacket, jeans, black boots, and his hair hung below his ears. He tipped his head backwards, closed his eyes, and chewed gum noisily. I realized that they were the boys Beth had talked to at the football game. I spun my combination as naturally as possible, but I could feel my cheeks redden under the blond boy's gaze. "Where's Beth been?" he asked, twirling a toothpick in the corner of his mouth.

"She said you guys are cousins or something," the other boy said, his eyes still closed. I realized they'd been smoking, and the gum did a bad job of masking the odor.

"Yeah, I heard her say that," the gas station attendant said. Barbie Robert passed with two other drum majors, each holding a baton.

"Hi Sally!" she said, and I whirled around, bumping into a boy whose clarinet case hit his knee.

"Watch it!" he said, grabbing his knee.

"I'm sorry," I said, and Barbie smiled like she knew I didn't mean to hurt the boy.

"See you," she whispered, fluffing a pom pom hanging from one end of her baton. Luckily, the pep rally was over, and the two hood boys fell into the swelling flow of traffic. I slammed my locker. "See you, Barbie," I said, watching her turn a corner. I wondered why she had said hi to me—it almost felt like she knew I was soon to become her, and she approved of the scheme. Things with Barbie weren't quite going according to plan, and for a moment I felt like screaming, like I was this kid I babysat a few times who screamed every time he didn't get his way. Could Barbie possibly want me to become her? I wondered, as I fell into the long march of kids to Homeroom, if everyone dreamed about becoming someone else. Barbie might be scheming to become someone else. With all the heads in front and back of me, I realized that finding someone else would be hard—maybe too hard. The word *impossible* raced across my brain, and my heart pounded until I persuaded myself that no one else thought about being someone else, and my heart calmed to the light flutter I'd become accustomed to. Barbie would laugh at the idea like was sure that the very notion of being anyone other than herself was a joke.

I practiced saying 'hi' just the way Barbie had, and then I told myself to never contemplate the confusion of people, other than me, escaping their own lives. I felt like shouting that I hated chaos; in fact, I hated the overloaded hallway with people jockeying for space.

Announcements dwelled on the World Series win, and no one complained or looked the least bored. Mr. Novak looked like he had returned to his youth. His graying hair appeared darker, and the bags around his eyes had disappeared. "If you're in my American History class, I'm giving an extension on the Hamilton paper—spread the word!"

I twisted around in my seat. "Where do you buy pom poms?" The girls stopped talking about having sex with their boyfriends and looked at each other for the answer.

"Not sure," one of them said and the other nodded.

"I have no clue."

I slumped in my seat and my hand shot up.

"Could I go to the nurse?" Mr. Novak scribbled off a pass and handed it to me as he talked to a boy I knew from elementary school about the beauty of Northrup's triple.

"Flood couldn't have caught it anyway!" The boy grinned and nodded. "He's a goat!"

A boy in the back row who always carried a briefcase shouted that Flood charged because he'd been blinded by the crowd. "That's what my dad said, but he's not a racist like the rest of you guys." The color drained from Mr. Novak's face and the whole class turned around in their seats. I made a fast exit, forcing myself not to turn around for one last look at Mr. Novak through the window, but Mr. Freds blocked my way.

"Sally Tallman—right?" I nodded, noticing that his pants hung loose. *He's probably lost weight since Stephen Fedkin's death*, I thought, noticing that he'd tightened his belt to the last notch.

"I have a pass for the nurse," I said, holding up the pink slip.

"Well, we can talk there—I guess," he said, guiding me by the elbow toward the nurse's office.

"I think I'm a little dizzy," I blurted once the nurse came in from another room. "Dizzy? Did you forget breakfast?" Nurse Hollenbeck rolled clean paper over the table.

"And, what's your excuse for skipping school yesterday? Dizzy?" Mr. Freds asked, and the nurse stopped shaking a thermometer.

"She was on her way here, so I just decided to get to the bottom of this—sorry for the intrusion," Mr. Freds said to the nurse. I handed the nurse my pass, and she widened her eyes. "We just caught it," he said.

"Well, I'm surprised—you're a freshman?" The nurse asked, and I nodded. Mr. Freds sniffed like he wasn't in the mood for a lot of talk.

"What's the idea of skipping?" Mr. Freds asked, glancing at the clock.

"I'll never do it again—I promise," I said, imagining Barbie Robert's horror at breaking rules. "My parents thought I could use a day off. My Dad's been kind of sick—didn't my Mom call?" I asked, my voice trailing off.

"As a matter of fact, she didn't," he said, raising his eyebrows above his black glasses. "You don't seem like the type to skip school," he said. "But don't think I'll let you off the hook again," he scowled, like I'd beat him at a game.

"Jump up, and I'll get your temp," the nurse said as the phone rang in her office and Mr. Freds left. She stuck the thermometer under my tongue and went to the phone. I slipped off the table, pretending to read a poster that explained the digestive system and nutrition. "No temp," she said. "Good to take your nutrition seriously," the nurse added, glancing at the poster.

"I'm thinking of becoming a nurse," I lied, eyeing the door.

"Well, stop in anytime if you want to talk about it. Have you considered signing up with the Candy Stripers? Sparrow Hospital has a nice program, and there's a bus right down Michigan Avenue."

I smiled. "Oh, I definitely want to get into that," I said, pushing on the door. "My Mom could take me when she's not busy with her sorority at MSU." I lied, imagining Mrs. Broadback organizing one event after the next for her sorority. The nurse looked confused, and I took this as a sign to leave. But then she nodded in a noncommittal sort of way.

"Sorority?" she said, raising her eyebrows.

"Yeah, the one for artists," I said, avoiding her eyes. Again, she looked bemused, and I could feel my face redden.

"How are you liking high school so far?" Without thinking I looked up at the ceiling—anything to avoid her eyes and her bland hopeful face. I searched the ceiling like it would magically reveal what I should say to this woman. She remained inscrutable, her eyes scanning my face like there was something inside me she needed to figure out.

I swallowed a couple of times, and after a minute, she handed me a Dixie cup of tepid water. Then the bell rang, and I started to leave. "Come back anytime, Sally," she said. I held the door, waiting for a lie to pop into my head that she'd like—a trauma I'd endured and could describe in a moment of fake confession—but nothing came to mind.

Dad would love it if I could come up with something dramatic, but I remembered Mom shaking her head at me after she'd heard I told someone I was adopted, and when Nurse Hollenbeck smiled and widened her eyes, I knew that I'd suffered nothing and that my actual life was worth nothing, too. I wiped away tears, and she looked surprised but then snatched a Kleenex from a box and moved towards me. I pulled back and then slipped out the door, grateful as I faced kids and wiped my eyes quickly, that the tears weren't fake. But as I dodged a big group of boys, I knew that it was too late to figure out how to be me, and of course Stephen would agree that we were both worthless.

I hurried to gym. "No need to change today," Mrs. Shafer yelled as a flood of girls headed down the long hall lined with trophies won by every team imaginable: JV basketball, varsity basketball, wrestling, swimming, track. I smiled and nudged Penny Stillwell, who also stared at the case that ran the full length of the hall. "Let's hope that our basketball team can do it again without John Fagan—did you hear he might be suspended?" Penny whispered. Mrs. Shafer was taking roll, and we hurried to the Health Room before she could give me details.

"Today, I want to talk about dating—something you're all going to be doing sooner or later—and, of course, marriage."

Penny smiled at me, and we both blushed. I knew she'd been to a movie with a boy from the youth group at her church. He'd inexplicably wet his pants right after he put his hand under her bra. "Do you still like that guy?" I whispered, but Mrs. Shafer shot me an irritated look, so we both stared straight ahead.

"One of the keys to a successful marriage is successful dating, and by that I mean knowing what a boy wants in a girl."

"We should take notes," Penny whispered as we stared at Mrs. Shafer demonstrating how to get in and out of a car without separating our legs.

Cindy Morton snickered and so did Anne, the girl who hated my dad for torturing horses. "Laugh if you want, but this week we're talking about things you need to know and I am sure you don't know," Mrs. Shafer pointed at Cindy in particular—probably because Cindy was fat and made fun of what she said were Mrs. Shafer's idiotic generalizations.

"Recently, Mr. Shafer and I were going out on a special date—it was our anniversary." She said the word *anniversary* slowly, like this would be an important word in our future vocabularies. "I was distracted and flung open the passenger door of the car and hopped right in," Mrs. Shafer said, raising her eyebrows and shaking her head. "Mr. Shafer was pretty disappointed, girls. He said, 'well we're getting pretty independent now—aren't we?'"

Penny turned to me, her eyes agog and I immediately widened mine. There was a general hush. "I hated myself for doing that to him," Mrs. Shafer said in a low voice. In my head, Dad laughed at her rules, and as girls in front of us continued to nod and Penny pinched my arm, I felt myself pull away, as if I'd begun to float above the room, watching everyone believe in what had to be a fake rulebook, this urgent advice of Mrs. Schafer. My heart began to race as I saw Mom and Dad floating with me, the three of us slipping through the windows behind Mrs. Schafer. Cindy Morton looked back at the clock and caught my eye, smiling at me as if she'd read my mind or thought we were alike. I looked away and my heart sped up. Stuck in the middle of so many nodding heads, I actually hoped Stephen might appear; at least I knew exactly what he wanted from me. He'd advise me how to get out of Health. But I remembered that boys weren't allowed into the Girls Health Room, even dead ones. "Can I get a drink?" I asked without raising my hand. Mrs. Schafer shook her head.

I calmed down when I thought of Barbie concentrating on twirling her baton, perfecting the toss and the little catch behind her back. For a moment, Barbie's graceful image blotted Mrs. Shafer's' tight smile. Penny looked at me anxiously as if she could tell I wasn't concentrating.

"This is important," she whispered.

"Girls, before we leave, I am going to end with a word of warning, and don't worry, I will repeat this all week as we continue our unit on dating. If a boy says that he loves you, he means one thing and one thing only. I think most of you know what that is, especially since all of you took part in the eighth grade class on sex education. Okay, that's all," she jumped down from her desk and pointed to the clock just as the bell rang. "Don't forget," she raised her voice, "your reputation is all you've got."

Period A turned out to be Period B, meaning that I'd drop Latin today. I twirled my combination after last period finally ended, daydreaming about the pompoms hanging off Barbie Robert's baton and remembering when Beth and I were obsessed with baton twirling, but only Beth could master the basic under the arm move. Maybe I could walk to Barbie's subdivision as if I was lost.

"Hey, for a change, I don't have to take anyone home, and my sister has Yearbook," the boy who'd touched my shoulder said. "Need a ride?"

I turned around slowly, like he'd disappear if I twirled around too fast. Before I knew it, he'd closed my locker and we stood at the passenger side of his car. I remembered Mrs. Shafer's warning about wounding a boy by jumping in the car, but Scott looked over the top of the car at me like he couldn't get in his side until I got in mine, so I took a chance and got in, swinging my legs without separating them.

"Those are new, but we never use them. My Mom actually ironed them the other day!" We both laughed at the smooth seat belts hanging over the front seat.

"Why do you have them?" I asked.

"Not sure," He laughed. "You are one of the few girls who gets baseball," he said as he headed out of the parking lot. I noticed his clean nails and the straight part in his dark brown hair. "Can't believe the series is over—seemed like it would never come, and then bingo, we took it." He shook his head.

We talked about the games—me doing my best to keep up. I wondered if he'd tell me he loved me, and exactly what he'd do then. Instead, he asked if I'd like to go to the Lansing Symphony in a few weeks. "I've got tickets through my Dad's office."

"I'd love to go," I said, hearing the words echo in the car as the two of us leaned slightly toward the middle of the wide seat. I remembered Mom coming home one night a few years ago, flushed and excited to have heard the symphony. She'd said we should all go, and I should study the violin, and then she went on and on about how the music filled her with hope. *Hope for what?* I'd asked, and she'd of course taken this the wrong way, throwing her program at me and then reminding Dad and me that we were like all the other hateful people who scoffed at her dreams of helping the world through art and making things.

I'd cried until my eyes throbbed and my shirt was soaked because truly I'd been curious about exactly how music would replace her distrust of the world outside of the house—the world I encountered in this car with its clean windshield and immaculate mats and especially this boy, Scott Noble, and his straightforward driving and the proximity of his hand on the seat. As I stared at his hand, I realized that if she couldn't have her own way, rule us all in some giant project to remake the world—she didn't want us to be part of the world, the one she hadn't created.

"Whatchya thinkin' about?" he asked as we took off from a stoplight.

"Was Driver's Ed hard?" I thought of Stephen absorbing the news that he couldn't take the class and would never drive.

"Nah, not really. You have to memorize a lot of braking distances. Stuff like that." He shrugged before making a smooth turn with both hands on the wheel. When he placed one hand back on the seat, I inched towards it. "We're moving in January, so this is the last time I'll go to one of the performances—my drum teacher is the head timpanist."

I nodded at the windshield, suppressing an impulse to ask if I could move with him. "You're moving?" I said in a low voice.

"Yeah, IBM is transferring my Dad to Chicago, and I'll have to be a Cubs fan!" He said, lifting his hands off the wheel for a second.

"I live right across from the new IBM building."

"I know," he said and then blushed.

"Would you mind taking me to Cedar Crest? I have to get homework from Barbie Robert, and I know her address."

I knocked on the Roberts' door after ringing the doorbell and waiting for what seemed like an hour as Scott Noble waited patiently at the curb. I hadn't told him to leave or stay as I got out in a daze, leaving the door open so that he had to lean way over to grab the handle and slam shut the passenger door.

Finally, an unshaven man opened the door and squinted his blue eyes—exact replicas of Barbie's. "She's probably at practice, I don't know," he said, still squinting as if he knew he should know Barbie's schedule. I looked past him into the house, trying to make out the layout of the first floor, but his wide body blocked most of my view.

"That guy looked kind of weird. Was that her dad?" Scott asked as I closed the car door.

"Wait a minute!" A pretty woman with a blond bubble cut ran towards the car. "Barbie's not home yet. Can I let her know who to call?" She wore a neat cardigan over a matching blue blouse, and I immediately thought of Mrs. Broadback.

"I wanted to get the Latin homework and talk about the next test—you know, to study for it."

Mrs. Robert smiled. "She's mentioned that someone from class is a real whiz and I bet that's you!" She backed up after I gave her my phone number. Then she smiled as she shut the door

"She seemed cool," Scott said, and I nodded slowly, wondering why Barbie's mother married her father, marring a sensible life.

The minute we pulled into our driveway, I sensed something strange. The Crafts' front door was open, and Mr. and Mrs. Craft were arguing. He clutched the sleeve of her green coat as she tried to move. I quickly slid out of the car.

"Bye! Thanks!" I waved, realizing as he backed into Michigan Avenue's traffic that I hadn't thanked him for the invitation. I watched him turn right on Cowley and ran to our front porch to listen from behind an overgrown bush. I heard yelling, and then Mrs. Craft screamed something I couldn't make out over the traffic. Then through the branches, I saw her walking backwards, shaking her fist at Mr. Craft who yelled at her from the steps. Mr. Craft wore a fancy green shirt and white pants—I'd never seen him in such a get-up.

I waited for him to go back inside when Mom pounded on the window, waving me to come inside. She vanished for a moment and then opened the front door.

"Come in," she said, like I'd finally made it to some kind of free zone—our house as a safety net. "Beth has food poisoning. She went to school, and Mr. Craft found her walking here just as it hit and gave her a ride." Mom pulled on her coat. "I'm going to run out for crackers and, I guess, ginger ale—can you persuade her to stay in bed? I guess she left a book at school and thinks the janitors will let her in. But she's in no shape, and I refuse to take her back to school."

"I think the Crafts were fighting," I said, waving my hand towards their house. Mom raised her eyebrows.

"I've never heard them argue," she said, searching her purse for money.

I found Beth slumped on her bed. "What's wrong?"

Beth looked around the room as if the answer was hiding somewhere. "Seriously, what did you eat?" I squinted at her, trying to find the young girl with the perfectly straight nose, the deep-set brown eyes and the curvy red lips—all of it buried now in a fleshier person.

"I think the meat was bad," she said, flopping on to her side.

"Well thank God Mr. Craft gave you ride. That would be so embarrassing to throw up with all the traffic zooming by." I took off my coat. "I mean, good thing you got to the bathroom in time," I said.

"I am going to tell you a secret, and you can't tell your Mom," she said hoisting herself up.

"She knows you stole," I said.

"Mr. Craft and I might go away—only because he wants me to go to a better school, like yours, but it would be hard for him to stay here because of getting fired and all."

"Is that why the Crafts were fighting?" I asked, staring at Beth's bracelet. "Where did you get that bracelet? Could I possibly borrow it for a date to a symphony?"

"It was a present, but you can borrow it," she said, slipping it off and placing it on the cardboard box between our beds.

"God, you're not going to believe what I found." I pulled from my back pocket the photo of Empress in the bathing suit. "It was in my Dad's stuff—so weird." Beth looked at it carefully and then shrugged her shoulders.

"That is weird," she said, tossing the photo back like it was the old days when we'd throw a slipper back and forth. We lay on our backs in silence. "You don't seem sick," I said, finally slipping the photograph under my mattress, hoping the metal springs would puncture it. Beth put her finger to her lips and then pointed at the door.

"Girls, I'd like to draw you." Mom gently tapped the door with her foot, carefully balancing two glasses of ginger ale and stack of saltines. Under her arm, she squeezed a large pad of her favorite paper. "Get comfortable," Mom whispered, squinting at us like we were miles away. Beth put her head on my shoulder, but soon the two of us fell back on the wall like babies propped up for a photograph.

It wasn't long before Beth snored and muttered in her sleep. "What's she saying?" I asked Mom, but she was too absorbed to answer, staring at us and drawing in short strokes.

The sound of the charcoal against the paper gave me goose bumps, setting me on edge. After a while I silently begged her to finish as I dug my fingernails into my palms. "Please stop," I whispered, drifting off and drawing in deep breaths, like all the scratching on the thick paper was suffocating me.

When I woke in the dark to Beth's snoring, I searched for Mom. Had my intolerance for the art-making she loved vanquished her? I yelled for her but again only inside my brain. Then as I vowed to stay awake and concentrate on becoming Barbie Robert, the dream I'd just lived through came back. It may have been only a chase through tight narrow rooms and hallways–some I had to squeeze through—but its ending made me beg off sleep forever. In the final room, Mom hung over a bathtub dripping blood from her toes.

CHAPTER XIII

Mrs. Broadback called early Saturday morning. Mom covered the mouthpiece and insisted in a hot whisper that Mrs. Broadback had recently ignored her in the checkout line of Prince Brothers Grocery, proving that Mrs. Broadback, like everyone else in East Lansing, hated her. *You want recognition anyway you can get it,* I thought, having no evidence that Mrs. Broadback hated anyone except maybe the carpet cleaner who couldn't get Danny's vomit stain out of the white wall to wall carpeting in her bedroom. She actually swore in front of Danny when she noticed the stain fainter but nonetheless still visible, still ruining the expanse of pure white carpeting that always made me think of heaven.

Mom and I tussled for the receiver, hip checking and pushing each other in the same way Patty Scott and her sister Susan once wrestled for control of Susan's new Princess phone. I wondered if it was wrong to feel so thoroughly the contours of Mom's body. We'd rarely hugged, never kissed nor even held hands, and now we bumped into each other with force like boys in basketball shoving each other around. "Get away from me," I hissed after losing my footing and falling into her hip.

She bounced me off and sniffed hard like she'd stop if I'd stop. "You're hateful like all of them," she whispered loud enough for anyone in earshot to hear, and I prayed Beth was nowhere near.

I was sick of sharing my family with Beth, even tired of sharing Mom. *Get out,* I said to Beth in my brain and then my heart pounded in my ears as it hit me that this sudden loathing of Beth was as weird (possibly sociopathic) as Mom's hatred of East Lansing. We'd learned about sociopaths in an assembly in sixth grade. A policeman talked about not getting into strangers' cars. Perhaps I was sick of mind, like the people who asked kids to get in cars. I don't hate Beth, I reminded myself and she could have Mom all she wanted, stating the obvious if only in my brain just to stop this barrage of associations and mind wrecking fear. A vision of a teacher I didn't recognize popped up in my brain. She wrote on a blackboard that disliking one person is not the same as hating an entire town. *Thank you*, I said in my brain. But the unknown teacher erased the board, signaling me to return to torturous thinking. *I like Beth*, I said, pleading with my brain to go blank; begging my brain to stop searching for ways to confuse me. *Beth is just Beth*, I said but Stephen sprang to mind, replacing the unknown teacher, and I thought he'd laugh and let me know that I'd better get used to a new life in which *nothing was not just nothing.*

I grabbed at the phone as Mom stuck a strand of hair behind her ear. She jerked away, and I missed the receiver, hitting her shoulder instead. We stared at each other, her with narrow accusing eyes like this wrestling match was all my fault due to my refusal to join her world, a world apart from everyone else where she reigned as a messy, disheveled queen but one I realized had quick reflexes.

Then I laughed, grabbing at the phone again. This insult must have hit her hard, announcing to the world, which was just our kitchen that she'd failed somehow. Defeated, head sagging, she handed me the receiver, untangling the cord until she looked up with a glimmer in her eye, remembering that her own kid did not believe the world singled her out, did not recognize who she really was, and she grabbed the phone back to her chest. But she'd lost her strength, and I wrenched the phone from her hand, sending her backwards and me onto the sink, landing hard and jolting me into the dreaded chaos of

Saturday—a day like the unpredictable Vesuvius we'd seen in a film script.

"Sorry that took so long. I was ironing my clothes for the upcoming week," I breathed hard into the receiver as if I'd run a mile to the phone. "I have all day," Mrs. Broadback laughed before letting me know that Danny was sick and probably infectious. "Oh, I see. All right," I muttered, desperately trying to sound nonchalant as the small under lit kitchen shrunk. Mom turned on the water full force, and I raised my voice, hoping some guy's method for persuasive speech they told us about on Freshman Day would change Mrs. Broadback's mind and she'd realize that she still needed me. "I hope Danny gets better," I said, enunciating each word as I stared at the rain dripping down the small kitchen window.

Hearing that Danny had the measles—that I wasn't needed—was worse than waking to a snow day. Babysitting was, outside of school, my favorite haven, allowing me to practice being someone else on a small scale. At the Broadbacks', I could be a mother, a rich person living in Glencarin, and a wife of a man with Playboys in his side drawer. At the Hurrells' I got to be a wife whose husband had fallen in love with a neighbor. I had discovered the news on the party line but still acted surprised when she told me he'd moved into the neighbor's house. I'd tried to cry when she sobbed one afternoon, but the most I could muster was some eye rubbing. Then she poured herself some vodka and me some apple juice and I listened to the whole story.

"If Danny gets better, I can still come," I said, again pausing between words. *Please, please,* I begged silently, picturing Mrs. Broadback's food, her furniture, her jewelry— everything I needed for a temporary change. For a moment, I wished Stephen's face would show up in the kitchen. *I need something permanent,* I whispered to him, like I could command him at will—torment him with what he wanted to hear and then back out.

"Measles lasts for a while—I think we're stuck at home." Once I heard the dial tone, I dropped the receiver and watched it dangle by its cord, a lifeline to the outside world that Mom, during dinner one night, had said we should get rid of. I had an urge to rip the phone from the wall in revenge for all her outlandish pronouncements, but for a moment as I kicked the receiver, I wondered why I had the right to hate Mom or anyone.

I hadn't been in a war or found myself stuck with a bed-ridden husband. I could see her now, shaking the white cloth out the front door, sending a shower of dust into the clouds of exhaust. If I rushed at her and pushed her under one of the many trucks that flew down Michigan Avenue, I'd at least have the right to be forever guilt ridden. No more confusion about what I should and shouldn't think. No more rage floating like a cloud about to burst and no more guilt trapped in the mist after the storm peters out. Killing Mom could lead to clarity— wipe my brain of everything except for one single horror.

As I dumped Tang in a glass and stirred under a stream of cold water, I saw Stephen in the foam and bubbles. It wasn't smiling Stephen but more like the photo of him in the eighth grade yearbook. His determined eyes reminded me of his obsession with drivers' ed and Mr. Freds thinking he was doing his job when he told Stephen he couldn't sign up for Driver's Ed—couldn't do what every kid waited to do since practically elementary school. Dad gave me my first driving lesson in about first grade, propping me on his laps so I could reach the pedals.

Mr. Freds, I thought, as I gulped the sweet drink, may never have had a passion or probably had given up on one. No wonder he forgot about the fixations of kids; a purpose that would monopolize the brain. As Barbie, I'd have real convictions, and nothing would throw me off track. I'd cling to baton twirling forever, unlike Mr. Freds who, like most adults, was neither here nor there, living because they had to, for some reason or another. Stupefying, I thought, that adults clung to halfway lives that ultimately added up to almost nothing. Then I heard Stephen warning me that I'd end up like Mom obsessed with something no one cared about. *Not on your life,* I shouted silently. And then I said it again, as sweat ran down my temples and my breath was stuck in my chest. I gulped the Tang and saw Barbie in my mind, twirling to an admiring crowd, and I saw her wave at me in the hallway, and I slumped, my breath normal, my mind clear of Stephen and worry about being Mom.

"Did you see the drawing behind the incinerator?" Beth whispered on tiptoe trying to reach my ear like she feared Dad even when he was safely upstairs in bed. "It's weird," she mouthed without making so much as a sound, but I read her lips and understood. Without saying anything, we hurried to the basement, me following and dreading what I couldn't imagine. "It's just a stick drawing," Beth whispered. Her thick brown hair swished side to side, and I couldn't help examining the texture and lushness. Why was she now making a mark in our lives, like a wet footprint on cement? When had she gone from the girl who dropped into our lives and left at a moment's notice, leaving nothing behind but memories of Dad disgruntled at her presence, some games we made up, and her dark eyes always probing but never appearing to drink in much beyond the moment at hand to someone at the heart of our family? "Remember sneaking down here with that cake mix you hid in your bag, and us both getting sick after eating it raw?"

"We did that? Wait till you see this drawing." Beth said, leading the way.

"I guess I should see it," I said as she led me to a narrow space behind the incinerator.

"That's it," she said, and I closed my eyes. "Maybe it was here before you lived here," she said, but we both knew that wasn't the case. I shrugged my shoulders and opened one eye. A black stick figure hung by a thick rope, and off to the side Mom had drawn a small hen and a nest of eggs. I knew this was Mom's drawing because of the eyes. The face was blank except for the eyes. I'd seen other drawings like this. I stood back, wishing I was alone and that Beth hadn't found it. Dad would hate the thought of Beth finding out something about our family. He used to invite foreign students he met at bus stops to our house, but he was a guard dog when Beth came around—like he was afraid she'd slip into our world and become a permanent family member if he didn't keep an eye on her.

"We shouldn't be here," I said, turning and staring at her puffy face and the rings around her eyes. "Don't you worry about looking like a typical hood?" I said, leading her away from the drawing as I tossed her a ball of twine I found on the incinerator. She snagged the twine, and I thought how much Dad would admire someone who could catch and throw— except Beth. "Don't get into our stuff anymore," I said. She ignored the remark, and we kept up this game of tossing the twine for a minute or two, while I thought about being meaner to Beth.

The allure of being mean, I realized, was that I half loved, half hated the way my heart turned into a rock—as Mom warned it would—when I treated Beth the way everyone had treated Stephen Fedkin or, in Beth's case, the way Dad had always treated her. He hadn't always dragged her around the house. Scowling whenever she entered a room got the point across that she wasn't wanted. His spontaneously mean face reminded me of the black dog's instinct for growling and sticking his tail straight up.

I imagined myself as Dad's substitute now that he couldn't treat her like the untouchables we'd learned about in a Travel Log at MSU. A sick heroism burned from inside my chest like I would act on something, throw caution to the wind for the first and only time I could remember in my timid life of dreaming and imagining. I guessed a murderer had the same sensation right before plunging a knife into someone's heart. At least he did something. The stone in my chest radiated a brave and noble fire--the thrill of danger, even destruction—as I caught the ball of twine.

"Why are you two down here?" Mom's kerchief was about to slide off her head. She held a rag in each hand, and her grey eyes widened, brightening under the fluorescent lights. For a moment I wondered if she contemplated suicide. She could be the hanging man or person; I couldn't make out the point of this drawing. At least she could make it clear: boy, girl, man, woman—who was this? Beth looked at me and then looked at the incinerator. I inched my way to the drawing, picturing myself smearing it with chocolate syrup from the can.

"It's my fault—I wanted to show her the drawing behind the incinerator," she said, shrugging her shoulders.

"If you didn't invite every strange person in the world to our house, this wouldn't have happened," I said, trying to keep my voice as even and cruel as possible. "I know not to come down here and look at all the weird stuff you do." Mom looked at Beth and then at me. For a second her eyes moved back and forth, and her lips parted, like she was about to defend herself or offer some kind of explanation, but no words came out. She motioned to the incinerator like we were playing charades, like the fire in the metal box or the ashes in its bottom drawer held the clue to the hanging person, or to a past event she couldn't describe. Beth looked up, exhaling loudly. Mom closed her mouth and wrinkled her forehead. "Oh god," I said in an attempt to diffuse the moment, but it came out mean when I'd hoped to lighten the situation. I kicked a rag stinking of turpentine at Mom's shins—another example of my failed instinct for bettering any situation. *I'd die so quickly in a concentration camp,* I thought.

"I'll hang myself too if you don't watch it. Do you want to find me the way I found my father in our barn?" She blurted these words, as if she'd been a different explanation but the truth had pushed its way forward, cutting in front of a gentler, calmer version of what happened one day on the farm. My stomach flipped like I was in the middle of a wave, and the room itself seemed to have no bottom or top, and I began to cry, first in terror and then, as I got back my equilibrium, in pure disbelief that a dad could be so cruel. I bent towards the drawing, getting face to face with the blank eyes. This can't be in my basement, I thought. Mom breathed heavily, and before I had a chance to linger over the drawing, figure out how she managed to draw even the noose without lifting her pen, she ripped the drawing off the wall, scrunched it in one hand and lifted the top of the incinerator. *Who are you?* I thought silently. *What kind of person would draw and hide in plain sight a morbid picture?* I stared at Mom's feet and then felt her breath on my neck and wondered if all people are strangers.

"This is all my fault, "Beth said as Mom dropped the drawing into the fire. When the top slammed shut, I cried harder, like a storm at its full strength.

"You're really good at drawing," I said, babbling and praying she would grant me the right to say nonsensical things without becoming suspicious of me or the world or even Beth, who for some reason chuckled and pulled on her bangs. Mom shuffled towards me, and I wrapped my arms around her waist, squeezing until she slumped into me, and we hung onto each other as I hiccupped. Beth dropped onto the cement floor and, as Mom and I clung together, I thought about the dirt that must be all over Beth's pants and blouse. Shouldn't Mom and I tell her to get up? I pictured beautiful Empress horrified by our pathetic standards of cleanliness, yet she wasn't around to teach Beth, and I felt bad that Beth was becoming a slob like us. Shouldn't a kid take on the ways of the parent? My heart twinged at the thought that I was like Beth, taking on the ways of another family, but Beth had no choice in the matter—unlike me running into the arms of Barbie and Mrs. Robert.

Mom smoothed my hair, dropping her hand again and again onto the top of my head like my skull was a drum. I winced each time it landed even though it didn't hurt. Then, like she couldn't brush away the moment when she entered the barn and saw her Dad's shoes above her head, she cleared her throat and took a deep breath. "He would've known I'd find him first. He'd have to know," she said, still stroking my hair.

I pictured her in the door of a barn I'd never seen, and my crying tapered off as I took her hand from my head and smoothed over its rough surface. "I'm sorry you found out," she said, staring at Beth like she was another person she'd come upon out of the blue, not hanging from a rafter but also in limbo. I stared at Beth, too. "Try to forget the whole thing. We don't want it to happen again." She whispered like I was Sleeping Beauty finding out about my fate, or maybe she was Sleeping Beauty. I wasn't sure who was most at risk for repeating the suicide, but as her face slowly reddened, I worried about repeating the past, especially events I'd forgotten to keep track of. I imagined myself recording each day in a diary as a way to control the future.

"OK," I said, and nodded, looking over at Beth, hoping that she'd help me comprehend the suicide of a family member and the possibility that suicide runs in families—something I'd never heard of but seemed exciting, as if our hidden distinction had been revealed. The next second it seemed scary and not anything I wanted to be part of but intractable, like I'd just received the prophecy foisted on Oedipus. I remember thinking the story terrifying—revelatory—while everyone else in English raised hands to say that the idea of an oracle was unbelievable. Now I could feel my face heat up, and I vowed never to descend to the basement again. Then both Mom and I helped Beth to her feet as she brushed dirt from her pants.

"Maybe we could go to the movies?" Beth said, like she'd had practice in resolving conflict or just wanted to do something other than hang out in the dirty basement near the blazing incinerator and the art propped everywhere while we thought about suicide and fate. The three of us hung on to each other as we walked to the stairs. I took the lead, planting a foot on each creaky wooden step as I focused on the light at the top peeking through the half-closed kitchen door. Had this experience bound the three of us together in a permanent stranglehold? I clung to the hope that it would wear off the way my tie to Patty Scott was now stretched thin. People, Dad said, were rarely trustworthy for the long run, and I hoped memories were the same.

CHAPTER XIV

"We could see *Rosemary's Baby*—it's at the Lucon." Like Dad, Beth seemed to know everything. I'd never forgotten the night she used my Barbie and Ken dolls to demonstrate something she said all adults do in bed every night. "The penis must be rock hard before inserted into the vagina," she'd said squeezing the two dolls together.

"What's the vagina?" I'd asked, and she patiently showed me as she had before, smiling wistfully like an adult who remembers the old innocent days.

"A movie would be fun," Mom said, motioning to a loaf of bread she'd made. "Butter and jam?" She placed her hand on my back, and it rested there like a rock. Her body, especially her large red hands, refused to melt the way Dad's massive hands and strong arms softened as he leaned into a person. He was like the stick of butter, barely able to keep its shape, puddling on a saucer meant for a teacup, resisting a permanent shape on which others could lean. Beth took her slice, and Mom buttered another before handing it to me. Beth and Mom looked at me like this was a big deal—not the movie but the bread, and I shook my head, realizing a moment later that I was starved and wishing I'd sunk my teeth into the extra thick slice.

I wondered if there was anything else I didn't know. Maybe they wanted me to take the bread, sit down, and then they'd tell me more things I'd rather not hear about. I shook my head again as I looked from Mom to Beth, wishing things were as they had been, with me figuring out how best to scorn Mom and belittle Beth. I pictured Mom scrunching the drawing and almost yelled at her for the image that I figured would haunt me. *Better not to know about my Grandpa,* I thought, but in the next second I wished she was Dad, describing in hideous detail his dangling head and the bulging eyes. "Can't you jazz it up?" he always asked when I read him a report I'd written.

"Will you be able to give us a ride?" I asked Mom as Beth slumped against the sink and nodded like we were finally making some progress, although towards what I wasn't sure— I guess the rest of the day.

"Yes, I will," Mom announced in a formal tone I'd never heard before.

"I'll get money from Dad," I said, remembering the moment at age five when I had jerked out of the hot nap and knew I had to get out of our empty house and find someone, even though I wore a slip, no underwear and it was the middle of icy winter. At first, I had wanted to find Mom, but like now I had wanted someone who never changed her tone of voice— like Mrs. Broadback.

"See if you can get enough for candy," Beth raised her eyebrows, and I looked at her and then Mom—the two of them reminding me of Gargoyles the French teacher had showed us as an example of architectural detail our buildings lacked.

"Sock drawer," Dad whispered from his bed where he lay like a mummy stretched out as usual on his back, toes straight up under the cream colored bedspread.

"Are you better, Dad?" I whispered in a pleading voice. "Do you want to practice ESP?" I leaned over the bed frame at the foot of the bed and stroked his feet sticking straight up under the covers. "Or the Racing Form? I can get a copy downstairs," I said. I stared at a bowl of old noodles floating in yellow chicken broth, wondering why I'd never tried to help him. I'd never be able to explain why I'd been so cold and uncaring to both of my parents, and my heart revved again as I saw myself alone for the rest of my life, or at least at high school—shunned by everyone for the next four years, until I could get to college like the girl with the super long hair who obviously loved college.

I walked to a chair near his head and moved a glass of water balancing precariously near the chair's edge. Perhaps I could become a real Candy Striper—a caring person. He puffed air out his nostrils like a dying dragon, and I backed away, imagining my hand stroking his head like Mom had stroked mine but not sure if he'd like it or if I'd hurt him somehow. If he died, I'd tell everyone at school that he'd had a heart attack. That's what Betsy Rover announced in homeroom when her father died, but Patty Scott told me at eighth grade graduation after Betsy's mom walked into the auditorium alone in a black dress that Betsy's dad hung himself because Rover Auto Parts was going bankrupt. Dad's life was going bankrupt, too, and Betsy's lie reassured me that lying to cover up the truth allowed her to face everyone. Then it hit me that Mom, as usual, got it wrong. She wanted me to forget the past, but that would never work. You have to change the past, the present, the future— make it up like Betsy did

But then I remembered Patty shaking her head and stroking my shoulder like we were still in her house on Kensington Road. "Everyone knows," she'd said. Everyone would know about Dad, too, I thought, and for a second, I imagined nodding as people lined up to tell me how sorry they were that my neglect had killed him. He dropped me first, I'd say and unlike Betsy Rover and her family, I hadn't pressured Dad to provide me with luxury cars and shopping trips to Detroit—other than a few coins from his sock drawer. *Our situations are totally different*, I thought as I stood at the door. I am not like Betsy and Mom—people who were directly linked to a death. Then, a voice told me that we never know how our actions affect other people. *You could be contributing to the death of someone right now and not realize it.* The voice kept going as I covered my ears. *All you care about is becoming other people*, the voice accused me, and I rushed downstairs. Then I saw Stephen's face hanging in midair, and I was relieved for the first time since his death that he still showed up like I was the most important person he'd ever known; like he cared about me and would probably never forget me.

Beth went outside, just as the phone rang. A man cleared his throat and then hung up. I thought it might be Mr. Freds, too afraid at the last minute to report my skipping and being late for school. The last thing he'd want was another Stephen Fedkin. Then I remembered that it was Saturday and he'd never call from home.

"Beth must be outside or something," I said as Mom emerged from the basement, and we went outside to the car.

"Who called?" Mom asked.

"A friend from Debate Club," I lied.

"I thought you'd join the art club," she said. Then she searched in her big silly pocket, drooping off the ugliest jacket I could imagine, and a piece of straggly hair fell across her face. I turned away, searching for Martins going in and out of the small holes in the white Martin house.

A bird erupted from a hole in the Martin House and I felt sorry for both Mom and the bird, living near me and expecting me to care about their lives and wanting me, in Mom's case, to be like her. No wonder Mom wound my hair in her fist after I laughed at one of her hare-brained ideas. I was cruel deep in my gut. I guess we were all disappointing each other, but the bird, released from the house, soared and banked, reminding me of Barbie's baton suspended for what seemed like an hour and her expert hand finding it midair. Then, like the warm air rushing towards the cold air, a tornado formed in my belly, and I spun around, fearing that Mom knew I would soon be Barbie. And then I pictured a door shutting and Mom looking out the window at me, brushing me away. She'd turn the tables, I thought. Anytime I thought I had the upper hand, winning a situation with her or anyone else, I'd lose. *People are so much cleverer than I am,* I thought, *except at figuring things out that no one cares about, like Latin.* But finally, as I imagined the list of Latin words we were to memorize, I breathed out loud, straightened, up as we'd done in the posture parade in gym and my body measured recently at 5'9" felt like it belonged to me.

"Forgot the keys," Mom said, adjusting her skirt as she went back inside. Beth appeared, hurrying away from the Craft's back door.

"Why were you there?" I asked as we slid in the car—the two of us in the front. Mom appeared, dangling keys and smiling at us through the window.

"Girls, let's keep our minds on positive thoughts today!" She smiled into the rearview mirror. "Holding onto negative thoughts or things from the past will kill your spirit." She turned around as Beth and I looked out the windows.

We sailed backwards with Mom expertly sliding the tail of the big finned car into Michigan Avenue. Operating machines brought out the best in her, I thought, while Dad always rammed the car into the stream of traffic, infuriated that the dopes in their dumb cars didn't give him the right of way, didn't automatically move over.

As we moved away from the edge of town and into East Lansing, the traffic thinned out. Shiny new cars glided toward the bright downtown. The main drag, Grand River Avenue, was lined with shops on one side and various gates and entrances to MSU on the other. Before, when Dad and I bombed around searching for stories, rousting one character after the next from stockrooms, alleys and always the soda fountain at the Rexall, Dad was king of the land. With Mom at the helm, the downtown glistened unnaturally, and our old Chevy looked out of place. Without warning Stephen appeared in the backseat, staring out the window. He sneered at the artifice surrounding us until he evaporated through the crack in the window and I could swear his eyes were full of tears like he wanted more than anything to drive next to the pretty bushes lining the boulevard and turn as Mom did now to the other side of the street where one bright shop after the next beckoned. "After the movie, let's make fudge, and if you want, I can teach you more about throwing pots, or we could draw a still life—I have some new gourds and interesting bottles."

"Sure," I said as a streak of lightning appeared far off.

"I have to go to the bathroom real bad," Beth said as Mom stopped in front of the Lucon on Grand River.

"Badly," I said under my breath as I leaped over a puddle to the curb. "Sorry," I mumbled.

While I paid for the tickets, Beth went to the bathroom. When she emerged from the Ladies Room, I stared at her breasts, bouncing beneath a burgundy V-neck sweater. When she ducked under the rope, I noticed that she breathed hard and that her greasy hair stuck to her olive skin. "How much did you steal, anyway?" She looked down and fiddled with the zipper on the jacket. I scanned the mirrored lobby, searching for anyone I might ditch Beth for without her noticing— someone I could imitate if only for a minute or two.

"I can't wait to sit down," she murmured.

I ducked under the rope and ordered two boxes of Dots, two Boston Baked Beans, two Jaw Breakers, and two Black Crows at the long candy counter. When I came back, there were two MSU students behind us, arms wrapped around each other, talking about how drunk they'd been the night before. Behind them, I recognized a hippie girl from Latin. "I wish there were other kids from school," I whispered to Beth.

"A lot of parents wouldn't allow their kids to see this movie, "Beth said, squeezing a Black Crow between her front teeth.

"How do you know that?" I whispered, thinking she was probably right, and when the man ripped our tickets, I gave Beth the stubs like I wanted no memory of the day so far—if I could just concentrate on becoming Barbie, I'd put everything so far to rest. Then, Mom's face popped up in my mind, and my stomach twisted. "I wish they sold malteds here," I said as we found our seats in the half empty theatre, and I envisioned a cool thick vanilla malted coating my insides.

From the first scene, I thought about escaping the giant screen and the evil characters. I longed for the day Dad and I saw *Fantasia*. Every weekend we'd raced around together to places he loved, but Fantasia he'd chosen for me—said kids loved it everywhere. I wondered how he knew about kids and movies, but I didn't ask him as we moved up the line, my hand in his grip. After we'd gotten into the lush lobby, he bought me at least five boxes of candy and popcorn for both of us, which he tossed into his mouth while we watched the black and white Newsreel. Dad loved the first part about horse racing, and then he leaned forward, staring at some bombs blowing up a country that he said reminded him of Guadalcanal. He flopped back in the seat and went on and on about the War and how much he hated the sweat and the mosquito netting, and the idiot army bosses, and also about hiding in foxholes. I held his hand, and then the usher told him to be quiet, and he left to wander the back of the theatre while I watched the dancing elephants and scarfed down the candy, which he replenished at some point. As we bolted into the bright glare at the end, I wanted to tell him that I loved him. Instead, I described every detail in the movie, and he nodded, but I knew that he was too far ahead to hear.

Now, Beth leaned away from me, sucking on a mouthful of Dots. A young blonde actress, with weird short hair and deep-set eyes like mine, reminded me of a runt guinea pig about to be ripped apart by its evil relatives. Why her husband and their neighbors picked her for this mysterious torture, I wasn't sure, but after her husband scratched her all over her body while she slept, she began to look like Beth, puffy and gaunt at the same time. I tried to think of something outside the theatre as this character, Rosemary, talked into a pay phone to a friend she hoped would save her from a circle of people about to make her their slave or their prisoner. But the movie beat out anything outside the Lucon, and I could only focus on her as she became more and more desperate. She was vulnerable, like Mom, and I vowed never to be mean to Mom again, and I threw Beth into this resolution and swore I'd treat Beth like a sister and stop praying to never see her again. And suddenly, as Beth sucked on the candy and placed one hand on her stomach, I blinked hard and saw an image of Beth pregnant, just like the woman on the screen whose deepening dark eyes were identical to Beth's eyes I gasped and choked on a handful of Boston Bake Beans. "Are you OK?" Beth asked, staring at the screen. I nodded. "It's just a movie," Beth whispered, and I nodded again, my head bobbing as my heart pounded, and then I opened my eyes. Rosemary's face filled the screen, and I realized that carefree Rosemary who'd tossed off her clothes in the beginning of the movie was now like Beth—pensive, quiet, and furtive.

I was scared for Beth—her pregnancy wasn't make-believe. Part of me was proud to have figured out why Beth looked different, and part of me wished that I'd never realized that Beth was pregnant. The burden of knowledge flattened me against the plush seat. I hoped that when Beth was a mom, she'd keep everything from her kid.

"I want to go," I begged Beth. Beth reached across to pat my shoulder while squeezing my other hand. A box of jawbreakers slid off Beth's lap, clunking to the floor.   "I'm so sorry," I whispered. "Shh! God, you guys, knock it off!" The college student behind us scolded.

I only half concentrated on the movie after the revelation, dwelling on Beth becoming a mother and thinking all the while that I'd rather spend my life being other people in my mind— imagining a different life—while always having me to fall back on. But soon, I guess, Beth would be a mother with responsibilities for a baby, and I couldn't imagine the finality of that. There'd be no changing after that. I shivered, and my heart raced at the inevitability of motherhood, and finally decided I'd kill myself before I would submit to it. Mom must feel stuck like the wheels of her old car stuck in a rut. As a young girl she'd had to push their Model A after it broke down while her Mom steered. She loved squishing her old shoes in the mud and she told the story with such relish I knew she wanted to fix things and have adventures. No wonder she seemed always deflated and trapped in our house on a highway, propping up Dad and saddled with me. For the first time, as the screen changed colors, Mom's addiction to art made sense. I imagined her caressing cloth and squinting at a still life— replacing all the hurt and doubt with the immutable truth of color and light. I should tell Beth to pay attention to Mom instead of just enduring Mom's classes. I winced as Mom's face appeared in my mind relaxed and defenseless while explaining various art techniques as Beth and I yawned and concentrated on the snacks she'd prepared.

When THE END appeared on the screen, we watched the credits roll, and I snuck a peek at Beth, realizing that she'd feel stuck too. I closed my eyes and imagined her holding a baby to her chest, but then she dropped the baby and walked over it, disappearing. "We should hurry," Beth said.

"Why?" I murmured. But she was up, and I followed her, vowing never to enter the Lucon Theatre again, except for reruns of *Fantasia*.

We blinked in the dull light as soft rain drenched our heads. Beth squinted at the cars filing by. "You might need glasses," I said, searching for a way to let her know that I'd discovered her secret. "I think there's an eye doctor in the new Frandor Shopping Plaza," I added, imitating girls I'd heard relaying important information as they changed out of gym suits in the locker room. She didn't answer; in fact, she turned away, staring down Michigan Avenue, I stammered something about feeling sorry for Rosemary and her baby. "When are you having your baby?" I blurted. We didn't move and Beth didn't look at me.

"Not for a while," she said." Please don't tell your mom and dad," she said, still scanning the street. "I didn't know you knew," she said, tugging at the bottom of her shirt. "I know I look like a pig, but I'm not what you think." She stopped and looked up at the sky like the rain would wash her face and rid her of the baby at the same time.

"Are you afraid?" I asked.

"There he is." Beth grabbed my hand and we approached a blue car I recognized. Beth jumped in the front seat.

"Thank you," I said, sliding to the middle of the back seat.

"Sure enough," Mr. Craft said, chuckling. "That *Rosemary's Baby* is supposed to be pretty racy," he said, looking sideways at Beth and then searching for me in the rearview mirror. Beth shrugged and turned on the radio, inching up the volume until Mr. Craft begged her to turn it down. She laughed like a brat, and I thought that nothing was the same anymore.

"Can you stop at McDonald's?" Beth asked. Mr. Craft nodded, turning right at MAC, expertly pulling a U-Turn with one palm.

"I have money," I said after he parked near one of the glossy yellow arches and Beth didn't appear to move beyond adjusting the radio.

"Oh, that's not necessary," Mr. Craft said, handing me a five-dollar bill. "Whatever she wants," he said, nodding towards Beth.

"Fries and a coke," she said.

"OK," I said. "Um, should I get you anything?" Mr. Craft looked in the rear-view mirror again, his blue eyes and white eyebrows filling the rectangular mirror, which he straightened with little tugs.

"I guess not," he said, letting his hand drop to the seat, next to Beth's. "You know, on second thought, I could go for one of their malts—vanilla would be great."

We sat in the car as the rain pattered the roof and streamed down the windows, each of us absorbed in the food I'd carried to the car in a white bag and a cardboard drink holder. I couldn't bear the sound of Mr. Craft gulping his vanilla milkshake. He said he never liked straws and had removed the top. I felt like the horrible short witch woman in Rosemary's Baby, producing a disgusting milkshake that I imagined coating his tongue and throat—poisoning him in a non-lethal way, but poisoning him nonetheless.

"I forgot about babysitting," I said, dropping my cheeseburger into the bag and jerking open the car door like Mr. Craft was about to lock the doors, imprisoning Beth and me. "Thank you for everything," I said, standing in the rain and peering in the front window. Beth waved and smiled, and I waved back, relieved that she seemed like an old friend.

"I can give you a ride—it's wet out there!"

I shook my head. "The place is near here--it's a short walk," I said, backing up.

He stared at me and then rolled down his window. "Oh c'mon," he said. "It's not good for you to be wet!" I knew I was imagining too much, letting my mind dash in all different directions, but he reminded me of Rosemary's husband.

Beth lowered her window. "Your favorite song," she said pointing at the radio. I forced a smile as she bobbed her head to *Wooly Bully*. I wondered if she remembered the day we'd danced to my 45 of this song, and Dad had appeared from nowhere with a florid face. In an astounding moment of raw strength, he'd ripped the record player out of the hi-fi, and we stopped dancing to watch in horrified awe. The black 45 flipped up into his face as he let the metal record player clunk to the floor, and I let out a laugh, which he thought or decided came from Beth. I had inched backwards out of the room as he had grabbed her wrist and whipped her around like she was nothing more than a jump rope.

Mr. Craft started the car, and I wondered if he would take Beth away to a better life, that is, if he had actually offered to do so. As she rolled up her window and slumped in the seat, I heard her say, *I'm not what you think,* and as the car pulled away, I thought she made up the story about Mr. Craft taking her away. When the car turned, she stuck her hand out, waving to me like Dad always waved—an easy transition to more amusement. In the next moment, I imagined Mom in her awkward outfit, helping both Dad and Beth despite haunting memories and a longing for real adventure.

CHAPTER XV

On the outskirts of downtown, three or four blocks from McDonald's, three tall, skinny boys came towards me. They all smoked cigarettes, wore some shade of blue, and walked purposefully, like they'd been searching for me. Maybe they mistook me for someone who owed them money or who'd ratted on them to Pinky and now were out for revenge. I prayed these boys would separate so I could squeeze through. A desperate voice inside my head told me to turn, run and hide somewhere. Where, I wasn't sure. No wonder Patty Scott dumped me; I hadn't a brave bone in my body. The most daring thing I'd ever done was run up and down Michigan Avenue in my slip when Mom took off during my nap. What was so scary about an empty house, even if I was five? Then I remembered the barren house, me outside barefoot on the freezing icy cement and the cars whizzing by—not one stopping to help me find Mom. The next day I changed for the first time into someone else; a doll in a red dress and an apron who'd stood on the shelf, the same every day.

As the boys got closer, I recognized the tallest one. He was the hood who'd hung out at my locker and wanted to know about Beth. His brown hair had darkened in the rain, and although I was sure he was the kid at my locker, the dark hair made him look older, almost like a completely new person or a deviation of his old self. *He's willful,* I thought, *confident and angry about being pigeonholed as a bad kid.* He said something as he nodded my way, and the boys laughed. Dad popped up in my brain like this was an emergency, warning me to avoid these kinds of kids, kids like Beth who want something from you; who invade your life and take what isn't theirs.

"You're so like your father," Mom had said in a moment of fury after I had snubbed a girl new to Mr. Craft's meetings, a girl too vague to lend me her life, and yet she peppered me with a million questions about my favorite this and that as if she might want some of me.

I had the urge to kick water, spraying it at these boys. It was all I could do to restrain myself as we came nearly face to face. I made quick plans to rush at them and bash through like a game of Red Rover. It reminded me of a morning when a kid had ridden his bike in front of our car, forcing Dad to pause and get stuck in his thoughts for a moment. In a split second Dad gunned forward narrowly missing the kid. I had ducked down, squatting on the floorboard as a man screamed at dad for treating a kid like that. I sobbed knowing the man was right.

When they were about a foot away, I took a deep breath, trying to squash the anger rising in my chest, but then one of the boys blew smoke at me. I felt a force erupting from inside, like Mom whisking plates off the table or throwing pots and pans at windows or doors in an impulsive release of emotion. Then the main hood, the one who'd asked about Beth at my locker, smirked and I yelled, "You got Beth in trouble. I know you're the one, and she's too nice to even tell you, but I will since she's pregnant with your baby." The words tumbled out along with spit that sprayed his face. He wiped it and laughed, but then he grabbed my arm, and I wondered what Patty Scott would do. She'd saved us both when the dry cleaner owner had accused us of putting snow down the drop box. I'd cowered behind her as the man pointed his finger in her face and said he was going to call the school.

"What are you talking about? Stupid freshman," the boy said, letting my arm drop. "In her dreams." The smallest boy ground a cigarette with the heel of his boot, and they all laughed. Then the kid blew smoke through his nostrils as he stomped on the cigarette, said they had to hurry, or they wouldn't make it to the tire sale in time. "I'm not surprised—she'd do it with anybody, but I'm not desperate," the boy said, and they all turned to leave as my face reddened, and I wondered what possessed me to accuse the kid of being the father. I felt dizzy and wished I was in bed plotting out Barbie's house or reading, anything to avoid this impulse to yell and accuse someone of disrupting my plans, ruining my world.

Everything felt dangerously real for a moment, and I thought of Mom threatening to hang herself. A voice inside told me to follow the boys and explain that I'd made up the story, but I couldn't move, and my breath felt stuck in my chest until finally Barbie's face popped up in my mind. As her smile widened, my shoulders dropped, my jaw relaxed. I imagined her twirling, and I knew that once I became Barbie it would be impossible to follow through on anything that popped up in my mind. I couldn't imagine Barbie kicking water at anyone. Ever since Pinky had announced Stephen's death, reality or things I might actually do as me, like kill myself, had clouded my thinking. *Just do it,* I heard inside my brain, but it was my voice this time and not Stephen's. *Just do it,* my voice said again.

"Where are you?" I looked up at the gray sky for a glimpse of Stephen but was blinded by the rain. If only I could tell him right then and there that I was going to become Barbie, hell or high water as Mom would say. "There won't be any of me to kill me," I said, and actually chuckled, but then my heart raced as I looked in a puddle, searching for Stephen, anyone—even me. But when my own face didn't appear in the greasy cloudy water, I felt myself dissolve into the puddle as if any vestige of the real me no longer existed. "I'm a puddle," I said and laughed again, but the laugh was jittery. I waited a minute for my face to appear, but when it didn't, I began to run until I couldn't catch my breath. I might as well be five again, I thought, picturing myself racing back and forth along Michigan Avenue. But at five I hadn't begun to worry about dissolving. I wondered what I thought about all day, as me. My breath and heart accelerated as I passed houses and an empty lot. It wasn't until I once again pictured Barbie twirling that my heart slowed, and I felt like I could breathe deep into my lungs. I cupped my cheeks and knew I existed, feeling a pimple on my right cheekbone that had erupted the night before.

As I headed away from town, I began to pass small bungalows, and I imagined wandering through them like Goldilocks. I stared at a man sitting close to a window, reading a newspaper. He looked out at me, and by the time I passed his garage I wondered if he'd keeled over and was now dead and alone. I willed myself forward, trying to forget about the possibility of his death. If I'd never considered his death, I'd never mull the decision not to check on him; run back and spy on him in the chair by the window. And if I'd never realized that Beth was pregnant, she could have delivered the baby secretly and perhaps given it up for adoption. I had to work harder at keeping my brain free of what Mom always calls the here and now, at least until I became Barbie. Better to work on higher thinking, she always said. But I was stuck with the news of Beth's pregnancy. Perhaps with a lot of will power I could convince myself that I'd never known. If only I'd worked on Barbie sooner, I'd know what she knows, and I'd live finally in this world as someone else, as Barbie. *Get out of this life,* a voice said, and this time I knew it was Stephen talking to me, but his face was nowhere. "Don't worry," I said aloud. "Don't worry. If I can't get Barbie down, I'm coming."

I turned around and hurried back towards downtown. Up ahead, none of the small buildings and shops—even the Campus Cinema with its bright marquee—appeared welcoming or like places where I could dry off. Steam rose from the sidewalks and the streetlight changed quickly from yellow to red like a warning to stay home. If only, I thought, I'd run into someone to talk with about the weather or other comforting, bland topics, like the new space program that the student teacher said was a sign of progress and important if we were to stay on top of the Soviets. "It's the next frontier," he'd said one morning, motioning a couple of boys to come to the front of the classroom. He pulled a globe out of a big box, attached to the globe were a sun and a moon. I eavesdropped, pretending to sharpen my pencil as he talked about the solar system, rotating the globe as one boy held the sun, and another worked the moon. He reminded me of Mr. Craft except instead of religion and systems of thinking he was obsessed with outer space.

"That is very interesting," I murmured as I passed the group on the way to my desk.

"Yes, it is," he said without looking up, and for a while I thought about becoming him or somehow getting him to fall in love with me.

At the corner of Grand River and Abbott I jumped when a door banged. "You stopped by to see Barbie!" Mrs. Robert, holding a plant in one hand and an umbrella in the other, ran down the steps of People's Church. "I told her you'd stopped by and she said you're quite the student of Latin," she said, smiling behind the flower. "You must come back—Barbie's at the barn in Haslett today, but I know she'd like to have you over another time—that is if," she stopped abruptly and smiled without showing her teeth. Then she shook her head and raised her eyebrows as if disbelieving that she almost told me something. We looked into each other's eyes like a game of who'd blink first. I gulped, but she lost, looking up at the inside of her umbrella. "Such an unsettled day." She held the flower out for a drink. "You're a brave one to be out and about."

"Well my Mom and Dad have colds," I said, picturing Dad getting information by offering a story of his own. My heart calmed now that I was making things up. I pictured the hood boy scorning my words, and I vowed to remember how dangerous the truth is. Beth might be able to hide the pregnancy—people might attribute it all to the weight gain we'd learned was not unusual in the teen years—but I'd announced it. I could imagine Dad shaking his head at my stupidity. How many times had he told me that the best reporters gave nothing away, and perhaps Mrs. Robert applied this wisdom to herself as well.

"Let's hope it's not going around," she said. I nodded, tilted my head and hoped she saw in my little head bobs and wide eyes a kind, shy demeanor.

"I'm out here to get medicine at the Rexall," I said finally.

"You need an umbrella," she said, brushing raindrops off the plant's leaves. "I'd offer you a ride, but I need to get to our shop." She walked on and then turned back. "Keep up the Latin!" she said. I smiled and waved Patty's pinwheel wave and then stopped, worrying she didn't want Patty Scott to be hanging around with Barbie.

"Vale," I said looking above her head where Stephen popped up as a signal that I was confused, I thought—confused about my chances of joining this family.

"Vale," she smiled and then chuckled. I chuckled too, but Stephen was talking in my ear about how unconfused I'd be after I suffocated myself.

The rain stopped for a minute before lightning flashed behind the thick clouds; after a long pause, thunder exploded like a sonic boom. Cold rain poured in sheets like the preface to the storm was over and we'd finally gotten into the heart of the story. I had no choice but to stand under a horse chestnut tree whose broad leaves offered some protection. In just a few minutes the leaves were sagging under the weight of the rain and I was forced back into the open. I made the mistake of looking up and was blinded for a moment. I stayed, face tilted to the sky, shutting out the world. Blotting out anything real, the minute after it happened could be the key. Uttering the word *key*, one of Dad's favorite words, helped me move forward with a lighter step in the drenching rain. But then the door to the church opened, and a woman stuck her head out. "Oh dear, it's really coming down!" She said. She held a silver baton, and I knew right away that it was Barbie's.'

"Is that Barbie Robert's?"

"Her mother left it. I hoped I'd catch her."

"I can take it to Barbie. We have Latin together." She thrust Barbie's baton into my outstretched hand, breathing a sigh like the silver baton had begun to clutter the massive stone church.

"You're a life saver!"

Right away I could tell why Barbie loved baton twirling. The silver shaft gleamed, and without being too heavy, it felt strong in my hand like we could work together as a team. I tried twirling it the way I'd seen baton twirlers make a figure eight in space, weaving it around a perfect bend in the elbow, but the rubber ball at the end wouldn't clear my jacket so I held the baton in front of my chest and walked on in the rain.

I saw my face in the baton shaft and smiled. I wished that Barbie and I could be twins, walking and twirling together, but becoming her, actually consuming her, was the plan. Twirling the baton was the key to blocking out people and their confusing actions and stories. Gleaming, I imagined the baton absorbing my life and everything I knew. I laughed a big laugh, almost a scream, at the thought of becoming a baton. "Twirl," I said, standing in a puddle. The rain continued as I finally got the figure eight motion down, and I promised myself I'd learn to twirl—somehow—if only to thoroughly become Barbie, join the here and now and forget Mom and Dad and especially my own life that I felt pulsing and pushing to emerge now as the rain poured, drenching me.

"Miss! How do I get to Sparrow Hospital?" A woman pulled her car to the curb and waved at me.

"It's in Lansing, that's all I know," I said, running over to the car and pointing in the direction of Lansing.

"You're all wet. Do you need a ride, honey? Where do you live?"

"No thank you. I live near here."

"How lucky you are. This is the nicest little town." Then she rolled up her window and drove on. She'd never guess that I was about to opt out of my life—drop it like a hot potato. My heart began to race as if the town was a gift I didn't deserve, and so was the baton. I should've run back to the church or even Robert The Florist, but instead I squeezed the baton and dragged my drenched shoes through another puddle, which was glazed in a slick of rainbow-colored grease. Stephen's face flashed before me, and I gulped, remembering the moment he had stood with the gum stuck to his pants. If only I could empty my cavernous skull, shake it like a saltshaker full of pictures, words, and of course my own accumulated record of experiences that always came back to torture me. But no amount of skull cleansing could erase the picture of Stephen crying or the picture that appeared next, of Mom in the man's clothing, dead in the window. Then a car stopped on the other side of the street offering I thought something like the reprieve we'd learned about in Civics. I threw my head back, picturing prisoners out of prison and let the rain cool my face and blind me for a second.

"You're getting sopped!" Mrs. Scott yelled from the Scotts' deep blue, bullet-shaped Tornado. "Get in this car right now, Missy!" Patty leaned into her mother, smiling and rolling one finger after the next in her signature pinwheel style wave while her Mom shouted through the barely cracked window of the shimmering car.

"I'm fine—but thank you so much," I called, holding the baton behind me.

"Don't be silly—look at your hair!" I hesitated, looking both ways as my wet hair slapped my face and neck. The streets and sidewalks were empty, but someone, anyone, might appear, and Mrs. Scott was right: it was super weird to be out with wet hair in the middle of a pelting storm.

"Thank you," I said, wedging myself behind Mrs. Scott as she hugged the steering wheel, pulling herself as far forward as she could without smashing her head into the windshield.

"I told Jim that a two-door would be a pain with all the picking up and dropping off I do of the girls and their friends. But he says that's what I've got the station wagon for."

I looked around the sleek backseat with chrome ashtray covers and gleaming door handles. I was tempted to press the automatic window button, but Mrs. Scott unexpectedly stomped on the brake, and I bounced to the ceiling and toppled over—a sign, I thought, to keep still and touch as little as possible. "The brakes are very touchy," she said, sounding her usual irritated yet upbeat self. "We just got this car—we must've ordered it six months ago! You'd think with the Oldsmobile plant right here, we'd get it sooner." I was about to tell Mrs. Scott that I'd heard two boys in biology compete over whose dad designed the new brake system for the Tornado. One of the boys had bragged that it was the most expensive Oldsmobile ever and that his grandparents had ordered one, too. But I hesitated, worrying that if I mentioned his grandparents, I might blurt out the news about my grandfather. I could imagine Mrs. Scott's horrified face as I described him hanging in a barn. The news could get to Mrs. Broadback. Perhaps she'd want to adopt me—shelter me from my own family. I pictured Mom in her housecoat waving from the driveway as Mrs. Broadback scooped me up. Guilt and relief swept over me, and I wished I could walk alone in the rain, talking to no one but myself as I tried out new people but mainly Barbie.

"Scott Hardy's is gold—I wish we could've gotten gold instead of blue," Patty said.

"Well, I like blue—although I'd prefer a four door," Mrs. Scott said, lighting a cigarette before accelerating too fast through the green light, whiplashing our heads into the soft leather. The smoke filled the car, making it hard to breathe, or maybe I felt sick because of all the movie candy.

"I can get out at this corner because I'm babysitting right near here," I lied. The rain had let up, so Mrs. Scott relented, and I thanked her as I breathed in the new car smell mixed with smoke.

"Next time, don't go wandering around in the rain!" Before I got out, Patty turned around and stared at me, her green brown eyes rimmed in lashes extended by a thick coat of black mascara, reminding me that I had to use some babysitting money to buy makeup. Barbie wore light pink lipstick most days, but otherwise she glowed without anything but a little blush. When she twirled and marched, her eyes, big and blue, flashed at the crowd under her naturally dark lashes and eyebrows, reminding me of the swirl of color and the black outlines the art teacher had pointed to in Cezanne's paintings. I thought about the girl I'd been in seventh grade—Susie Allen. She adored her three golden retriever dogs and always wore dark colors, like she didn't want the dogs to confuse her for one of them. Mom made me slacks and blouses out of navy blue, and I wore them every day. After school I helped feed the dogs, and we ran them around her yard, the two of us like the black ink outlining Cezanne's apples. But her mother died, and her aunt insisted she get rid of the dogs, and I guess her clothes because she started wearing pastels and all kinds of colors. After that it was as if someone had pricked her with a needle and the air had whooshed out of her plump body. She never even asked why I stopped following her everywhere and hanging out in her yard every day. No one would take twirling away from Barbie, I thought, clutching the baton.

"Let's hope we get a class together next year," Patty said, looking more concerned than hopeful. Mrs. Scott ground her cigarette in the ashtray. "Good for you two to catch up—does that weird guy who got fired from our church still hold those oddball services next to you?" I shook my head. "Well he was a little too interested in the girls, and of course the whole thing with Jean Maxwell. I don't think her husband's ever recovered—that's adult talk," she said to Patty, who raised her eyebrows and smiled like she knew all about Jean Maxwell and Mr. Craft—something I'd never heard about. I remembered Mrs. Maxwell's beautiful dresses when she played the piano for our school play, and that was all I could remember about her. I wished Mrs. Scott would say more, and I stared at both Mrs. Scott and Patty, wondering what else I'd missed. The three of us froze for a minute, waiting for more news or for some kind of ending, but we'd shared so little in the past years, we came up with no saying, no goodbye ritual, and those we'd had long ago had died like everything from the time they lived nearby and Patty filled me in with her know how.

"See ya," we said in unison and laughed, Patty's a natural kind of laugh and mine, my old goofy laugh—the laugh I still associated with Patty and the times she'd nurse me and I'd fake illness just to get her hovering above me and stroking my forehead. "Hey, are you learning to twirl?" She pointed to the baton. I shrugged my shoulders, afraid after the meeting with the hood boys to talk without contemplating (contemplare was on our Latin test) what Barbie would say, but a little bit of Barbie came through and I smiled without plumping up my cheeks because you can't smile broadly or with too much force while you're twirling, or you might drop the baton. Why else would Barbie keep her face still but outwardly happy?

"Yes, I am," I said, the way Barbie talked, without hesitation, and we all waved as Mrs. Scott gunned ahead into the empty street. I waved again from the curb, teetering back and forth, so that Mrs. Scott wouldn't see me in the rearview mirror head off in any particular direction. Finally, the blazing blue car turned, sending up a big spray, and I jumped off the curb and ran across the empty street, fearing she might make a U Turn, roll down her window and ask me more questions about Mr. Craft, who, according to Mom, had been booted out of People's Church because he didn't care about things like the color of a Tornado or the number of doors a car had. Mom said the superficiality of People's Church had run amok, and no one liked Mr. Craft pointing out that the church wasn't a place for social climbing and showing off one acquisition after another.

As I hurried along Michigan Avenue, I remembered the day Mr. Craft had written *covetousness* on the big pad of paper with such a flourish that the pad fell from Mom's easel and I saw her face redden like it was her fault, like she'd deliberately given him something faulty; like, perhaps, she'd tried to ruin the lesson. Suddenly she was up hurrying across the driveway, and everyone in the meeting heard our backdoor slam. I stayed put, picturing her red face and not listening any longer to Mr. Craft's lesson. Later she told me that she could do nothing right. But now, coming through the backdoor, I felt as I did back then, that her fault might really be my fault for mingling in the world, in the here and now and not shunning or hating people who liked to shop and think whatever popped in their mind. That's why Barbie was the answer. All she cared about was twirling, and there couldn't be anything wrong with twirling.

"Well you've had quite a day!" Mom stirred stovetop fudge, holding back a piece of hair with her free hand. I put the baton down and wrapped my arms around her shoulders, pressing my wet blouse against the housecoat she'd slipped back into, like the day could be the night if she so willed it or, like she couldn't resist the mini death of nighttime and that's why she often spent the whole day in her housecoat and pajamas. I scanned the house, empty of everything but the few necessities, like the old dining room table Mom tried polishing with walnut halves she and I shelled. "It's not shiny," I'd said as she rubbed the nuts into the scratched and pitted table. With her hair falling into her eyes, she rubbed harder, hissing that she didn't want anything fake, but as I turned to leave, she banged the nutcracker onto the table and brushed the shells onto the worn carpet. Then a few days later, the table disappeared, and now in its place I pictured the shiny interior of Mrs. Scott's car, and I wished I'd stop making comparisons that only make me question what I should like, what I should prefer, whom I belong to—more than myself, of course. If I could just become Barbie the way I'd been other people, I knew I'd feel less nervous and addled. Then the chocolate reminded me of how hungry I was. I dropped my arms and breathed deeply, promising myself to better organize weekends from now on with non-stop babysitting. "I bought graham crackers," she said as we both watched her pour the chocolate onto a plate of crackers.

"Thanks, Mom," I said, wishing that I could cry, beg her forgiveness, instead of envisioning so clear-eyed that she'd no longer be my mother once I was Barbie. I guessed this was the transition leading to a separation, a time when we wouldn't even know each other, and I must be stoic. She didn't turn off the burner, and a strand of her hair drooped near the flame. Neither of us moved, and then a red streak moved up a strand of her hair like an inchworm as I watched it silently. She wrapped her hand around the flame, and the odor of burning hair mixed with chocolate filled the kitchen with an acrid smell. My face heated up, and I thought that as Barbie, I'd never again feel responsible for anything other than perfecting my baton twirling, unaware of anything else while I concentrated on twirling nonstop and perhaps horseback riding. I'd never again return to this life. I'd never again witness turmoil of any sort.

"I'd like to just walk some more outside—if that's OK." Mom blew on the fudge. "This will harden in a jiffy, and we can watch The Ed Sullivan show—go tell Beth."

"She's here?" I felt angry, the way I'd felt encountering the hood boys, and for the first time Stephen appeared in our downstairs. *You're never getting out of this,* he said.

"Of course! After skating, she got a ride with that nice girl whose parents run the Organic Gardening Club we visited that time. Beth said you wanted to skate more." Mom blew on the fudge.

"Don't you know that she's lying? Mr. Craft picked us up and took us to the new McDonald's—that's where she's been eating anything she wants and just getting him to be her slave, and you don't even care about makeup or anything I actually need!"

I choked on the last part, wishing I made more sense or at least had a longer list of things she'd neglected but were crucial to me staying alive. Stephen disappeared as I stood red-faced, waiting to dodge the plate of fudge, hoping actually to catch it, run with it, and devour every last bit. Instead, she waited, like a teacher with inquiring eyes, gripping the plate with both hands, waiting, I supposed, for more information, more details. We stared at each other as I wondered if I should divulge everything about Beth. My face reddened as I pictured Mr. Craft backing up down the driveway with Beth so fat she could barely fit in the front seat. Mom looked into my eyes without blinking or squinting as she did when she was about to begin a drawing. For a moment, I stared back but then looked at my wet socks and swallowed, fearing that her response would be something violent. I could imagine her collapsing and me fleeing, once more out in the freezing rain. I may not even find Stephen out there since I figured he was getting pretty tired of begging me to kill myself.

"Beth's taking a bath," she said finally, and I nodded, wishing Beth would go away, disappear with her new baby.

"This is someone's," I said, propping Barbie's baton against the wall. "Please don't touch it." Mom glanced at the shiny baton and then looked at me without moving, and I thought for a moment that her unwavering eyes didn't seem to actually see me but rather were glued to me, confounded by having to relate to someone and their desires, that she hadn't the capacity (a new vocab word) for hearing and comprehending the words of others. In fact, my words—anyone's—seemed to set her face on fire. Angry people carry torches I thought recalling a scene some movie Dad and I watched. But she became a dangerous weapon so much so that her staring began to burn my face like her eyes could shoot flames, and then she laughed at the baton, tilting her head at it like looking directly at it would be to affirm the worth of something she hadn't made.

I was relieved to find my bedroom empty. I could hear Beth running water in the bathroom. Before Dad had dissolved into bed, the sound would've been enough to engulf his mind and send him into a stampeding rage. *Too bad,* I thought, wishing he'd give Beth some of the old treatment he wasn't capable of right now—if only to establish the old order. Wishing again that not only could I opt out of my life, but that the few people in my life up to this very moment would repeat the same patterns, so that I could count on something—something to ditch for good. *I want everything to be the same,* I ranted in my head as a flood of fear consumed my head, arms—even my hands tingled with heat, and for a moment I slipped out of my body. I touched my face and ran my fingers through my wet hair, anything to assume a form I recognized before I became Barbie. Anything to know that there was a time when I was real. Then I flounced on my bed, and my heart calmed, I guess because it knew the hard mattress hadn't changed.

I ran through some declensions, smiling at the neat categories. One of Beth's magazines caught my eye, and I practiced a lecture I'd give her as soon as she slipped through the door. But instead of composing what I hoped would be a definitive list of her pitiful transgressions, I imagined Patty

Scott, leaping over waves and finally lunging at the red raft we'd shared. "I got it!" She'd screamed, and I didn't know who to hug, the raft or Patty after she tossed it on the beach. I threw my arms around her, and she squiggled away like a slippery fish. "OK, OK—enough hugging already!" Embarrassing tears welled up as I snuggled deep into the raft before hitting the hard sand. Then she came back with two Sno-Cones, and I forgot about her rebuff as we crunched on the ice and sucked on the sweet cherry syrup until the air had completely leaked out of the raft and we rolled off, burying the limp white paper cones in the sand.

Beth slipped through the door and slumped on her bed, her hair wrapped in a towel. "I don't think McDonald's agrees with me," she said, tossing off the towel and drawing her small fingers through her wet hair. I narrowed my eyes, trying to hate her or at the very least make her squirm. She shook her head at the fudge, and I shrugged, putting the plate on the cardboard box as near to her as possible and stared at her small squat body.

"Do you do anything but lie and steal?"

She fell back on her bed, coughing.

"I bet the skating rink isn't even open yet—did you ever think of that?" I bit into a square of fudge, licking my fingers and smacking my lips. "I saw the boy—the one you did it with." She looked at me blankly. "Of course he won't admit it. That's par for the course," I said, angling for the name of the father of this baby as I pictured the cute boy in the Health movie they showed us in gym. He and a girl with the weirdest name—Phoebe—rolled down a sand dune like the one at Sleeping Bear Dune our eighth-grade class visited on Class Day. In the movie, their bodies were locked together in an embarrassing embrace. The next scene showed her kneeling before a toilet, vomiting a lot, and then we all trooped out into the gym where a nurse told us never to use a tampon, only sanitary napkins. "Will you get me some water?" I asked.

"I'm sort of sick," Beth said, still twisting the ends of her dark hair. "And, well, Mr. Craft is going to help me get better. I just want you to know."

"The Crafts are moving—ok? Will you ever just go live where you should? No one wants you," I said, turning over to face the wall. "First it was my Mom you mooched off and now poor Mr. Craft—you've obviously cast some spell on him. No wonder you picked that movie." I stared at Beth's impassive face, thinking about Rosemary and how I was going to be nicer to Beth and everyone, including Mom. But it was the movie that hypnotized me, I decided, forcing me to bypass my real goals of getting away from people like Mom and Beth and now, Dad.

I thought about Scott giving me a ride in his car and asking me to the symphony. Why was he moving? Why did I have to lose everyone? But then I realized he didn't matter. It was all Barbie now, and I could feel myself on the precipice of invading her life since her Mom seemed to like me and admire me.

Beth and I both jumped when the phone rang. Tearing off to the kitchen, I got to it on what might've been the final ring before the caller gave up. *Who calls on Saturday night? Maybe Scott*—I said hello in the cutest way I could imagine. There was silence, and for a moment I thought the caller hung up, but then I heard breathing.

"Who are you?" I said after the same man from yesterday cleared his throat. "This isn't funny," I said and hung up. Then, the breathing or the throat clearing reminded me of someone familiar, and I ran to the back door and searched the Craft's house. Mr. Craft stood in the kitchen near their wall phone. I put my hand to my mouth when I realized that it wasn't the hood boy who did it with Beth. It was Mr. Craft, who I guess also did it with Jean Maxell.

CHAPTER XVI

Sunday morning I woke starved, wishing I knew nothing about Beth and Mr. Craft. There had to be a way of erasing from my brain the thought of them doing it. My stomach growled, but the last thing I wanted was to see them in the kitchen or anywhere beyond my bedroom. Instead of flinging off the covers as I often did to get the day rolling, I watched the words *Mr. Craft and Beth* blow up in my brain, squeezing out other words like *get dressed, eat,* or *read your book.*

I flipped onto my back, and Barbie appeared flying around the room like Tinkerbell. She landed on Beth's pillow just as Mr. Craft arrived in the Barbie Car I still played with from time to time. He jumped out of the front seat and circled Barbie, jabbing at her in the quick boxing-dance Dad said was Cassius Clay's calling card.

I squeezed shut my eyes, and behind my lids Barbie grew to her normal size, leading the marching band between the beds. I wanted to join the band wherever it went—around the room, out the window, wherever Barbie saw fit. I'd have to keep track of the whole enterprise, the best way would be to get in the middle somehow, the way I'd once gotten in the center of a Jewish family and learned about special foods, no driving or lights on certain days, and other rituals. I'd begged the girl I was trying to be not to move to Detroit where her father would finally be a regular cantor and not just a visiting one. Losing her meant losing her whole world, sort of like the marching band. We cried, holding hands before she got into the back seat of a station wagon. It pulled away, and her mom lowered the window, pushing away a kid as she yelled that they'd loved having me as part of the family. Nodding, I'd teetered on the curb, desperate to memorize their faces. Thank god Barbie would never move.

If I could get to Barbie's house today, I knew her mother would welcome me. *This could be my last day as me*, I thought, humming to block out Beth's snoring as I threw off the covers.

Downstairs, I gathered some boxes of cereal, a bottle of Fanta, and a half-eaten pop tart and headed to the basement. While I waited for the world to wake up, I'd transform the basement into Barbie Robert's bedroom—vanquish everything Mom had accumulated. All the canvases, odd shaped clay pots, and vases scattered everywhere had to go to make room for Barbie's canopy bed, the side table, and princess phone, plus her many batons. At one end of the basement, the loom and pottery wheel blocked the washing machine and dryer. It was hard enough for me to squeeze by the contraptions on the rare occasion I helped Mom fold laundry. I wondered how she managed, but then again, I could imagine her directing movers to block the appliances so that she could now and then blow up and hurl the clean laundry onto the dirty floor.

I leaned against the loom, nearly tipping over a clay bust that sat on an old yellow stool. A man from Greece, Demos, had sculpted my perfect likeness when I was about six. Mom had met him during a pottery class at MSU and had invited him to our house one afternoon. "She's so beautiful," he'd said, squinting at me from the doorway, where he stood in a black suit. Most of the time, I avoided the old sculpture, although there was a period when I'd tried to destroy it or at least ruin it somehow.

One evening after dinner, Mom had handed me a soggy bag of garbage. I rushed to the incinerator, tumbling down the basement stairs and falling at the bottom onto a bare knee. "Scheisse!" I yelled imitating Mom's now and then explosive use of German. Then, like her, flustered, boiling with anger and with liquid leaking on to my shorts, I flung the garbage at the perfect likeness of my face. Mom never said anything, but when I checked the next day to see if a bread crust still hung on my nose, I found no trace of the garbage, not even the coffee grounds that had stuck to the wall in a mosaic pattern I'd found sickening.

As if Mom and I were engaged in a silent battle, I now and then assaulted my likeness, scraping it with my nails, dribbling laundry detergent on the nightgown. Other times, I looked for ways to camouflage the sculpture, hanging on it rags that smelled of turpentine, arranging them so that I looked like a nun. Another day, I poured water over the top, hoping to dissolve the clay. Nothing worked, and slowly it grew dry and ashen so that it blended into the wall and the yellow stool. It became easy, especially if I kept my eyes straight ahead during errands to the dryer or the incinerator, to completely ignore it.

But today I felt transfixed as if Demos and the time we spent, me sitting in my nightgown and him staring at me throughout the process of turning clay into my bust, should be resolved somehow in my mind, especially now after discovering the secret about Beth and Mr. Craft.

Some memories I worry I've made up. For instance, I couldn't imagine accusing Patty Scott's sister, Susan, of cruelty, or worse something icky, when she had demanded that Patty and I run naked around the Scott's house wearing Mrs. Scott's jewelry while she took pictures with Dr. Scott's expensive camera. She might say I made the whole thing up, and so could Demos if I told the story, about him and me.

I chomped on some puffed rice and swigged the Fanta, wiping my chin as I remembered Demos holding my hand as he led me up the basement stairs to the living room. He'd asked

Mom to get something at the art store downtown, and I thought he was going to put me down for a nap. "I don't nap anymore," I'd said, and he'd laughed. He adjusted a blind and asked me to lie on our davenport. "My bed is upstairs," I'd said, and he'd laughed again. Then he blew on his hand for a long time and I giggled. I'd never seen a grown-up blow on a hand or anything other than hot soup. We laughed together, and I moved over when he sat down on the davenport like he might feel my forehead or sing me a song. Then he waved his hands before my face, and I kept laughing. I continued to laugh for no good reason as he slipped one hand beneath my shirt and gently massaged my chest and nipples while I stared at his black curls and his deep brown eyes, laughing and then scowling—telling myself that he should stop and leave.

If Mom found us, she'd think I asked him to do this, I thought, *and if Dad found us, he'd stab him in the back*—at least, that's how I imagined Dad, toppling Demos, bringing him to his knees. I guessed Demos heard my voice or read my mind because he disappeared after that, and the bust was left unpainted, unglazed, and it crumbled a bit, since it had never been fired, either.

Mom had explained the process of firing to me one day as she gazed out the front window, looking for Demos like he might materialize out of nowhere. I didn't listen but held my breath, praying that he'd never reappear. She turned red at the end of the explanation, angry because I hadn't listened and was just fooling around, holding my breath to show her that I had better things to do. "You hate art and everything I love," she'd yelled, reaching for me as I crawled under the only chair in the living room. Luckily, she couldn't reach me, and I stayed there for a long time, figuring out if I hated art or not but certain that she was a monster with a red, almost purple face.

I swigged more Fanta and choked spewing red pop on the cement floor. I wiped my mouth as I stared at my long hair falling in curls around my shoulders. Demos had curled the ends with one hand while he sculpted with the other—sometimes with his fingers and sometimes with a sharp metal tool. I felt tears rise, imagining how scared I'd been to be alone with Demos, and then I wondered if Beth had been afraid the first time she was alone with Mr. Craft, and if he fussed with her hair, and then I held my breath, imagining him stroking her nipples and her much fuller breasts. *These two men, both with eagle eyes and beautiful smiles, could almost be related,* I thought as I squeezed my eyes shut, willing my brain to forget them both.

I dropped the bottle of Fanta when I heard the doorbell. Red pop spewed over the cracked cement floor. The doorbell rang again, and I pictured someone standing on our porch in a nice coat and hat, wondering if Mr. Craft's church still existed and was our house the place? I picked up the empty bottle and placed one of Mom's turpentine soaked rags over the trail of pop as I waited. The hum of the incinerator grew in my ears like the noise of traffic throughout the house.

"Probably the Watch Tower lady," I yelled when the bell rang again. "Or the Fuller Brush man, or that weirdo selling potholders," I said, hoping that a persuasive salesman had arrived to pull me away, fill my brain with anything other than images of Mr. Craft's hands inside Beth's shirt and Demos stroking and gently pinching my nipples.

But as I hurried upstairs, I feared the worst. Mr. Craft may have realized that I had figured out the truth about him and Beth. Maybe he wanted to blame me for neglecting Beth. Maybe he wanted to blame me for sending negative thoughts her way or just harboring all kinds of bad thoughts. What a mistake I'd made dwelling on Demos. I thudded up the basement stairs, hearing in my brain Mom use the word *dwelling* like it was an evil trap, like to dwell was to slide into quicksand of the brain pulling a person into the muck of thoughts.

Mom stared at the front door with a perplexed look I knew and hated. "It's OK to just open the door," I said, searching for nicer ways of talking to her about the world outside of the house. "Open it," I said without moving. She stood frozen and then turned the knob like her life depended on opening the door without hesitation, with skill and acumen she brought to her drawings and the patterns she cut for outfits she never wore.

"Empress?" Mom choked. We crowded into the door frame, our toes side by side on the threshold, and Empress, sparkling in a pool of sunshine, froze as if she wanted to give us a moment to take in the details of her attire: dark sunglasses, black high heels, and a yellow A-line wool coat. Best in my mind was her pale, yellow hair pulled away from her creamy face, like a thick coat of vanilla frosting pinned in a spiral at the back of her head, a tip of hair peaking over the top. I nodded, remembering the art teacher explaining that sculpture intrigues because of its three dimensionalities. You can walk around a statue to discover its delights, but from any angle the viewer imagines its entirety through the hints of what lies on the other side. Kids laughed at a boy who pretended to be a sculpture when she turned away from the class. No wonder the new art teacher said she'd gone back to art school so she could teach college kids.

A cloud passed over the sun, the porch turned grey, and Mom's stomach growled. Empress didn't flinch, and we stared at her, in our mismatched pajamas and bathrobes, too dazzled to speak.

"How's she doing?" Empress asked, adjusting her sunglasses. Mom cleared her throat. "She sleeps a lot," I said. Mom looked at me, and I pulled back, my eyes going from the washed-out clothing bagging around Mom's tall frame to the pressed panels of Empress' yellow wool coat and the beautiful detail of a glass button at her throat.

"Not that much," Mom said, and I was about to disagree but thought twice about riling Mom up, asserting myself for no reason other than the truth popped up like the best option as I drank in the blatant unashamed adornment of Empress' s get up.

"Well, hopefully you were able to put a kibosh on the stealing," she said, adjusting once more her large black sunglasses. I narrowed my eyes, willing Empress to apologize to Mom or at least admit that improving Beth wasn't Mom's responsibility. Perhaps she could thank her, I thought as I continued to squint and stare at my reflection in her sunglasses. In my new life, I'd refuse to like or not like people according to categories such as needy or not needy. Mom was blind to the wiliness of Empress, all because Empress and Beth couldn't function, and like the broken machines she brought back to life, Mom found comfort in the nonfunctioning—even if it meant being a slave. "Go get Beth," Mom whispered. I nodded but then didn't move, worrying that Empress might leave before I came back, or worse: criticize Mom. "Hurry," Mom whispered.

"You have to get up. Your Mom's here," I said, shaking Beth's shoulder even though she was awake, staring at the ceiling. "Did you wear eye makeup to bed?" She sat up, lightly fingering the black circles under her eyes.

"I don't think so," she whispered like she was Rosemary confounded by what had gone on during the night. "Maybe."

As she pulled on jeans and a white low-cut peasant blouse over the bra she'd slept in, I stared at the faint scribblings on the wall behind her. Long ago, during a nap, we'd experimented with ballpoint pens. I'd ripped the pen out of Beth's small hand and told her to stop ruining my life and our house. I'd pushed her down and sat as hard as I could on her stomach, bouncing up and down as I waited for her to scream in agony. Eventually, her resolute blank stare wore me down, and I rolled off.

"Your Mom likes us to draw on the wall," she'd said like I knew nothing about our weird family. From the beginning I hated the way Beth wormed her way into our lives.

"She just says that," I lied as I considered pulling her hair, anything to get her to stop revealing the truth about Mom and her eagerness to destroy the sanctity of our house. "When we get our new house, you're not welcome," I'd whispered in her ear.

Later I'd apologized even though I wasn't sure I was sorry. "Anyway, we're not moving," I'd admitted.

"I know," she'd said, and I hated her all over again, until she gave me a box of Junior Mints, and I vowed once more just to let Beth come and go, accept her in my mind like the leaves that wafted past my window.

"I've got your bag," I said, holding the straps apart as Beth tucked in clothes and a couple of comic books. "Doing it— whatever—with Mr. Craft is gross," I said.

"It's not what you think; we didn't do it," she said, her eyes fixed on mine. I followed her, and when Empress moved aside, staring at Beth as she chewed on the tip of her sunglass bow, I clutched the handles of Beth's overflowing bag. I didn't want them to leave before Beth explained the mystery of getting pregnant without doing anything, and I wondered if Jean Maxwell and Mr. Craft hadn't done it either. I stared at Beth's cleavage, thinking that perhaps I should steer clear of boys. After the health movie, I'd ruled out hugging. And, of course, rolling down dunes clamped together was out of the question. It might produce a dizzying affect, the way having my nipples pinched and stroked made it so hard to stand up after Demos took off. When Mom came home with the art supplies Demos had asked for, she'd whirled around, searching the house like I'd lied, and he was actually hiding somewhere. I'd struggled to stand as my heart raced. Looking at her red face from below made me feel little and trapped, plus I was too disoriented to make up a lie. When she hurled the bag of supplies, I ran to the yard and spent the rest of the day on the swing.

"Beth—take that bag," Empress growled. I backed up as Beth pulled on the handles, and I clung for a second before letting go. Mom and I waved from the porch as the old white car ambled into the sparse Sunday traffic. Beth waved, staring at me, and I waved back. Then she continued to wave, like she didn't want to lose sight of Mom and me. I ran to our bedroom, tripping hard on a step, crashing onto my knee, and ripping my plaid flannel pajamas. I slumped on the step, staring at pinheads of blood springing to my skin. I pictured Beth running off for a band aid. She loved to take care of me, just the way Patty Scott played nurse to my patient. I hoped that when I was fully Barbie, I wouldn't lose every friend who had my best interest at heart—who cared about me. At school I never saw Barbie with anyone. but the trade off, twirling endlessly and leading the band, was worth it.

CHAPTER XVII

I don't remember falling asleep on the davenport, but Mom had to shake me when Penny Stillwell called asking if I could go to her youth group. "It's Bring-a-Guest Day, and finally you'll have a chance to see him," she said. I glanced down at my ripped pajamas. "Also, there's at least one other boy who doesn't have a girlfriend—he's from Grand Ledge, but no biggie; he's got a car." I pictured riding in Scott's car, but in a flash, I imagined Beth in the front seat with Mr. Craft. "So, can you come?"

We agreed to meet at McDonald's before heading over to the youth group meeting at the Methodist church across the street. "Come early. We can watch him park his gold Jet Star 88; be sure to pretend it's a coincidence, you know, like how funny we got there at the same time." I nodded into the phone, wondering who the heck Penny thought I was and if she herself was anything more than human wallpaper or a run-on sentence. I could imagine that in a year or two she'd call me about another boy, another steady, and his car. Then in a few more years there'd be news of an engagement—some guy with a fleet of Oldsmobiles. A kid in homeroom said East Lansing had more cars per household than any other town in the United States.

"I'd wear a skirt if I were you; show off your great figure," Penny said before hanging up. Beth had the figure, I thought looking down at my small breasts. I hung up but clung to the receiver, frozen and sucked inside a pose—ear pressed to receiver, forehead pressed to wall—imagining myself walking on Michigan Avenue in clothes I'd seen in Mom's *Women's Wear Daily*—chic attire. I'd wear a lot of make-up, so that no one recognized me, a vision of the movie star everyone said Mom resembled. But then, like the rabbit who grew wings, I'd return home in this guise, but unlike the rabbit's Mom turning away her own child she failed to recognize, I envisioned Mom, barely out of her bathrobe, welcoming this new person while Dad would tear down the stairs, a towel wrapped around his hips, yelling that I should get out.

I shook my head but couldn't come out of this mini trance. *Stick with high types,* Dad said in my brain as the two of us cruised down Michigan Avenue, him repeating a story about an army higher up with IQ of one, a guy who hadn't heard of Shakespeare. In my mind, I slid into him, felt the protection of his strong thick body—my own high type—until someone honked at us, our big finned car skating across lanes as I flew into the door handle, wincing in pain while Dad let out a barrage of swear words.

My face flamed, watching Mom scrub the sink as I let go of the receiver, my mind still overheated from the nap, trying to remember all of Penny's directions and suddenly flooded with worry about things I'd given little thought: bomb shelters and being trapped forever underground, getting pregnant without even doing it—like Beth had said—and Mom leaving us like she'd left me places, left the burner on, and would have to leave the world if she continued to believe that everyone hated her.

But then I remembered Stephen, realizing that those other worries were a respite from the central worry of Stephen and Barbie and who to be.

I must remember never to nap again, I thought as I pulled on wool pants Mom made and a blouse with a round collar she'd said had taken her most of a day. The nap's derangement began to wear off, replaced by a determination, almost a desperate need to make a change. I had the urge to tell Mom to leave, flee with me. I'd become Barbie and she could move to a place where there'd be other artists. "I hate Empress," I said, lingering by the back door, hoping she'd smile when she saw me in a coat she'd designed and made of navy wool. "That Penny girl sure hates me," she flung the dishrag over the faucet. "Can't you pal around with that Patty Scott?"

I grabbed Barbie's baton. "You don't know about Patty Scott—you don't know about anyone," I said, my voice high and unnatural, and then I left, slamming the door in a fury that immediately produced a slew of guilty thoughts. As I flew down the steps two cars without mufflers raced towards Lansing and in the wake of the old cars' putrid exhaust, one guilty thought stuck out: would Mom fling herself into traffic the way she'd just tossed the dishrag, an abandoned old cloth she'd left dangling limp over the faucet?

I'm no dishrag, I thought, gripping the baton in both hands and tilting it slide to side like a ship's captain at the helm. Against the grey sky I envisioned an algebraic equation in which Mom and I were the same variable, making it impossible for her to be a dishrag if I wasn't. "Math is everywhere," Miss Stokes said last year, and I guess she was right. The equation disappeared as I breathed deep, relieved that Mom would still be alive tonight. For a moment an airy bright light expanded before me, like I could remain free of worry if I believed in the truth of something like the equation and its sensible outcome. In the sheen of the baton I saw my worried eyes and I tried widening them and unfurrowing my brow, but I dropped the baton and couldn't get it to work like a mirror after I wiped it on my skirt.

Maybe I could go to Barbie's after the youth group meeting. I practiced twirling as I walked towards McDonalds, but the image of Beth, waving to me from the car was like Stephen, someone I couldn't shake, appearing as she now did on the sidewalk and then in the trees. My stomach twisted, and then my face flamed, and I felt like throwing the baton at a passing car or at a squirrel that ran in front of me. I tried to squash the anger quickly because it reminded me of Mom, always furious at people for doing things to her when it was Mom and now the two of us who couldn't control our own minds and thoughts. I twirled with more confidence, and the smoother motion helped banish Beth from my mind or from lingering in front me no matter where I looked.

Penny probably regretted inviting me, or at least she was annoyed that I didn't moon over the hulking boy from Williamston. But from the minute the husband and wife leaders called us into a group, I fell under their spell and hardly noticed Penny or any of the boys. The young couple welcomed me by shaking my hand and then in a circle we sang *The Sound of Silence* to the husband's guitar playing. Afterwards, as we discussed the song and the isolation we all felt, I had an urge to talk to them about missing Beth and even about becoming Barbie and how lonely Mom would be, living her days without Beth or me.

Just before we left, we went around a big circle so that anyone who wanted to could describe an experience of feeling isolated. Luckily, the minister came in just before they got to me, and he announced that another group needed the room. I swallowed hard and breathed out like I'd just run a race. I knew that if I tried to speak, I'd falter. I hadn't even come up with a specific memory, and I'd barely listened to anyone else but had watched people speak while I listened inside to Beth try to convince me that she hadn't done anything with Mr. Craft, and then out of the blue I imagined Stephen Fedkin's swollen face inside a plastic bag. *Please use me as an example,* he said. *Someone you knew.*

"Please come back," the wife said as we filed out.

Her husband nodded. "We'd love to have you join us." They smiled at each other, and I nodded, torn between asking them if I could stay and help clean up or running out for good. Then Stephen told me that they were desperate for more members.

They ask everyone to join. Not many would put up with these get-togethers. I looked around at the bare basement, the old chairs, and the dirty white walls with tilting pictures of former ministers. Even the snacks were pale and tasteless. *Aren't you above this?* Stephen asked. Then I told him that I couldn't wait to become Barbie so that I'd never face a barren world again, one I was expected to fill in or just plain improve, and he'd be forced to go away forever since I wasn't sure Barbie even knew him.

"Can you get home on your own?" Penny asked, tilting her head towards the boy who stood staring off into space with dull eyes. "I told my parents we were going to the library," she whispered. I nodded and then asked if they could drop me off at my babysitting job. This could be a perfect time to knock on Barbie Robert's door; it wasn't too late, and I had the baton for an excuse. I didn't want to waste time walking. And I didn't want Stephen to appear in the clouds telling me to forget Barbie.

"You're babysitting here?" Penny said after I thanked the boy for the ride. "It's a long story, I whispered. "Are you meeting someone? You could've told *me!*" She giggled, and they drove off.

I stood outside the Robert's front door for a few minutes, rehearsing what I'd say to Mrs. Robert when she opened the door. I was about to ring the bell when the outside light came on, and the next moment Mr. Robert peered out the screen door. I hesitated, looking over his shoulder for Mrs. Robert.

"Yes?" He asked, his large blue eyes—Barbie's eyes—widening.

"I-I-I have Barbie's baton," I rushed, barely getting the words out.

"Hi Sally!" Barbie pushed the door open, and I slipped in sideways. "I had no idea you were coming now," she said.

"I couldn't remember what time we said," thinking how Dad would fill in the gaps and make something appear real or intended. She grabbed the baton and smiled. "Your Mom left it at the church downtown," I said. Once in her bedroom, I tried to stay calm and nonchalant as I took mental notes. The room was more beautiful than I'd imagined. "I love your wallpaper," I said running my fingers over the pink and green stripes. Next to her bed was a beige Princess phone sitting in the middle of a white table with gold trim. I thought of the box between Beth's and my bed and imagined Barbie's horror at something so makeshift.

My favorite part of her room was the white bedspread and matching canopy with light pink fringe. The pillowcases were also light pink. Everything went together, I thought, in a way, that perhaps Mrs. Broadback would admire and figure out but Mom would hate. I pictured Mom's haughty face, but immediately her image disappeared, and I heard her ask if I really liked Barbie's room. *It's so fake,* she said, expecting me to agree and on the verge of killing herself if I didn't. I wanted to plug my ears.

"Thanks—some people think it's over the top," Barbie said as she searched for the Latin book in her stack of textbooks. "I bet you don't need to study all the time." She said. I shrugged my shoulders as I stared at the plush carpet, hoping to appear oblivious to my own intelligence. Barbie motioned me to sit on her bed. With our backs propped against a wall, we looked at the grammar until I realized she wasn't concentrating. "Everything makes sense if you see Latin as a puzzle. But first, do you get the cases?"

"Not really," she said, twisting her hair. My face began to heat up. She seemed to resist Latin, I thought, and I'd never win over her parents if I couldn't teach her at least the basics. I scanned the room and saw a medal for baton twirling and next to it was a photograph of a girl twirling a jump rope. "Who is that cute kid?" I asked as Barbie slid off the bed.

"She lived next door until she moved to Florida. I miss her so much." Barbie smiled, and I stared at the photo, imitating Barbie's smile as I relaxed into the line of pillows against the wall. Barbie found paper in her desk, and I was about to make a detailed chart when Barbie's parents began to argue. I stopped for a moment, holding the pencil above the paper. "Go on," she whispered. She found a ruler, and I continued to make the chart as she nodded and now and then muttered an "okay," as the fighting continued beneath us. Finally, she looked sideways and took a deep breath. "Sorry, it's embarrassing," she said, and I stopped writing, searching my brain for an answer as I realized staring at Barbie's pearl pink nails that her family was perhaps falling apart. "I hate it and it's not, I don't know, right," she said, like she suddenly understood that I wanted to become her—the perfect version of her.

"She needs to leave," Mr. Robert burst in. Barbie grabbed my hand, and as her Latin book thudded to the floor, we rushed passed him and down the stairs. He bounded down after us, and on the last step Mr. Robert slipped. "God damn it," he yelled as a bunch of Barbie's batons slid to the floor. He grabbed one with silver streamers on each end, tossing it so that the baton bounced across the kitchen floor on one end like a kangaroo. Mr. Robert swore again, reminding me of Dad throwing things that got in his way. Barbie shook her head, and now, reminding me more of Mom, Mr. Robert left through the back door, letting in a burst of cold air.

"I'm so sorry." Barbie said, tucking her hair behind an ear as she looked backwards towards the staircase.

Then she led me to the front door, where I told her I'd help her somehow. "At the library?" I smiled and shrugged my shoulders like together we could solve any problem.

She nodded, and then Mrs. Robert, holding a Kleenex to her nose, came to the door and waved to me as I walked backwards away from the house. I hurried across a big road with no sidewalks. When I reached the other side, I slipped on a shallow ditch, catching myself before falling to my knees. My hand covered in mud, I ran towards a street where I hoped to find a sprinkler on or a hose left out on someone's lawn. I must have run five blocks before I thought to wipe off the mud on a thick lawn overseen by a black jockey holding high a lantern.

The next thing I knew, a car drifted across the street like the driver was confused about which side of the road we drove on. I turned the corner, and the car followed. Then the driver tapped his horn, and I stopped, peering at the car in the early darkness. The window scrolled down, but I looked above the car at the stars peeking through clouds. "Need a ride?" Mr. Craft looked different, younger and glitzy with his pure white hair slicked into place. I pointed to Michigan Avenue a few blocks away and shook my head. "We love that new doughnut place in Frandor—have you tried it?" He pointed to a bag of donuts sitting in the passenger seat where Beth had sat the day before. "Say, is Beth still at your place, or has she gone somewhere?"

"Her Mom came," I said, eyeing a doughnut coated in powdered sugar on the dashboard.

"Take it!" He laughed. "Will she be away for a while?" I took the doughnut from his outstretched hand, bit into it, and struggled to swallow as I wiped my chin of powdered sugar.

"I'm sorry—what?" He laughed, and I noticed a single gold filling in one of his bottom molars.

"Will Beth come back to you all? That's what I meant," he said, chuckling and waving one hand so that his gold wedding ring flashed under the streetlight that had just come on.

"I'm sure she will." I tilted my head like a teacher, advising a parent. "She does, usually," I said, holding the donut close to my face like I'd gulp it down as soon as we stopped talking.

"Oh, good, good…"

"Why did you do it?" I asked, imagining the moment I kicked water at the hood boy. Mr. Craft smiled and nodded, rolling up his window like I'd said goodbye. Then he pulled ahead and I stayed put, staring at his taillights until the car turned onto Michigan Avenue, but his car wasn't in the garage when I got home, about five minutes later.

I stood at the end of the driveway, imagining Mrs. Craft inside her darkened house. I thought I saw a shadow moving in the front room. Beth should live with the Crafts; let Mrs. Craft keep track of her stealing and other things. I began to inch my way over to their front walk. If she saw me, perhaps she'd come outside to their porch and ask me if I knew the truth about her husband and Beth. I imagined her talking to me from the porch but not inviting me to sit in the wicker chairs with the nice flowered cushions. But then I heard metal crashing into metal, cars colliding at high speed and glass shattering on the other side of Michigan Avenue. Before I could get to the boulevard, another car screeched and bashed into one of the cars, hitting it so hard that it rolled to one side, and in a moment, sirens filled the emptiness of a Sunday evening.

Before he took to bed, Dad would've been out in a flash, but like they were deaf, neither Mom nor Dad appeared. A bunch of students from Brody Dorm hurried out, some in pajamas, some with hair in curlers. I ran to the boulevard, remembering when I'd stood by Dad at the edge of a big fire in downtown Lansing years ago. He'd begged people for information, and I wished I could do the same now. "Get back," a fireman yelled. But then the car lying on its side went up in flames, and the fireman shoved a student and raced to the fire truck parked diagonally across one side of Michigan Avenue. I jumped back as more flames shot up and sweat sprang to my face and neck. The guys from the ambulance dragged a woman from the car as two firemen sprayed the flames.

Everyone pushed back as the air filled with black clouds of putrid smoke, but I stayed put, staring at the woman whose head dangled to one side, her eyes wide open and her hands grazing the cement. A fireman rushed to the guys carrying her as he screamed about the other car. "It might go; it might go!" The men struggled, and I thought they might drop the woman as she slipped closer to the ground, her weight dead and her head twisted far to one side. Her hands dragging along the cement made her extra heavy, I thought. But then the stretcher arrived, and they dropped her onto it. Nothing about her changed; even her eyes, focusing on nothing, stayed open, and I knew that she must be dead. One of the men put her arms across her body, and then they hoisted the stretcher and were about to take her to an ambulance when someone yelled for them, and they put her down, running to the other car.

Before I knew it, my stomach heaved, and I threw up on the old grass that cropped up here and there on the boulevard. In my mouth I tasted the doughnut Mr. Craft had given me and punch from the youth group. I was about to go home when I saw a student with a golden retriever. She was kneeling and petting the dog, comforting it I guessed. She caught me staring and waved at me. I waved back and without thinking went to her.

"My friend had that dog," I said petting it again and again. I wanted to whisper in the dog's ear that I was telling the truth. "She loved her dog. She did," I said, again wanting to tell the dog and I guess the owner that I wasn't lying. I wasn't telling them something to get a story out of them or to become either of them.

"They're great dogs," she said.

"Yeah," I said, kneeling by the dog. "My friend's got in the sewer, and they found him drowned in the Red Cedar." I motioned to the campus and the river that runs through it. My stomach calmed down, and I sat wishing I could tell this dog and this girl a million true stories about Patty Scott or anyone, but I couldn't think of another story, and besides, she was tugging on the dog's leash.

"I have to get back to studying," she said, and before I could apologize for telling such a sad story as men scurried about with stretchers, she was gone. I looked for the dead woman on the stretcher, but she was gone, too. Only one ambulance was left, and a fire truck. A couple of firemen hosed the street, getting rid of glass and maybe blood; I couldn't tell. When I turned to go home, I saw Mrs. Craft through a window on the second floor. When I got closer, the window darkened, and she disappeared.

CHAPTER XVIII

I awoke to the chirping of a few birds on the windowsill above my bed. For a while I listened, imitating the sounds in my head until I willed my inert body to flip around and face the ceiling. I tried squinting the way Mom stared at a still life with half closed eyes. Sorting out the darks and the lights, she always said under her breath. But the technique was useless without an object—a bunch of dying flowers or a gourd--to copy. I searched the shadows in the ceiling for a shape like the bunny Beth and I had found during our first nap together. But the room, except for a faint streak of light, was neither dark nor light, and nothing appeared. Could this be the preface to death? My heart quickened and then took off, like I'd wandered into the boys' gym class and was running splits instead of sitting around in girls' gym learning about dating and avoiding early marriage. Fast as I could, I dragged Dad's gray army blanket over me and sunk underneath the covers, figuring hot darkness might set the scene for a comforting vision, like sledding or swimming or anything effortful and bright. But again no image materialized. My brain went blank, and I could see or feel nothing except for the jackhammer in my chest.

I threw off the covers, swung my feet to the floor and stood up over Beth's unmade bed. Without thinking, I smoothed the sheets, plumped the pillows, and tucked the corners as I'd seen Mom do many times. The effort cooled me down, made me feel like I was contributing, somehow, to the workings of the house and the world. If only Mom allowed more stuff in the house, I'd fill my days dusting and vacuuming and in the process ward off the tortuous wanderings of my mind.

I remembered the night I had wandered into the kitchen for a glass of water and found Mom folding clothes as the black sky turned grey. It was always there, she'd said, the scrubbing, ironing, folding. "We're lucky to have work," she'd whispered, thrusting a rag at me like it was a weapon for killing thoughts that pop up without warning. "Help me," she'd said, and I didn't know what to do as tears rolled down her cheeks, so I dropped the rag and ran back to bed.

I slid two copies of LIFE magazine from under Beth's pillow. I couldn't imagine Beth reading LIFE, but then I saw they were Mr. Craft's; it hit me that maybe he'd tried to help Beth, show her a world with purpose. On the cover of one was the skater Peggy Fleming and on the other two stewardesses boarding a plane. I stared at Peggy Fleming as I pulled on the day's outfit. She had dark hair, but other than that, she reminded me of Barbie, skating instead of twirling a baton.

I left the magazines on the bed, hoping that Mom would find them and figure out for herself that Mr. Craft and Beth were having a baby. Harboring the secret irritated me. I wanted my mind free to work on becoming Barbie. I clutched at Beth's pillow, squashing an urge to rip off her sheets, rip up the magazines, and stomp on the stupid cardboard box we used as a table. Mom could take care of Dad and Beth, running between the two of them as she doled out advice on thought control.

Then on the floor I saw the glint of the silver bracelet Beth said she'd loan me, and I thought how little I had done and perhaps would do with my life. She may have stolen the bracelet, or it may have been a present from Mr. Craft, but at least she knew what she loved and had seized it—made it her own. Jewelry, accoutrements of any sort baffled me. I couldn't imagine that as me I could figure out how to decorate a life. I pictured a Christmas tree with no ornaments.

And what about bigger things? Khrushchev, fall out, and the poor kids who lived in Tower Gardens? I heard these kids picked fruit and lived on the other side of the wall the rich people from White Hills had erected; someone had nicknamed it the Berlin Wall, and it stuck. I knew I should go beyond myself, and yet even Beth, a girl no one cared about made me want to flee deeper into my own mind.

I imagined Dad hearing the splash when one of the guys died at sea and was sent down a chute on the war ship he took back from the Pacific. When he finally walked off the ship, the doctors said he'd go blind. "Bombs got to my eyes, but worse, the malaria kept coming back, hobbling me like an old man." I could see him splashing the bathwater as he told me about the war in a series of tales like the fables with tragic endings I loved. He had an excuse for hiding from life. I could imagine Mom picking fruit with the kids from Tower Gardens, her kerchief covering her thick hair as she lugged baskets of fruit. I hesitated at the door and then went back to Beth's bed and hid the magazines as she had.

During the trek to school, I practiced smiling like Barbie. When the telescoping building finally appeared, I ran to the parking lot where I hurried through rows of cars and straight through the lobby without stopping at my locker. In Homeroom, Mr. Novak was adjusting a shade that fell on his head as I quietly shut the door. Someone left a black comb on my desk, and I drew it through my tangled hair. Soon, I'd make my entrance into Latin and firm up plans to meet Barbie at the library after school. I needed to be prepared. She wasn't the type of girl who wouldn't notice tangled hair.

"Don't forget today's schedule is altered," Mr. Novak said, rubbing his head as he slumped in his chair, which skidded backwards into the blackboard. I wasn't sure what he meant by "altered," and everyone in the front rows looked side to side, like they were confused too. On the board, in big letters, he'd written: SEIZE THE DAY! Next to it, he'd drawn a baseball. I stared at the words, hoping to do just that.

My goal was to get Barbie to sneak me to her house so I could begin memorizing the lay out. Sweat dripped down the sides of my body as I continued to comb my hair and her father's unshaven face appeared in my brain. He was a huge *impediment,* I thought, grateful to Mrs. Bell for putting that word and a big list of words with the root *ped* on our Latin test. *God, I love Latin,* I said silently as I imagined bashing into Mr. Robert the way I'd imagined crashing into the hood boys. It dawned on me that Latin gave me courage. The opposite of nerves and dread radiated throughout my brain as I unscrambled sentences, parsing them carefully to reveal meaning and also to revel in a sentence structure that, while not straight forward, was never arbitrarily complex. Unlike solving a math problem, you're rewarded not with one answer but rather a sentence that provides multiple meanings. No wonder Dad loved Latin, although he said he wasn't good at it. He probably pictured himself as an orator when he lolled in the bath for hours making up speeches he'd never deliver to anyone but the people he imagined listening right there in the steam and fog.

Mr. Novak, facing the board drew another baseball like he'd forgotten he was teaching and decided to perfect his rendering of baseballs. After he finished, he turned to smile at the class like he welcomed inserting a little absurdity into a job that seemed to baffle him. Then he copied the week's schedule on the board, careful to avoid ruining the baseballs he'd drawn and the caption, SEIZE THE DAY. I wished I could sneak between him and the board, replace the English with CARPE DIEM and then fly off to Latin before the halls filled up. If I were a teacher, regardless of subject, I'd show how Latin pops up all the time, even though it's dead. *Weird that this dead language lives forever, teaching us stuff*--bolstering *our language*, I thought as I smiled at my correct use of a word from the vocab list. Latin's not going anywhere, I thought, and copied CARPE DIEM on the ditto about after-school clubs Mr. Novak passed out. Getting into the middle of Latin reminded me of getting into the all-encompassing world of a person's life.

"I've heard rumors, even that she's pregnant. She is from Lansing after all." The girls behind me had scooted their desks together, blocking the aisle. *News traveled fast*, I thought— another reason to become Barbie quickly before anyone associated me with Beth or Mr. Craft. But then I pictured Beth slumped in our basement by the incinerator, waiting with her typical patience for me to stop crying, and I wished I could see her after school in the safety of our house. I heard Dad's voice once again telling me to help someone like Beth. Even though he hated Beth, I bet he'd appreciate me coming up with something to get her out of this jam.

"I guess she'd do it with anyone."

"Oh god—anyone?"

"Well, don't you have to do it a lot to get pregnant? That's what Jim said," one of the girls whispered.

"She's gross! Her reputation—if she ever had one—is ruined."

I flipped around, my face heating up. "She's not gross," I said, looking at one girl and then the other.

They raised their eyebrows. "Like you'd know," one of them said, shrugging and chuckling.

I swallowed, searching for a comeback. "She's nice, I'm telling you. She's a nice kid," I said, blinking hard. "I guarantee she's nicer than either of you guys. Plus, she has a brain in her head," I said throwing the comb to the floor, and then as I reached down to pick it up, I pushed my desk into one of the girl's desks and she pushed hers back, bumping my chair. I whipped around, holding in tears as Mr. Novak waved his hand at us.

"You know about keeping aisles clear," he said, raising his voice and then letting it drop like he hated enforcing rules and was actually embarrassed by the list of rules he'd posted by the door. I breathed hard, smoothed my hair, and listened to the whispering behind me as they moved their desks. I thought about telling them that Beth didn't have a father; actually, I felt like making them feel guilty for talking about someone like Beth. But I knew they'd never understand the difference between their lives and hers. I was relieved when the bell rang.

I ran along the near empty hall until I came to the language wing. "Okay, okay, c'mon!" Mrs. Bell smiled at me as she scanned the hall, her black curly hairdo streaked in silver, peeking out the door to the Latin room. I slid into my seat next to Barbie, who was busy, cycling through her three-by-five notecards.

"Hi," she said. "Are you ready for the quiz?"

I nodded, questioning whether the truth—that I knew the vocabulary and the grammar—was what she wanted to hear.

"I don't understand the declensions that well," she said, tucking her thick blond hair behind her ears.

"Let's meet at the library," I said, tucking my hair exactly as she did again and again. I timed it so that we tucked and smoothed in unison. Then in a low voice I said, "Maybe after the library we go to your house?"

Mrs. Bell widened her eyes as she placed the quiz face down on our desks. "Okay girls, enough talking," she whispered. Barbie flipped over the paper and pressed the tips of her long fingers into her forehead. I copied this, frozen in worried concentration until my patience ran out and I flipped the quiz over and began to fill in the blanks. Barbie picked up her pencil, too, and slowly turned the quiz over, but made no marks. I'd hoped we'd finish at the same time, so I erased my name and rewrote it a bunch of times. Mrs. Bell, pointer in hand, loomed over Barbie. I quietly placed my pencil in the pencil holder at the top of the desk as I watched Mrs. Bell frown so deeply she began to resemble an angry cartoon character. I couldn't hold back a laugh, and neither could John, who sat behind me. But Mrs. Bell ignored us and said something to Barbie that I couldn't make out. Like a magician pulling a rabbit out of a hat, Barbie produced a bunch of three-by-five notecards. Her tears also appeared out of nowhere, streaming down her cheeks, and landing in big splotches on her quiz. Everyone surrounding Barbie leaned towards her while Mrs. Bell awkwardly bent down to gather up the notecards lying on the floor near Barbie's purse.

Then Mrs. Bell pulled Barbie to her feet, holding high her pointer like she was about to strike Barbie. "Open the door," she said in a fierce whisper to a senior girl. Mrs. Bell backed into the hallway, holding one of Barbie's wrists as if Barbie was her prisoner.

The senior hopped up and closed the door before turning to the class. "I think we should wait before turning in our quizzes," she said. "Just to show some respect."

I turned my quiz over and slumped, remembering the day, a few weeks into the school year, when Barbie had told me her parents wanted her to study Latin because it helps with everything. I distinctly remembered her saying *everything*, and then Mrs. Bell had said that Latin was a dead language and we shouldn't worry about pronunciation the way we had to in modern languages. A girl had whispered loudly that Mrs. Bell had a terrible French accent, and Barbie giggled into her hand and looked sideways at me. I did the same but out of the corner of my eye, I caught Mrs. Bell's sagging ankles and her wide hips underneath a dull gray dress. My stomach twisted, wishing that I didn't have to laugh at her, too. She deserved protecting, I thought, from kids who'd always stick together. None of them appreciated her brain full of beautiful patterns and words. Lisa Jamrich, a smart girl from Okemos I'd been during the time our families had dutifully attended Mr. Craft's meetings, would have had the guts to say something to this stupid mob but I couldn't if I hoped to be Barbie. I pictured Lisa giving me a knowing look, and then it would've been even harder to go along with the laughing and the scorn for Mrs. Bell. Barbie wasn't naturally mean, I told myself. When I became her, I'd erase this part of her life.

But now Mrs. Bell was back, strangely without her pointer, and then Barbie came back with swollen eyes and one of Mrs. Bell's Kleenexes balled up in her hand.

"Quizzes, please," Mrs. Bell said, facing the class with her hands clenched at her sides. Her dark moustache matched her sideburns and her lips curled as she spoke, and I remembered Dad describing the army bosses he detested because they only cared about rules. But Mrs. Bell, shoulders now shaking, seemed genuinely upset and angry, probably, I thought, because she trusted us and never made us turn our desks away from each other or do other things like mix up the seating arrangement to prevent cheating.

Outside the classroom, Barbie drew me towards a group of lockers recessed between two drinking fountains. "I know you've seen me cheating before, and you never said anything."

I shook my head and immediately regretted my honesty—maybe she liked me because I'd supposedly kept her cheating to myself. My response didn't seem to register as she rambled on about what her parents were going to do once they found out. "I have to start learning this stuff. I have to, or my Dad will kill me." I saw myself in the middle of her bed, drilling her on all the cases. "You get it, you really get Latin," she said. "What should I do?" she asked, and it dawned on me that Barbie mistook me for competent and savvy.

I stared at her sweaty face, while listening to a voice inside my head laugh and make fun of me for not seeing this side of Barbie. *Besides*, the voice said, *you should try being honest for a change. You just stuck up for Craft,* the voice reminded me. Then I realized that I missed Beth and found Barbie irritating for complicating all my plans with this episode of cheating. As I stared at her elegant competent fingers hanging beneath a couple of bangles and a cute pink watch, I thought that banishing chaos was impossible. I'd like to burrow into myself and design my own world of tunnels and rooms, never to worry about dishonesty and fakery.

"Do you have any ideas?" Barbie broke into my thoughts, tugging on my wrist. I nodded without speaking. She looked different at this moment, not the expert twirler but a child begging for help. I wondered, staring at the clock hanging above Barbie's head, if I could go on living, if it was somehow mandatory that I remain inside myself, enduring each day as the person I had to admit I'd neglected to fill in or even get to know. I saw myself trapped inside, struggling to communicate with the real Barbie, who now stood before me, her outlines fuzzy where they'd once been so clear. You could scrutinize Latin, I thought, but it wouldn't change. Its complexity was set. Could I trust Barbie—the real Barbie—not to lash out at me one second and then cozy up the next? I looked at Barbie for the answer, but she was waving at a boy who was in the marching band and telling him that they had practice at three fifteen. My heart pounded as I realized that I might have to be me negotiating with the streams of people jostling us as they moved to the next class. If only I could go back to a time before I became other people, I'd beg myself to stay me so I could remember what I like and don't like and how I react to things before I think too much. Stephen Fedkin's distorted face in a plastic bag flashed before me as someone touched my shoulder and I jerked away.

"Sorry," the nurse said. "I checked your schedule and gym is next so not to worry. Let's go to my office for a second or two." Her breath smelled of coffee and her teeth glistened.

"Her or me?" Barbie said, eager to follow the nurse. The nurse smiled and pointed to me. "Are you OK?" Barbie whispered. I nodded, pressing my fingertips into my forehead. She waved her long graceful fingers, and I immediately copied this beautiful wave, which reminded me of a Ferris wheel with seats of pearl pink—nothing too garish. Then with his bright pink face, Mr. Vandervelde rounded the corner, bumping into the drinking fountain. He held a pointer, which I imagined was Mrs. Bell's, and pointed it towards his office at the end of the long hall. Barbie turned to me, pleading for help as she headed off with Pinky in a different direction.

"So how's it going? When a freshman skips school, I usually look into it—did you do it on a dare, or were you a little overwhelmed and wanted a break?"

I thought hard, reddening as I hesitated and stuttered, trying to get out words I hadn't decided on, never having prepared for this encounter in her stuffy office. The truth swirled somewhere in my brain as my stomach burned, and I thought that if I threw up, she'd figure out that I wasn't telling the truth when, in reality, I wanted to tell her the truth, at least some form of it. But instead I asked an unrelated question, hoping to throw her off, the way Dad turned the tables on people who dared ask him a question.

"Do you get suspended for cheating?" I asked, imagining Barbie stuck at home twirling batons in her backyard while her Dad whipped her occasionally. The nurse smiled like she wasn't fooled by my tricks.

"Do your folks know you skipped school?" I swallowed a fake big swallow, hoping that maybe she'd think my parents were bad parents and that a story, I'd think up on the spot, would substitute for a nuanced description of why they wouldn't really care, too much. She'd never sympathize with the waywardness of the truth, and I couldn't resist creating a story of perhaps not horror but the amount of clear-cut neglect necessary to garner empathy and even love. *She might want to adopt me,* I thought, and then I pictured Mom staring upwards at her Dad's feet in dirty boots, twirling in small circles, and Dad teaching me how to read *The Racing Form* when I'd just begun to read. I shook my head, not in response to her question, but in response to a little voice asking me why I directed my life to the past or to the future and never to the moment at hand, which, like the real Barbie, demanded my participation. *Gut level participation*, the voice grew in volume, practically yelling the last part.

"My father's going to die," I said, looking straight into the nurse's eyes and swallowing this time for real because he might, I realized for the first time, be preparing for death. *Nothing so real should happen to me,* I thought. Part of making up life was warding off a real occurrence—an event I could not reconcile and would haunt me forever.

I'm never going away, Stephen said his face appearing above the big E on the eyesight chart. The next minute I remember Pinky announcing that Stephen had taken his own life and it felt like the whole school fell quiet.

"I'm sorry," she said, handing me a Kleenex. I took the tissue but didn't cry, dropping it on the floor as I felt a storm swirl inside and chaotic thinking take over my brain. I almost slid off the table to begin pacing the small office when I grabbed the Kleenex and twisted it until the nurse's probing eyes found mine and I breathed out, praying that I'd never again feel deranged at school. "Is your dad in the hospital? It must be hard to concentrate with him so sick," she said, handing me another Kleenex even though I hadn't shed a tear and still clutched the first one.

"He's home in bed," I murmured. "He might not die—no one talks about it. Neither of my parents knows about the skipping, and I promise I won't do it again," I said, blowing my nose even though I didn't need to. I wanted to talk with her about perfect, idealized Barbie and all my hopes to become her, and how the whole plan was falling apart, and how if it did, I'd probably follow Stephen. She said something I didn't hear because I imagined Pinky over the PA announcing my death and how I'd also taken my life.

"Come by anytime if you want to talk," she said. "It's okay to be confused. All of us are sometimes." I looked up at her relaxed face and big eyes, waiting, I thought, for me to agree about being confused as I basked in sympathy that I hadn't earned. And yet rather than set the record straight, let her know who I actually was on the inside, I encouraged her kind thoughts and the empathy Miss Knowles said readers feel for tragic characters like Juliet. She could be a different kind of Mrs. Broadback. A woman who saw me as fragile and I could visit her every day.

I wondered if she was clairvoyant. But regardless of whether she could or couldn't read my mind, I wasn't about to let her know that before the cheating incident I hadn't been confused whatsoever about my goal of becoming Barbie. A picture of Barbie tossing her baton in front of the whole school flashed across my brain and then I saw Barbie's worried eyes searching mine for help, wavering for the first time since I'd decided to become her. *Yes, I am confused* I said in my brain. *Is it possible to become perfect Barbie anymore or must I settle for regular Barbie?* And if everyone is regular as I was beginning to suspect, I might as well stay me and forget Barbie.

Who are you going to be? Stephen said, chuckling as he popped up again, his goofy face looming over the eyesight chart like he was the new point of reference for the eye test we had every fall.

"I hope your Dad recovers," the nurse said as we both realized it was time for me to leave. At the door, I hesitated. A fragile me didn't seem a safe choice. I imagined her analyzing my thoughts in a relentless effort to find out exactly what I was up to, accessing me bit by bit and eventually discovering that my only real goal was to become someone else. I eyed the examining table as I felt myself spinning away into infinity, a black hole that terrified me. Pulled apart like a shattered jigsaw puzzle, I'd be stranded as nobody nowhere. Then I thought of the scarecrow in the Wizard of Oz, stuffing straw back into his depleted nearly empty body. I loved the way he kept talking throughout, almost as if his voice and mind were about to shut down and he needed to hear his voice as long as he could.

"I don't think he will," I said, noticing that the nurse stared at me without blinking. With one hand on the doorknob I pictured myself across from Mom at the kitchen table, me screaming at her to stop staring at me. The nurse did more than just glue her eyes to me. She examined me like a doctor, unwilling to give up until she got a proper diagnosis.

Jump, jump! In my brain I heard the swim coach yell at the kid stranded on the high board, and I almost thought about sitting in her office and beginning a process of becoming myself. "It's easy once you do it," the coach had yelled. But the time between jumping and landing in the water, or in this case the two or three steps to the chair in the corner, that terrified or seemed at least unendurable.

She raised her eyebrows as if to warn me that this would be a different relationship and one I couldn't tackle, one I couldn't master on my own terms. I nodded, and she tilted her head like she'd like to hear my thoughts. But I couldn't tell her that I might need her, the way Dad could need real help. "Why?" she'd say, and I'd be caught explaining lies mingled with what might be the truth, and I could sense she'd never rest until she figured it all out. Like Dad, I was now beginning to hate her psychologizing, especially as she seemed impenetrable, allowing her to work on me without having to give anything herself.

"Bye," I said, and she nodded, still looking at me as I backed out.

In the hall, I felt a tug on the back of my blouse. "This has been the worst day of my life," Barbie said as I whipped around, knocking my biology book into her elbow. "Ow!" she grimaced.

"Oh sorry!" I said.

"Par for the course," she said rubbing her elbow.

"Are you suspended?" I asked, wishing I could rub her elbow or at least get her an aspirin, anything to make her what she was before the cheating.

"Because of the pep rally tomorrow and because of the game next weekend, Pinky said he'd give me a break, but now Mrs. Bell hates me," she said, letting her arm fall to her side. I pulled back as far as I could without actually moving so I could see her from a distance. I even tried squinting like Mom, reducing Barbie to the lights and the darks. But she leaned towards me, and I had no choice but to focus on her face, still puffy from crying, and her messy straw-like hair.

For a second I looked at the floor, hoping to see the old perfect Barbie in the shiny linoleum. When I looked up, her usually determined face reminded me of Dad, weak and vulnerable. "I know I can help you," I said, twisting my hair as she twisted hers, but realizing that this version of Barbie bored me. I could see none of the confidence and drive for perfection. The thought sent me searching for the old Barbie like the way I looked for the old Dad to pop out of bed.

"Do you think you could come over this weekend? I'll make Toll House cookies!"

I couldn't speak for a moment, absorbing her outfit: an A-line navy wool skirt, nylons, navy flats, white blouse, and a small silver circle pin at her throat. "We could go over Latin from the first day in September, and I'll get it—I hope."

I nodded slowly, still taking her in and willing the old Barbie to materialize under the glaring lights. Instinctively, I memorized the squint of her eyes and the slight blush— probably left over from crying and the terror of being caught cheating, but that would fade and, hopefully, the incident as well.

"I'm not good at baton twirling, but I'd like to try!"

"It might take me a little longer to remember everything from the first day so. . ." She puckered her lips and I did too. "You could definitely spend the night," she said, brightening. I smiled, almost laughed with relief as she cocked her head to the side and the old Barbie shone through. "You'd have to put up with some practice, though, because next week I'm performing with fire batons for the first time," she rolled her eyes as if she couldn't believe the school was going to allow fire batons. "I am so nervous but so excited."

"I can imagine," I said exhaling as if I'd been holding my breath ever since she dropped the cheat cards to the floor. Then, it dawned on me that the time had arrived to take a chance, and I really wanted to ask if I could stay for the weekend or even for the rest of the school year, but I nodded instead, picturing me holding a suitcase, unpacking my toothbrush and all my things. I'd control my thoughts from now on, I thought.

At the last bell, I gathered a few things from my locker and then flew home. The traffic on Grand River whooshed at my side and the houses on both sides of Kensington Road blurred. The mean black dog appeared, wandering through a yard at the corner of Chesterfield Parkway. He let his tail drop, and I smiled. "Stay!" I yelled, and he turned around and went up the hill. *This neighborhood will be history,* I thought. No more mean dog and no more racing traffic on Michigan Avenue. No more Dad on his unicycle or Mom setting up an easel in the backyard drawing the Martin House Dad struggled to erect and all the horrid black birds.

In no time, I rounded the corner at Michigan Avenue and saw that the front door to the Craft's house was propped open, and a man whose pants slid embarrassingly low balanced a big chair above his head as he backed out the door yelling, "Slow down, slow down!" A Fritos bag floated along the driveway, and I picked up an envelope with the Craft Family printed in big letters on the front. *Strange for such neat people,* I thought as I grabbed a pencil box I recognized from our days in his meetings, taking notes with perfectly sharpened pencils.

"Are the Crafts moving?" I yelled at the empty kitchen after bursting through the back door. I yelled again and heard Mom in the basement.

"Is that you?" Mom called and I pictured her squinting at a still life as she painted a still life she'd set up. I tore down the stairs.

"I think the Crafts are moving," I announced, out of breath. Mom had moved my bust into the center of the basement, and I closed one eye to blot it out.

"Oh," she said, tilting her head towards a large canvas she'd covered in yellow oil paint. "Are you sure?" she said, and I remembered that gathering news, comprehending the lives of others didn't interest her.

"I think they are," I said, imagining Beth pining for Mr. Craft. Mom went back to spreading paint, and I stared at the brush going back forth as I heard myself reveal Beth's pregnancy inside my head. "Mom," I said aloud and paused before switching gears. "I need a wool A-line skirt. Can you make it by tomorrow?" She turned to me, and her eyes gleamed. Her wide smile revealed beautiful straight teeth, and for some reason she looked not unkempt, as usual, but of a piece in her paint splattered pants and the kerchief holding back her thick hair. I realized there must've been a moment when Dad first got to know her after the War that she had radiated a beautiful calm. I could picture him riding his old bike around the empty lot next to her house in Adrian madly catching butterflies in a net as she watched through a window intrigued. Her distrust of people's motives masked behind high cheekbones and the classical beauty we learned about in art. "Your face is perfect—symmetrical," I said. She widened her eyes and shook her head like the news would hem her in, make her something prescriptive instead of completely conjured by her own design. I followed her to the old ping-pong table where she kept her drawings, and we looked at a sketch she'd made of an A-line skirt that hit daringly above the knee.

"Hems are going up," she said, squinting at the sketch of a stick-like girl, not unlike myself, in black flats and a new kind of blouse Mom said was called a "nothing blouse" because it had no collar or cuffs.

"It's perfect, but we need navy fabric, or I guess burgundy would be okay. Can you make the blouse, too?"

"Let's hurry. We can always find the right material at Clark's Dry Goods." The movers were gone when we tore down the driveway. Mom was on a mission and didn't mention the Crafts. I was sure she'd forgotten the news for now, so I pretended to forget all about it. But I felt the news of Beth's pregnancy in my throat, and I squirmed as she bombed down Michigan Avenue towards the fabric store in Lansing. We pulled into the parking lot, and I saw someone in the window pull down a shade and then switch the sign in the door to 'CLOSED.' The next second, the lights flickered out.

"Oh shoot," Mom said after she threw the gear into park. "Darn, darn, darn," she said pursing her lips, and without thinking I moved over so our shoulders touched. She didn't move until I pointed to a Little Caesar's Pizza a kid in Latin had talked about.

"Let's try it!" Mom backed up, and as she palmed the wheel, I put my hand on hers, like she needed help steering. She froze, and I cleared my throat.

"Beth's pregnant, Mom."

CHAPTER XIX

Mom must have stayed up all night because by the next morning, she'd cut out the skirt and sewn it together, including the darts and the interfacing. We didn't bother with breakfast, hurrying to the basement instead, where she showed me the opening for the zipper. "Thanks, Mom," I said. She nodded, running her finger down a seam as if she'd stitched the news of Beth's pregnancy into the skirt. Yesterday in the car, she'd said almost nothing to me, too embarrassed, I guessed, to discuss the particulars of getting pregnant. But as she digested the idea that Beth was going to have a baby her eyes widened and her chin dropped, realizing perhaps that no amount of positive thinking could alter this irrefutable news. For a moment, I thought we were going to talk about doing it, and maybe I'd tell her about Mr. Craft. Then her face flared.

"You do that and you're nothing but a . . ." she fumbled for words. Her eyes narrowed. "What are kids thinking? Your generation's on the wrong path," She said, barely able to spit the words out. I turned away, vowing never to tell her anything again.

"I'm not like that," I said to the window, coating it with my breath. I heard a sigh, like relief welled from the place where she stored the deep feelings she had for me. I turned to her, and our eyes met, hers pleading, and for once I lost my resolve to hate her for fearing the world we actually live in. She asked if I knew the father. I shook my head, perhaps too vigorously, but she nodded like she believed me and was once more relieved. Then before we left the car, she put her hand on my arm and said that she'd call Empress, and I thought, as her face softened, it was the closest we'd ever come to sharing something other than some clothes she made me. Once inside I hid on the stairs to the basement, straining to hear her whisper the news to Empress. Instead of divulging the truth about Beth, she told Empress that she'd accidentally dialed her number. "So sorry to bother you," I heard her say before hanging up. Maybe her lie cancelled out my lie about the father, but I knew hers was smaller.

"I can get this zipper in right now and baste the hem. You'll have to be careful, but I think you can wear it today." She'd talked me into some checked wool we'd found in a little closet behind her pottery wheel in the basement. "You can't really see the checks," Mom said. I knew she was right, but I also knew that getting a person, Barbie, embedded in my brain and body demanded perfect copying. I gave in, praying Barbie wouldn't dwell on the checks and then neither would I.

I slipped on the skirt and stood on a low table. With pins poking dangerously from her pursed lips, she began pinning the hem. Out of nowhere, Dad called from the kitchen. "I need help; I need help," he called in a hoarse whisper. Mom struggled to stand, and I froze, imagining Dad barefoot in rumpled pajamas, drooling and sweating.

"He's up," she mumbled through the pins, her eyes focused on the hem.

"Can't we finish the skirt first?" I asked, staring down at my own bare feet.

"I'll be right back," she said, and I took a breath, relieved that she had ignored my selfishness. We were on the same track, and I brushed aside a little voice warning me that there would be consequences to faking this alliance. If she kills herself, I'd worry for the rest of my life that she had discovered this deception and that it sent her over the edge. Then I told myself that I did, truly, love the way Mom made things from scratch. But I knew that was a lie. You're only nice to get what you want. My brain swirled, waiting for Mom to return, and praying that she no longer held pins between her lips. "You always told me to use the pin cushion," I said silently.

"I can't stand it anymore!" Dad was wailing, and I heard Mom cooing over his moans and yelps. I willed myself to think of Barbie, how she'd smile at me as I walked into Latin with my black flats, this nearly perfect skirt, and a white blouse—unfortunately, not a Nothing blouse. (Mom had made a pattern for the Nothing blouse, but we found no material in the basement even close to the light cotton blend necessary). Everything's going in circles," Dad moaned, and then the doorbell rang.

I grabbed my blouse and slipped out of the skirt, picking a stray pin from my underpants. I had no idea who was at the door, but I knew enough to put something on before rushing upstairs. After struggling with my bellbottoms, I hurried upstairs, imagining the rare pedestrian on Michigan Avenue responding to Dad's desperate cries, pushing Mom to the floor. "Mom! Don't open the door!" I yelled. "Wait for me!"

Dad raised his index finger to his lips while Mom unlocked the front door. We stared at each other, and then I squeezed shut my eyes for an eternity, and when I opened them and saw his probing deep set eyes looking beyond me, I realized that anyone could've followed him around town, encouraging his stories of mangled bodies and cars; anyone could've memorized his story about the Jap prisoner shot for target practice. I knew by heart this lurid tale with great dialogue between Dad and a stupid guy from Alabama who thought it his duty to practice his sharpshooting on defenseless Japanese targets. Dad hadn't chosen me for this honor as much as I just happened to be there. My face flamed, and then everything inside drained and

I felt the terror of disintegrating now that my memory of being loved and cherished was a false construct. I wished I'd known that one's history could vanish in a flash of understanding. But I wouldn't be sucked in again. If he recovered and needed a receptacle for his seductive storytelling, he'd have to find someone at a bus stop or somewhere on Michigan Avenue. We stared past each other, Dad like a balloon floating out of sight. Before he blended completely with the shifting clouds, I wanted to yell up to wherever he was that I understood I'd been a convenience, not a chosen ally or, God forbid, a loved one.

"Dad," I said, groping for words that might elicit the truth from his curvy, rose-colored lips. But then the yelling started, and without thinking I put my hand on his shoulder. He grabbed my upper arm and squeezed hard.

"She's going to have a baby! Is this your idea of how to take care of a kid? I never should have trusted people like you. Never, Never!" I recognized Empress' loud voice immediately, but Dad cocked his head to the side like a bird. Instinctively, I cocked my head, too, listening to Empress bark at Mom about how she never should've trusted Mom with her weird ideas and that I was a spoiled brat who got away with murder. For once, I was glad we lived on a noisy, indifferent highway. Dad got up from the table, pushing his chair back into the wall and jostling the kitchen table so that his big spoon dropped to the floor and the half empty milk carton tipped. I grabbed it in the nick of time and followed him.

"You floozy!" He pushed Mom to the side like he had no option—like Empress would evaporate in the time it took to make a polite request that Mom move out of the way. As Mom bounced against the wall, I pictured Barbie Robert horrified. I bet she hadn't experienced this kind of fighting, even though I could see that her father had a mean streak. But I couldn't imagine him pushing and shoving like Dad, back to his old violent self. I wondered, as Dad got closer to Empress and Mom pushed me aside, if I'd ever want to get married.

"You get the hell away from my house!" Dad was moving quickly as Empress backed away, tripping on the last step and falling backwards into the mangy evergreen bushes, smacking something on the pitted cement but not her head, which she held high as strands of bleached blond hair escaped the French twist she always wore.

Mom ran down the steps, gasping. "Empress, Empress," she said, and when she looked back at me with eyes telling me to stay quiet, I knew that she didn't want to bring me into the mess. I felt like throwing my arms around her just for that look.

Empress, her hair half down, pressed her hands to her ears as she limped towards her listing white Cadillac. A car honked and swerved into the other lane in order to avoid the Cadillac's bumper that stuck into Michigan Avenue. Another car honked and Empress crumpled like she might topple forward. Mom squeezed past Empress and blocked her path, repeating herself, "I told you I'll help, Empress!" She bent down and tugged on Empress' wrist, pulling her to her full height, which in her sleek black high heels made her taller than Mom by an inch or maybe two.

"What am I supposed to do? Do you realize that she can't have an abortion—she's probably way too far along! Do you realize that? I don't have money to send her to Colorado anyway," she said as Mom brushed dirt from Empress' buttercup yellow dress before hugging her. I looked back at Dad in disbelief—I'd never seen Mom hug anyone before--but when Empress mentioned Colorado, he scowled.

"A home for unwed mothers?" he asked. "Just like that, you'd foist off a daughter where she'd be all alone?" Mom shook her head while Dad and Empress looked at each other as if they'd discussed this in another life.

"Her life is doomed, you know," she said. "And I can't afford even the plane to Colorado. Everything costs," she said, her voice trailing off as she searched Dad's face.

"Let's think positively," Mom said, and I tried to catch her eye. Should I tell her somehow that it was Mr. Craft, even though Beth said they'd never done it? I thought of the hood boy grabbing my arm after I accused him of doing it with Beth, and I stood mute as Mom gently led Empress to the passenger side of the car.

"Are you leaving?" I called to Mom as she hurried around the front of the car.

"I've got to go," she said, and then I blurted, "Mr. Craft should pay for the trip to Colorado."

Empress straightened up, and all three stared at me while the traffic zoomed in the background. Then Empress looked at Mom, waiting for her to admit that this was the truth. Mom was the first to move, helping Empress—who seemed fully recovered from the tussle and fall--into the car and then getting in herself.

"That's not funny, Missy," Empress leaned out of the window and pointed her finger at me.

"I'm not trying to be funny," I said, waiting for Mom or Dad to announce that I'd never make up something like this, but they said nothing. "It's the truth, and he should pay," I shouted over the roar of a motorcycle.

"Stop it!" Mom shouted and started the car.

"That can't be right," Dad muttered and then went inside. Mom and Empress left, leaving me on the porch in my bell bottoms and white blouse without any sense of when Mom would come back to finish the skirt.

Bye, I said silently, my stomach flip-flopping at the thought of Mom anywhere but the house or the occasional art class and me alone with Dad after pointing the finger at Mr. Craft.

The trip to school on foot in the cool fall air was rather uncomfortable because of the pins sticking into my waist, but I willed myself to stop feeling the pricks and mini stabs, picturing Mia Farrow in *Rosemary's Baby* discovering scratches all over her body. Even though a lot of kids milled in the parking lot, I walked as fast as I could, sucking in my stomach to keep the pins from pricking me. "Wait up," Sue Miller and Jane Noble called to me like twins with identical voices. Then out of the blue, Penny grabbed my arm and dragged me along.

"Ouch," I yelled, feeling the pins loosen on one side and the skirt slide lower onto my hips—as if I actually had hips.

"I have so much to tell you about the ride home, and what he said to me!"

By the time I got to homeroom, I realized that wearing the skirt had been a mistake. The pins refused to stay in place and as I struggled to sit down, I thought how easily Mom would've solved this problem by basting a quick stitch as a temporary solution. I sat motionless, fearing the skirt might slip off if I moved. For Homeroom's half hour, I listened to the announcements but remembered nothing as my mind replayed Empress falling and Dad unshaven wearing pajamas outside in full view of the traffic.

After Homeroom I hurried to Latin, praying that Barbie wouldn't notice the faint silver glimmer circling the hemline. The minute I arrived, she waved to me and pointed to my empty chair like I might've forgotten that I sat next to her. I smiled in a grateful, shy way—without showing any teeth. "Sally, come to my desk," Mrs. Bell said, standing and then walking around to the front of her desk. I held on to the pins on one side of the skirt and raised my eyebrows at Barbie as I made my way to Mrs. Bell, who smiled broadly at me, revealing a silver wire affixed to some upper teeth. "Do you like Latin?" Mrs. Bell asked.

"Oh, I love it," I said. "And, I want to help others—if that's all right with you." Mrs. Bell knitted her eyebrows like I'd gone off in a direction she hadn't anticipated.

"Well, I don't know anything about that, but I've talked to the freshman counselor and we've worked it out so that you'll move up to Latin II!" This time, Mrs. Bell spat as she spoke, and I instinctively wiped my chin. She frowned, and I felt like I was ruining her announcement. Pins pricked my skin and sweat rolled down the sides of my ribcage as she raised her eyebrows and wiped the sides of her lips, erasing some of her lipstick.

"Oh, but I can't—I mean isn't Latin II during one of my other classes? You know, that I must take?"

Mrs. Bell regained her high spirits. "Well, that's the wonderful part," she said. "Latin II is during your gym period and art is during Latin I—everyone felt that you could easily move into another freshman gym class as well as another period of art—isn't it wonderful? Your quizzes are perfect, and the last one was no exception! Besides, this class is too big, and Latin II is half the size."

Her eyes widened and shone as she handed me my new mimeographed schedule with blurry purple letters. Stephen Fedkin's face inside a plastic bag appeared floating over the page and for a moment I heard nothing Mrs. Bell said until she patted my shoulder. "Scoot over to Art—she knows you're coming. Here's the pass," she said. "We got it all ready for you."

"But I like it here so much," I murmured as I looked at Barbie, who was staring into space. Her blank eyes reminded me of Dad retreating inside, and then I thought of Mom leaving with Empress. "You might need help in here," I said, staring at my new schedule—the room shrinking around us.

Mrs. Bell smiled, patting my shoulder. "Oh, you'll like Latin II much better. I don't mind telling you that you're one of the best freshmen I've ever had." Then she turned to the class, motioning a girl who sat in the back row to move up to my old seat. "We have someone advancing to Latin II and in all my years teaching, I've never moved someone from Latin I to Latin II as early as October!" Then she mimicked clapping, and everyone clapped for real.

"Now, I can help you even more," I whispered to Barbie as I passed her desk.

"I think I need someone in Latin I," she said, frowning.

"Can we meet after the pep rally?" I asked, turning the doorknob with my sweaty grip. I pictured my hand stuck to the knob and then my feet unable to move—anything to stay with Barbie. But the door clicked open as Barbie shrugged her shoulders in a doubtful way, and I clutched the side of my skirt.

That dance is over, I heard Dad's voice as I stared at one of the large clocks that hung in the hallway outside the Latin room. It seemed cruel of Dad to say that after visiting his old editor at Sparrow Hospital moments before he died, and I know he'd say it again if he'd seen Barbie's shrug. His getting into bed for what seemed like the rest of his life was beginning to make sense. But I couldn't give into failure quite yet. I stood alone on the polished floor, mesmerized by the red second-hand making a slow round of the big clock. In the silence, my mind raced through an encyclopedia worth of survival ideas. The best was to deliberately flunk the first Latin II quiz.

My face flamed, and I leaned on a locker. The loss of real hope of becoming Barbie drained my energy, and besides that, the pins stuck me unmercifully. I wished I could rip off the skirt, but more, I wished I had a better plan than flunking a quiz, which seemed like a long shot. Of course, the success of my suicide loomed as a good alternative to becoming Barbie, but now suffocation just seemed like another failure. I wanted to achieve, to act—anything to give me the feeling of chasing Dad up seven flights of stairs in the tallest building downtown. Once I got to the top in my blistering Mary Janes, I'd beg Dad to do it again. "Please, Please," I'd say, and he'd chuckle already halfway down the stairs, more than willing to do it again or as many times as I'd like.

"Hey, I hoped I'd run into you!" The nurse came from behind. "There's something going on tomorrow evening at the new coffeehouse downtown. Should be a fun get-together for teens," she said, eyeing my hand holding the skirt. "I'm picking up another kid and could swing by your house if you'd like to give it a try. Teens tell stories or sing, anything, or you can watch, have a pop." She wrote her number and ripped the page from a notebook. I nodded, trying my best to convince her that she'd hear from me. "Hope you can go!" she said, walking backward as if she wanted to get a good look at me before I disappeared. The minute she turned the corner, I pushed on a door by the janitor's closet and stepped outside into the gloom and drizzle.

I thought of Mom in her housecoat and unkempt hair slapping me across the face after I had begged her never to come to my classroom—a nice shock that encouraged my sense of being unjustly abused, not unlike standing on this empty sidewalk, staring at the rows of empty cars in the parking lot as the cold air circled my head. But the chill didn't heighten my sense of being wronged or persecuted. I felt powerless with Barbie sitting in Latin I next to my seat while it was filled by someone else. Without thinking, I counted the cars, envying them of their purpose. I let out a small yelp when a black squirrel raced across my black flats. I watched it run under a car and then up a box elder tree, crushing the stream of red and black box elder bugs that were marching in a thick formation on the corrugated black trunk. I suddenly had no desire to be outside at all.

CHAPTER XX

Hurrying along Grand River, I turned at Harrison, picturing in the cavern of my brain a purposeful stride. I imagined my hair cut and ratted to match that of the bubble haired girl. For a moment as I got her down, I stopped in front of a small brick building to stare at my reflection in a window. Under my breath I said hello to this new me, me as the bubble haired girl waving not in a friendly way but in an official, tight way. My stomach relaxed, and I considered answering an ad hanging on the doorknob for a room to rent. *Should we knock?* I asked the bubble haired girl. She didn't answer but rather announced that she was late. I took off, the two of us picking up the pace: me smiling at nothing except the idea that I could be someone at the drop of a hat—a solution to all the turmoil surrounding becoming Barbie.

Just as I turned off Harrison and onto Michigan Avenue— now void of the rush—a car pulled over. I paused while a man struggled to roll down the window. Finally, he shook a white paper bag out of his half-lowered window. White and yellow hamburger wrappers wafted in the still air, and a McDonald's cup, its top skewered by a striped plastic straw, thudded onto the highway, spewing thick pink liquid in the wake of the car's black exhaust. I itemized the junk, annoying the impatient bubble haired girl who took off in a huff. I watched her run between the dying Dutch Elms bent over the sidewalk—the few remaining trees along Michigan Avenue where there'd been so many before the blight that Mom said was a sign of the times. And I guess this fleeing girl was a sign too that anything offering instant relief, this solution of acquiring a person to be at will without lengthy preparation, wouldn't work. After all, the theorem we just memorized in Algebra wasn't going to fly off the board but was there for good; had been since someone worked on it night and day, testing it again and again. I hated the bubble haired girl, I realized as I turned back to the litter drifting across the lanes on my side of the boulevard.

A car flew by on Michigan Avenue and then made a U-turn, careening on two wheels towards the outskirts of MSU. Most likely heading to the lakes of cement Mom and Dad remembered as farmland—parking lots an unchangeable encroachment on everything free and improvisatory—a symbol of my diminished time.

The car disappeared, as did the litter absorbed by sewer grates and the like. With no more commotion, I turned towards our house blocks beyond, and the dying elm trees, like sentinels along the sidewalk, ushered me forward. I pictured myself freezing to death on the back porch, holed up in the listing Lazy Boy, but it was too mild for freezing. Suffocation was the only way, I thought, now that everything seemed to be ending. I squeezed harder on the wad of fabric at my waist, feeling somewhat sorry for the skirt only beginning its life. Perhaps I'd be buried in the skirt, giving it fame or some purpose.

At the back door, I peeked through the windows. Dad's cereal bowl was still on the table next to it the LIFE magazines Mr. Craft had given Beth or she'd stolen from his house. The phone rang. I pushed through the back door, grabbing the receiver before the caller hung up, before I faced another ending like this was the day of nonstop endings—warning me of my own. "Hello!" I shouted, panting into the receiver.

"Pauline?" A man whispered. I hesitated.

"I'm comin' home," the voice whispered. Perhaps it was Dad, but I wasn't sure. I heard a siren and then the dial tone. I ran upstairs, my knees quaking, until I saw their empty bed. *Why would Dad leave the house?* I wondered, picturing him on his bicycle, or worse, on the unicycle in his pajamas, challenging the traffic on Michigan Avenue and then calling home from the pay phone a few minutes away by the new, about to open Dairy Queen—checking in with Mom like a kid. If only Mom would come home, I could go back to planning my suicide and put Dad out of my mind. But then I heard the backdoor slam, and I ran to meet him.

"I always hated Craft! Taking her in his car, giving her magazines and clothes," he said, pointing to the LIFE magazines on the table. "Now he's disappeared, Jayne says, but she's covering for him. I could tell." Sweat poured off Dad's cheeks, splotching a white tee shirt he usually wore under his crisp work shirts. I slid between him and the door, gripping the doorknob and readying myself to flee. Terrified as I was of his brutish wild look, I wanted to know where he'd seen Mrs. Craft; where the Crafts were now. I hesitated as he searched my face, bracing himself against the sink

A pin pricked me hard in the waist and I yanked the skirt apart, marveling at the gleaming pins I'd woven together. I squeezed my eyes shut, but in the blackness I saw the points glistening and the pins overlapping like surgical instruments laid out in a harsh, mechanical pattern. I waited for Dad to head upstairs so I could slip off the skirt and hide it in the garbage. But he poured a glass of milk and slumped onto a kitchen chair, gulping and wiping his mouth with the back of his thick hand.

I felt so dizzy and overwhelmed by losing Barbie Robert to Latin I and all the events of the day, like real life had caught me in a web of its own making—a tangled mess of intractable realities. Who would take care of Beth's baby? Would Mrs.

Craft leave Mr. Craft? As usual, my mind raced from one worry to the next, leading me to the question I couldn't ask Mom: could she ever forget the image of shoes swinging above her head? As I watched Dad drain the glass, I imagined myself asking him for answers, but before I could speak, the pin pattern popped up and then just as quickly was swept away by images of Dad in bed moaning, Mom defiantly stranded in a desert, and me nowhere discernible. Then I got scared, really terrified, because I felt the urge to blind myself with the pins, and I knew that the resulting darkness would send me even further into nowhere. I had to get somewhere recognizable and stay there, forever. Clutching the skirt, I moved towards the door when Dad cleared his throat and said I needed to be nice to Beth. "Help her," he said, and then holding his head, fingers threaded through the curls I wished were slicked down as in the old days, he told me I had to stick with her through thick and thin.

"Why?" I asked, hardly believing we were exchanging words like two people solving a problem. I was about to sit across from Dad when we heard pounding and Mr. Craft yelling for Dad.

"Louis! Louis!" Mr. Craft screamed and banged on the backdoor so hard I heard the shattering of a clay figurine—a cat I'd made in elementary school that had stood on a table in the corner of the porch for years. "Open up!" He demanded, like Dad was a fugitive.

"Bastard!" Dad yelled, and then Mr. Craft appeared in the kitchen, shouting and spit flying as he tried to explain that he hadn't meant to fall in love with Beth. I could feel my eyes bugging out of my head, and when Dad got as close to Mr. Craft as possible without actually pushing him into the door, I hoped he might hit him. Pins pricked me hard as I pulled on Dad's shoulder.

"What kind of jerk are you?" Dad asked, shaking me off.

"She needed guidance and I was helping her, Louis," he said. "Love is something you can't predict," he added.

"Bastard," Dad said again, stepping backwards onto my foot, and when I yelped, he did nothing but clench his fists. I only wished one of them would look at me. When they didn't, I backed up and nearly fled to the basement to find a new outfit, and then I'd go somewhere to comprehend that Mr. Craft loved Beth when I'd been sure he loved me. Losing Barbie Robert was much worse than losing Mr. Craft—a stupid old man. Still, I hated Beth at that moment for effortlessly luring people like Mr. Craft and the hood boy. I grimaced at the thought of squishing my body into Mr. Craft's and rolling down a dune. Still, how could Beth be on the road to a new life, one with a baby and Mr. Craft? Even Dad seemed in her camp now. She had so many people, and I—no one. If I killed myself, would anyone know me well enough to feel guilty, or at least really bad? Patty Scott would hopefully come to the funeral, I thought—if she wasn't drunk or cheering.

"She's a kid for god's sake," Dad said as I hurried to the basement. I heard Mr. Craft bang out the back door, and quick as I could I tore out the front door to watch him pull his car into the traffic. As I walked along Michigan Avenue, I heard Dad yelling my name. I swung around, smiling to hear my name, relieved to hear him yell my name like he had a plan for the two of us because I had none. I ran back, hoping to hear him beg my forgiveness and that I was his favorite, always had been.

"I'm sorry," Dad said. "You don't deserve any of this," he said, waving his hand at the traffic like Mr. Craft would be forever cruising in his sleek car. Then he hugged me. "Oh, god," he said. "I'm sorry, Sally." I let my head fall on his shoulder.

"It's not your fault, Dad," I said, thinking about Dad yelling at Beth from the first day she arrived.

"Take this to Beth's house on Cowley—right over the line in Lansing. You remember. Give it to Empress," he said licking a white envelope.

"What is it?" I asked. "Will you come?"

"Take it," he said, and then he backed into the house, still holding onto the envelope, making me grab it before the screen door shut. I pulled and he let go. "Wait," he said. "Tell Beth's mother this is it."

"Why are you helping her?" I asked. He stared at me through the screen, his eyes dark and his lips squeezed together. Then he said something I couldn't hear through the screen. I moved closer to the screen, struck by the softness of his features. His apologetic demeanor reminded me of softhearted Mr. Novak. Then he tried to speak, but instead tears rolled down his face, and I thought he was about to tell me how much he regretted hating Beth. Just as I was about to make up something about Beth not remembering, he said something I knew I must've heard wrong.

"She's my daughter," he said. "She's my daughter, too."

The sky was gray and empty. I turned my back to the door, heading away automatically, feeling everything behind me evaporate. I was tempted to look over my shoulder, but I resisted and kept going, imagining our house collapsing in on itself. The time had arrived to run away, I thought, and suddenly my heart pounded envisioning the world empty except for people like Mr. Craft and the man who'd palmed my bottom right on Michigan Avenue. I felt an angry rush at my brain for bringing up the sound of the man's heavy steps and the feel of his massive hand cushioning my bottom which held onto the feeling for I think all of third grade—standing for the Pledge, his hand was there, and at recess too.

At the corner of Cowley and Michigan Avenue, I dawdled, circling the stop sign like I was waiting for someone to show up who'd listen to me. I lost track of time, my stomach growling as many more cars sped past, leaking strains of pop music and the tortured rhythm of gears staying too long in first or second before moving into higher and more forgiving gears. But I couldn't move on, couldn't decide on a course of action, couldn't begin a new plan, couldn't do anything.

CHAPTER XXI

I have no idea how long I lingered at the bus stop, clutching the envelope in one hand while the other hand did its best to keep the skirt together. If only I could've buried the envelope or tossed it into the traffic and watched as a tire ground it to nothing. But I clung to the envelope just like I clung to the skirt. The obvious responsibility to deliver it competed in my mind with a calculated decision to get rid of it and flee.

I waved the envelope into the traffic. Maybe I'd take up hitchhiking now that my family had fallen apart. A truck barreling towards my outstretched hand slowed to change lanes, and I nearly let the envelope fly onto his windshield. The driver beeped and waved. My heart stuttered. Something told me, as I snatched the envelope to my chest, that Dad expected me to keep his secret to myself and that in the envelope was a note to Empress, begging her not to tell Mom or Beth. Part of me hoped Empress had already blurted the truth.

I imagined Mom, barely able to comprehend the news, wandering towards an expanse, like a desert, that even she'd find too stark and isolated. One thing I felt for certain as our histories crumbled: Dad had kept the facts to himself. If he confessed to Mom, he might begin to heal. I pictured him out of bed and back to work, not as his old self, but subdued and wary of the consequences of pumping up reality.

I bet along the way, while deceiving Mom and I guess me, he'd convinced himself that the news would destroy us. Told himself that he didn't want to kill Mom's search for a nirvana or destroy her commitment to positive thinking and art making. I'd heard him brag that she could paint anything, render a face so detailed you couldn't distinguish it from a photograph. But really, the silence on his part was only self-serving. He was afraid she'd abandon him if he confessed. Unstable or not, she'd been at his side.

As I shifted my feet and stared down Michigan Avenue, pretending to search for the next bus, I saw nothing but a blur of traffic, and Mom's face popped up in the branches of the dying Elms. Her unflinching stare convinced me the revelation wouldn't crush her, wouldn't quench her underlying whirl of determination and defeatism. Perceived slights and unfounded fears about our little world destroyed the logic she applied to making things while real situations, like the truth of Dad and Empress and Beth, might focus her on how to proceed, at least for a while, like the way she made a dress without a pattern.

I envisioned Mom clearing her mind once she was in the desert or perhaps out to sea and then returning home, standing on our porch, suitcase in hand, ready to do what she could. After she implemented her grand plan, (who knows what that would entail, but I bet a lot of positive thinking, drawing, and maybe staring into the distance without the aid of glasses, which she told Dad were nothing more than a man-made crutch), she'd smash plates at the wall and throw chairs, not because of what actually happened, a betrayal, but because the scheme hit a snag, a pothole in the road proving she didn't have the powers of a god. Obvious, I thought as a pin stabbed my thumb, that Dad's nearsightedness would not be cured by blindly staring into the distance as she'd suggested.

I breathed in but moving on proved tough. The walk over the border into Lansing seemed impossibly long. The afternoon traffic whirring without a break, like a window fan, did little to push me forward, and instead I sank into the little strip of dead grass meant to beautify either side of Michigan

Avenue. Inside my head I heard Dad uttering the truth about Beth and Empress. I wished I'd mocked him as payback for changing our lives without even hints to prepare us. I could've asked him whether this was another one of his stories I was supposed to memorize and perhaps store for him. Instead, I took his note, said I'd do his bidding—and now I was stuck replaying the announcement against the backdrop of screaming tires. I congratulated myself that at least part of my brain knew to keep track of the shifting skirt. Finally, I gave up pretending to wait for a bus to take me to Lansing or beyond and headed, stumbling on the curb and gripping my skirt, towards Cowley and Beth's house. In my head, I continued to hear Dad's words, his tearful, barely audible announcement.

Before turning at Cowley, I stared at Dad's big scrawl, *Empress Martin.* My mind reeled, picturing the two of them together, holding hands and walking somewhere I couldn't identify—a park perhaps. Mom appeared in the picture, tall and stiff in paint-splattered art clothes while Empress and Dad were dressed in fancy clothes, Empress's hair in a smooth French twist. The vision of Dad and Empress rather than Dad and Mom gave me goose bumps, bringing to mind, as I teetered at the edge of cars whooshing about an inch from my toes, that Dad liked her verve and her mission-less life. I bet Empress never mentioned the shapes of the clouds or lamented all the bad thoughts floating and penetrating our brains without warning.

Barbie Robert seemed like a memory. Only Stephen hung around my brain at the edges, observing what neither he nor I expected. *You'll have to wait,* I whispered, like finally I could justify a hesitation to follow Stephen or anyone for that matter.

I looked at Dad's handwriting, trying to find out more about him, parts of him I didn't know, and then I tore open the sealed envelope, finding a check for five hundred dollars and a note that read:

Empress, This is all I can give you now.
I am sorry about Beth and Craft. He will pay.
Please leave us alone now.
—Louis

He obviously didn't care if Empress told Mom and Beth the truth. Probably hoped she let it slip out since he'd been too afraid to tell Mom himself. Shifting the responsibility to Empress reminded me of all the times Dad said he couldn't find a parking spot near the car wash so could I just run in, find out whether his horse lost or won? I knew where to find his bookie behind the big hoses, so no big deal, he'd say as he patted my arm. And if the horse lost, just blurt it out, he'd tell me— "I can take it," he'd say through the open window. I'd run into the car wash, afraid, as our car turned the corner and I couldn't see it anymore, that he'd never come back.

I hoped that he hated Empress as much as he hated Beth— the way he used to—but I sobbed at the thought that he probably loved Empress's lipstick and her clothes. I remembered Dad in his black suits and white shirts, combing his black curls flat to his head, staring at himself in the big mirror as he admired his cufflinks.

I recognized the house, despite the fact that I hadn't been on Cowley since the day we delivered Beth to her mother, the two of us coincidentally on matching tricycles. Now I saw that nothing had changed on the outside—peeling paint and a dilapidated garage--but I'd never been inside. Never played at Beth's throughout the years. She and her mom were so often gone or missing—a random life no one could keep track of. When she'd showed up on our front porch clutching her pink bag, it was like the annoyance of finding someone else's mail in the mailbox. *Don't you belong elsewhere?* I wanted to ask.

After I rang the bell, which made no sound, and then knocked on Empress's front door, I peeked through the front window. The house seemed dead. Had Mom, Empress, and Beth escaped to Texas or somewhere far off? I panicked for a moment, my mind racing ahead to a future alone with Dad. I knew Dad so well at one time, but now we were like strangers. We'd have to relearn each other's lives, and I'd have to forgive him for lying and betraying Mom.

Then Empress stood in the door.

"You're here," she said and opened the screen door. I handed her the torn envelope and then followed her inside. In the foyer, she read the note and examined the check. I watched her carefully slip the note back in the envelope along with the check. "I suppose you opened this?" She sniffed, and I looked down. "Honestly, I don't blame you." We walked along a hallway, and I wondered if Dad had been here, and, for a moment, I felt dizzy and nauseous.

Empress led me into a suffocating living room. I wasn't sure where to look. The house appeared lived-in, much more than ours, but at the same time, it felt frozen and waiting for the truth to come out about who lived here and who paid for it. A clock on the mantle had the wrong time, and two snow shakers were on their sides, longing, I thought for someone to put them upright, but I didn't want to leave a trace of me, not even a fingerprint. I looked around quickly for gifts from Dad, things people gave him for writing a nice obituary—vases and what not that Mom mocked and usually whisked away without even waiting for Dad to forget about them.

I squinted at a framed photograph hanging near the door and then quickly looked away. My face reddened, and I thought of running outside in the cool fall air, but the small photo drew me in. *Stop staring at that picture,* I said, looking down at the patterned carpet, which was deep blue like the night sky with yellow stars and crescents scattered throughout.

Without thinking I got close to the photograph of a much younger Empress. She and Beth looked nothing alike, the way Mom and I could be sisters, people said. How was it possible I'd never noticed that Dad and Beth had the same smile, the same nose and eyes? Then in my brain I heard Beth chuckle at someone's absurd behavior, and realized she sounded like Dad. I immediately looked down at the fake nighttime sky and then out the window at the wind blowing the few leaves left on a tree. My eyes watered, and I turned back to the photograph of beautiful Empress staring back at me.

She is part of your life now, I heard myself say, and I didn't think anyone would deny this. *But I won't let her in,* I said to Dad, whose face filled my brain like I was between them now, entangled and knowing that the refusal to let her into my life would take a lot of determination that seemed at that moment, in the dim light of the only lamp in the room, impossible to muster. Then the little photo I'd discovered buried in Dad's cufflink box flashed before my eyes. I'd rip it into shreds if I ever again went back home.

For a moment, I thought that Empress might try to be my mother—worm her way deeper into our lives—and I pictured the two of us in a convertible with identical French twists and lipstick, laughing about something unimportant like we preferred laughing to worrying about anything—giddiness to any striving to make the world better. I wondered if I could sit down. But I couldn't form the question and instead leaned against the wall.

Empress came through a swinging door from the kitchen, her silk robe whisking about her figure. She pointed to a door off to the side that led to a small porch, where I could see Beth asleep on a davenport covered in a bright red afghan. "Beth feels like crap," she said, jiggling her drink, the ice cubes clinking against the glass.

I winced. Mom never used words like 'crap,' and I thought again of Dad and Empress together, wondering what he thought about her manner, her way of talking. I wondered if he'd lied about high types, if he hadn't meant a word of his advice to steer clear of people like Empress. Find the best sorts, he always said. Like they'd protect us since we couldn't manage on our own. Then I blinked hard, realizing that I needed to fixate on the here and now and stop obsessing over the real meaning behind Mom and Dad's words and ideas, like how to get through life, make something of it, rise above as Dad said.

For instance, did Beth and Mom finally know the truth about Dad and Empress? Maybe I should have given the envelope to Mom. Was I wholly disloyal at heart? Handing the envelope to Empress like I trusted her, believed in her more than my own Mom? I swallowed and envisioned myself running away, finding somewhere else and not someone else to sink into—shutting down my brain forever.

Mom came through the swinging door holding a glass of water. Her face sagged. Her hands, big and rough looked awkward rather than strong. She'd just lost, I thought, all her ambition for transforming the world through thought control and art and it would be up to me to help her get it all back. Everything I'd resisted and hoped would go away I'd work to recover, work to pat it back into her tall big boned body like she was the scarecrow in The Wizard of Oz.

She tried to smile but hardened her face like she'd start crying if she didn't remain motionless inside and out. She glanced over her shoulder at Beth still asleep on the porch and put the water on the mantle next to the snow shakers.

My heart raced as I saw myself leaving now that I'd delivered the money and the note. The three of them seemed to have sorted out everything, and I had no role. Beth needed Mom more. But Mom moved towards me in one awkward step, her foot squashing my toes, and stroked my arm. We stood across from Empress who sneered and shook her head. And then Mom took my hand, and I remembered a photo I'd found snooping in one of her drawers of me sitting in her lap. Her hand was on my cheek in the photo, like we were models and the photographer had told her to put her hand there. Empress, gloating over this opportunity to finally disrupt the unity she assumed we enjoyed, blurted out that Beth and Mom knew that Dad was Beth's Dad. "I had to tell them. It's time your Dad grew up and took some responsibility, for God's sake."

She looked at Mom, who stared ahead, her cheekbones hardening; her face rebounding. And her grey eyes, for once, not narrowing to see the lights and darks but fully open.

"There were times I almost told you, Pauline," Empress said. "But I'll be frank; the money would dry up, and if anyone would help with Beth it was your family—of course little did I know this would happen right under your nose."

She went on about Mr. Craft and how we should've known he was despicable, and I was surprised to hear her use a word we'd had on the vocab list. I'd depended on Beth and Empress being less intelligent than us, but now that we were related, I was glad Empress had a brain in her head. When she paused, I saw the glass of water and suddenly craved a drink. Empress looked at the glass too and then laughed and pointed at Mom. "You were Louis' crutch, and I a thorn in his side."

My fists tightened, and I imagined socking Empress or throwing the water at her beautiful hair. I imagined grabbing Mom's hand, pulling her outside where she'd see the translucent clouds she loved, and I'd try to see their shapes as they adapted to the unseen vapor flying upwards. I closed my eyes, picturing an afternoon in elementary school when we'd memorized the cloud types and learned about the process of evaporation with the weird mom who'd volunteered to teach us all about weather.

"I guess Dad wanted it all hush hush," Mom said like she was putting together pieces of a simple puzzle that still eluded her even after Empress made it all quite clear.

"He didn't think the two of you could handle much," Empress said, like Mom and I could now handle the news along with a heap of scorn.

"This is a lot for us," I said, staring at the glass of water.

"Well, I have feelings too, and I got sick of protecting Louis. Got sick of you having everything. East Lansing this and East Lansing that."

Empress pointed her finger at me. "Well, you got it all started, didn't you?" Empress stared at me, sitting erect in a rocking chair with her legs crossed and the envelope in her lap.

"No, you did," Mom said, her face bright red. "Besides, none of us knew about Beth and Tom Craft until it was too late--I never thought she was a sneak. But maybe Beth needed someone who'd be loyal, wouldn't shunt her off. Too bad the cards she drew were, well," Mom paused, "unlucky."

Empress trembled and her creamy skin turned pink and then red. "All I hoped was for Louis to be a good Dad to Beth. It's what you got, Sally, isn't it? Beth's no less his daughter."

Mom stared ahead but the brave comeback seemed to drain from her body, and finally, as the silence filled the small room, she looked down, and I wondered if she was holding back tears. "I'm sorry," she murmured and without looking at me I knew she spoke to me. I pictured myself at five wandering the Chicago train station. I closed my eyes, hoping no other pictures showed up in my brain and in the blankness of my mind I felt relief that for Mom's sake I hadn't been kidnapped.

"Is Tom going to be in trouble?" Beth stood in the door with the afghan hanging off her shoulders. "Can I see him, please?"

"Mr. Craft to you," Empress said, rolling her eyes. Then she got up, leaving the room like we should figure out how Beth would deal with the pregnancy and her future life as a mother.

"I wonder why your dad never told me he was my dad," Beth said, looking at me as I thought a sister might, with natural irritation and jealousy I'd never seen before. A streak of sunlight shot through a window, illuminating Beth's olive skin and deep brown hair and eyes. She had the luck of beauty, but as if she'd lost a coin toss, she got nothing else, while I got it all. I looked down, ashamed for a moment that I'd spent my life wanting to be someone else.

"We need to go," Mom said, still looking down. But then she looked at Beth like they'd just met. "I wouldn't give Tom Craft another thought." Empress returned holding a glass of wine.

"But you have a husband, don't you? Dads may not matter to you, but you two are set, and Beth's got a big problem, and what have I got?"

Mom's grey eyes narrowed, and I thought she looked like a wolf or a predator that had restrained herself and would now pounce.

"I suppose you didn't want something to drink?" Empress looked at Mom with a resigned expression, and then after she took a long drink, she slumped into the chair and smoothed her hair. "I never wanted this," Empress said. Beth went to Mom, standing next to her on the other side. I thought the three of us in a line across from Empress could be a firing squad.

"You mean me," Beth said, and I looked at Beth—her eyes wide like she wanted Empress to say what was obvious, that Beth had never been wanted by anyone. Empress sipped her wine and muttered something I couldn't hear. "I love him," Beth said, looking at me and then at Mom. I couldn't imagine Mom abandoning Beth, but she grabbed my hand and led me to the door.

"It's time you figured this out, Empress but you know we're going to help," Mom said, pulling open the door. I wished she and I were home, where I could finally take off the skirt. I hated Empress for looking so much better than Mom and me.

We stood on the sidewalk in front of the house unable to speak. In the silence, I forgot about the skirt and about everything except Dad and Empress. Mom, I thought, dwelled on them too as she at last took a step. Then she stopped, and when she looked at the clouds it was without awe.

"What will happen to Beth?" I asked, hoping to erase from our minds' images of Dad and Empress. Mom, without a jacket, remained silent and impervious to the chill. I tried to see inside her brain, but after a while I gave up, allowing images of Stephen to float across my brain, his big smile and crooked glasses fading with each iteration of his goofy face.

It seemed like forever that we stared at the wide street, naked without the Dutch Elms that had once decorated the whole town, like hundreds of candles on a sheet cake. We could, I thought, stay here forever, worrying about how to go on until eventually we'd starve or freeze to death, following Stephen naturally, without a plan, our remains found on a dull street at the very beginning of Lansing.

Mom shook her head and sucked in her lips.

"I don't know what will happen to Beth, it's up to them now." The sense of failure hung heavy in the air. I took a deep breath, afraid that if I took a step, we'd move out of a mutual wariness into our old sparring ways. "She was such a cute kid," Mom said, and I nodded, remembering her bangs and her deep brown eyes.

"They have the same eyes," I said under my breath, testing the waters of spontaneous exchange without the constant gauge of mistrust and fear of attack. Mom nodded slowly.

"I never noticed," she said. I straightened up and stroked her hand, lying on the seat like an old rock on the beach. Maybe I could help her understand what's going on in the world before she lost her way and found someone else she hoped to save in a web of art-making and higher thinking. Becoming other people had filled my mind for as long as I could remember, but in the vacuum once filled by Barbie Robert, I pictured Mom asking me questions on how to operate in the world. I envisioned myself as the surrogate mother, not resenting Mom, but helping her. I hated to admit that I'd gleaned a few ideas on how to be a woman from Empress, the worst of all mothers yet a vision of toughness and elegance I couldn't forget.

CHAPTER XXII

"There's Mrs. Broadback." I pointed at Mrs. Broadback's green station wagon, half in our driveway and half hanging into Michigan Avenue. A driver honked and then beeped over and over while swerving into the far lane. Mom stopped short of the driveway. "Is it OK if I babysit, Mom?"

She turned my way, her eyes roving over my face, not to see color and shape but to glean information about me. I looked away, embarrassed by her gaze and worried about what she'd find. "Sure," she said in a far-off tone.

I fumbled with the door. "Bye."

"Bye, Sally."

I settled into the front seat of the Brodbacks' station wagon, gripping the skirt and praying Mrs. Broadback wouldn't notice my hand keeping the skirt together. As she struggled to shift the gear into reverse, I wondered if I could run upstairs and change my clothes. But as she backed up into Michigan Avenue, biting her lip and wincing, I stared at the window on the second floor and thought better of confronting Dad. "I don't know how your folks do that every day," she said. "And soon you'll have to!" We both laughed, and I turned around to make sure Mom had pulled into the driveway and hadn't decided to keep going—abandoning us for good.

"I thought I'd find you closer to the school—you got home fast!"

I nodded, as the memory of me slipping out of school flashed before my eyes. My mouth felt dry, and a response stuck in my throat. Finally, I choked out something about early dismissal.

"Lucky for you," she said, and I smiled at the sound of her voice and at the white light shining through a crack in the clouds.

"Can we get something from the Good Humor truck?"

Mrs. Broadback raised her eyebrows. "If we see him, but I don't have time to race all over like yesterday." Mrs. Broadback checked her mirror, searching for Danny.

In my mind she gasped when I admitted to skipping school. Then I felt the news of Beth and Dad rise in my throat like I was about to blurt everything, and it was all I could do not to jump out of the car and run to some place where I'd never see her again. I took a deep breath through my nose, pinched my lips together, and then like someone took pity on me, I relaxed, and we headed away from Michigan Avenue to the comfort of the winding streets and the deep green expanse of the sloping lawns in Glencarin. I wished we'd tour the neighborhood for a while.

"I have something to ask you," she said as telephone repairman signaled for us to stop.

"I'll get right to the point: Dick has gotten word that IBM wants him to head up the new London office. It's a year assignment at the least, and I'm wondering if you'd consider going with us. I told Dick I can't manage Danny alone in a strange place, and we both thought of you. I think Danny needs you." I looked back at Danny, who dangled a plastic dinosaur by the tail. "Your hair is tangled," Danny said. I smoothed my hair with my free hand trying to understand what Mrs. Broadback had just said.

"Can we get out and watch the work man?" Danny jumped up and down on the back seat like it was a trampoline.

"Danny!" She looked at me for sympathy. "See what I mean?"

"Would I live with you?"

Danny reached over the seat and waved the toy in front of my face. "Be nice to T-Rex or he'll bite your arm off!" Danny laughed and fell onto the back seat.

I heard threads rip in the skirt and felt tears rise. Living forever with the Broadbacks could solve all my problems, I thought as I squeezed the skirt at my waist, ignoring a pin sticking into my skin. But not it she knew about Beth and Dad. I sensed the news was about to explode straight up from my gut, and this time I wouldn't be able to squash it.

I pictured Mrs. Broadback's wide eyes as she heard about my family. And once she saw my skirt, she'd never put so much trust in me, a person who'd go outside, let alone to school, in something so clearly unfinished.

"What did you ask before Danny began his jumping routine?"

I gathered my thoughts, hoping my voice wouldn't quake or that I wouldn't burst into tears. "I just wondered if I'd live with you?"

She laughed and reached in her purse for her cigarettes. "Of course! We're not going to put you on the street!" She dropped the cigarette pack back into her purse, and I wished she'd give me specific jobs—anything to help me melt into the family, the house, even the car. For a second, I considered asking for a cigarette.

"We'd talk to your parents—if you're interested—and we'd get all the information on the schools. But we'd go soon. I just can't face this all alone. I've just been elected Recording Secretary for my sorority, and I'm going to be very busy winding that up, and, well, I've just got to figure out how we'll manage things over there—even the holidays will be different." She pulled into the driveway and let her hands slide off the wheel while Danny began to jump again. "I mean it's a big promotion, but it's a lot for me to handle with Danny. Dick has no idea how much goes on every day." She shrugged, and I copied her. She could be Barbie Robert's older sister, I thought.

"Oh, I really want to go with you," I blurted.

Like a weight had been lifted from her narrow shoulders, she let her head fall back and closed her eyes. Danny slipped out of the car and ran to the button for the automatic garage door. He reached on his toes and pushed the button manically as we stared through the windshield at the door sliding up and down.

"I have a sorority sister who knows someone at State who went on something called a sabbatical. Their kids loved living in a different country and going to school there—although the kids might've been younger than you. I don't know about their ages, but she said you might get a lot out of the experience. You know, different customs and all that. Of course, each of us would have to get a passport." We continued to watch the garage door slide up and down until finally I got up the nerve to ask if she could take me back home so that I could change clothes. "Oh, you look fine," she said, finally slipping a cigarette from the pack. After she lit the long menthol, she blew smoke and shook her head. "I do hope your parents go for the idea," she said, sucking hard on the cigarette.

"But if I am staying tonight, I think I'd like some pants," I said.

Inside, she offered me a stack of slacks. "I think these slacks will fit best," she said, pointing to a navy-blue pair she'd placed on the top. "Looks like that skirt needs some serious repair."

I ran off to the bathroom and locked the door. Finally, I could let go of the skirt. In my underpants, I stared into the mirror, enamored of the curve in my delicate lips and the straightness of my nose. I closed my eyes and lightly placed my fingertips over my eyelids. When I finally opened them, I saw the harshness of my bones, jutting from my cheeks. My face transformed into Mom's, and tears immediately poured down my cheeks as I thought of Dad and Empress instead of Dad and Mom. I closed my eyes again, wishing I'd never looked at face so closely.

If only I could tell Mrs. Broadback everything. I looked at the doorknob, imagined myself flinging it open and telling her the news without taking a breath. A calm voice told me to forget telling her. *You have no one,* it said, and I nodded. For a moment, I begged Stephen to show up, but got dressed fast so he couldn't show up. I knew I couldn't think about killing myself in Mrs. Broadback's bathroom with Danny waiting for me and Mom perhaps waiting for me to call to check in or just let her know when I'd be home. Maybe Stephen had met his match with London, and that's why he wasn't around. Would London at least delay my death, now that I'd failed at becoming Barbie?

Mrs. Broadback left plates of fish sticks on the counter before she yelled goodbye. Danny and I yelled "Bye," as we watched Lassie on the Broadback's new TV, nestled safely in a wooden piece of furniture with doors that hid the TV when you weren't watching it--a home within a home. Our metal TV sat somewhat precariously on one of Mom's narrow sewing tables.

"Ruff Ruff!" Danny shouted in my ear and then leaned on me. The warmth of his body felt good, and for a moment I forgot that I was babysitting and slipped off my shoes and put my feet up on the coffee table. Then I closed my eyes. "Mom doesn't allow feet on the table," Danny said.

I got my feet off the table fast, hoping Danny wouldn't tell Mrs. Broadback, especially now that she'd asked me to join them in London.

"We should stop watching TV—it's very bad for your eyes," I said, standing abruptly so that Danny toppled into the soft cushions of the Broadback's huge davenport.

Danny buried his face in a pillow and began to sob. "I want my Mommy, not you!" His back convulsed with each sob and like staring at the traffic; I found the wave-like motion a thing apart from the body producing it. In fact, his brown pants and yellow shirt blended with the davenport so thoroughly it appeared that the davenport sobbed right along with him. As if he couldn't comprehend that anyone would care so little about his distress, Danny flipped onto his back and stared at me; our eyes locked in mutual curiosity. "I miss my Mommy because she's only here when I'm asleep and that doesn't count."

"That's a lot for someone your age to figure out." I said, oddly wishing I could teach him some Latin. Barbie was too stupid to get Latin, I thought, and I remembered Mrs. Bell so happy to announce my promotion. My stomach twisted when I realized that Mrs. Bell wouldn't be my Latin teacher if I went to London with the Broadbacks. Mrs. Bell translated Latin sentences so easily, reminding me of the way Barbie twirled the baton under one arm without ever hitting herself. Then Danny grabbed my hand, and I held onto him while he jumped on the davenport. After he landed in my arms, I told him that I hoped he had Mrs. Bell for Latin when he got to high school. "She's really a good teacher," I said, dropping him on to the thick cushions.

Danny said he hated nursery school because you had to sit in a circle. He told me about some other things he hated about nursery school, but I didn't listen because I was thinking about Mrs. Bell and how from the first day I'd wished everyone had been nicer to her because, like Mom, she had a passion. I leaned against the fridge, worrying that I'd miss Mrs. Bell if I went to London.

After dinner we read books, Danny snuggling once again. I moved away, and he moved too until I leaned on a wall by his bed and his head dropped into in my lap. "Your hair is long," he said, reaching for the ends of my hair, winding it around his small fingers.

"I might have to get it cut," I said, picturing Mrs. Broadback's short hairstyle.

Danny finally fell asleep. I waited outside his door until he stopped humming and calling for water. Mrs. Broadback had told me not to bring water because he could still wet the bed. I tiptoed downstairs and lay down on the davenport. On the ceiling, I tried to bring into focus Mrs. Broadback. Instead I saw Stephen Fedkin. For once, Stephen appeared smiling inside the plastic bag. *It's an option to kill oneself*, I thought, and smiled at Stephen as I tried to imagine what the moment was like when Stephen decided to go through with it, when he had taken the final step. If only Stephen had found an outlet, an avenue to become himself and not someone else like one of the dumb guys who rams around town in a fancy car.

I swallowed, thinking how Barbie had hardly noticed me when I had left Latin after the applause. Stephen needed something that never changed, like Latin. I wished I'd brought my Latin text home so I could get ahead. I flopped back on a cushion, surprised at how quickly things changed. I'd been devastated when I was promoted to Latin II, leaving Barbie behind. But now the promotion, translating texts, and the very world of Latin, with its intricate structures and history, spoke to something inside me, a longing for inquiry and logic. Barbie's house flashed before my eyes like the Barbie house I'd wanted so badly when I was young but never got.

My eyes felt heavy, and I knew the Broadbacks expected me to stay awake. What if Danny got sick, or the house began to burn? I scanned the bookshelf and pulled down a book called *Entertaining Elegance*. The table of contents listed meals from around the world. I searched for one from England. The only somewhat related chapter was on food from Scotland. I read about the best methods for making oatcakes and wondered if Mrs. Broadback would make things like oatcakes and another dish called haggis. I closed the book, and as the clock ticked in the otherwise silent house, I thought about living without Mom and Dad in London. I remembered a kid from England visiting our fourth grade class and her matching sweaters and skirts, like what you'd wear to meet someone important. I imagined myself dressing like Mrs. Broadback, becoming Danny's surrogate mom, and maybe we'd stay on forever. Maybe I'd wear pumps like I'd seen in a window downtown; I'd see what Mrs. Broadback wore for shoes. Of course, Mom wouldn't approve of shoes and clothes bought and not made, but Dad would love to hear that I had a new life somewhere he'd only dreamed of. Then I thought of Patty Scott. I hardly talked to her anymore, but would she forget me entirely if I went away? Would Penny Stilwell write me, or would she find someone new to divulge all the goings-on at her youth group and her experiences with the weird boy?

As sleep began to overtake me, I pictured a chasm and me slipping between huge rocks. I jerked to sitting and thought about boarding a plane and leaving everyone behind: Mom, Dad, Mrs. Bell, even Penny Stilwell. Beth might want to talk to me, and I choked back tears at the idea of Beth alone with horrid Empress. I wished that I'd been nicer to her. I guessed I could write her, and of course Mom and Dad, but as I sat in the near dark, I already missed Mrs. Bell, and I couldn't imagine writing Mrs. Bell.

***

"I'll get back to you probably this week on what you'd need for a passport, and I want to talk to your parents," Mrs. Broadback said, idling in our driveway after she drove me home. I nodded, and before I pulled on the door handle, I told her that Danny was smart. She laughed, reminding me of Barbie Robert with the graceful wave of her hand. I waved and stumbled backwards into a hole in the driveway that I always forgot about. We both laughed, mine a laugh I didn't recognize. Where it came from, I didn't know, except that it just sprang from me and hung in the air.

I dawdled on the front steps too afraid to go inside--unable to picture the three of us together. Who'd break the silence? Beth had once called me a fraidy cat because I wouldn't lie down in Michigan Avenue during the still hours of a Saturday morning. "Just for a second or two," she said after she'd lain motionless on the lane marker for a full minute.

"You can do it," I'd said out loud, and then I'd told myself that taking my place between Mom and Dad wasn't as scary as tempting fate by lying down in an empty highway. I tiptoed along the driveway to the backdoor. If Mom sat at the kitchen table sipping tea, I'd ask if I could fold clothes or scrub the sink. I hadn't imagined myself part of my own family. Our beings never overlapped, but now that it was falling apart my family might need me, to pull it together. Once inside, I'd start on a list of strategies for getting along. One thing for sure, I wouldn't mention London, and if I could remember where I'd hidden the picture of Empress I'd found in Dad's cufflink box, I'd tear it into bits.

"I should leave, and you should come with me," Mom said after I quietly closed the back door. She stood in the middle of the kitchen, glued to the pitted yellow linoleum, perhaps waiting the whole time I'd been away for me to come home. "We should go," she said, and this time my stomach flip flopped, and my head whirled like I was on the merry go round with Dad running and grunting, turning the world into a nauseating blur while I begged him to stop.

"Where would we go?" I asked, and she slumped onto one of the kitchen chairs.

"Whose slacks are those?" she asked, and without thinking I squeezed her hand.

"Mrs. Broadback's," I said.

"Oh, that was nice of her," she said, tears rolling down her cheeks.

Chapter XXIII

"I heard you're a brain in Latin," Penny said, grabbing my hand the next morning as we walked to the language wing. "It's perfect because I have German now. We can always meet after this period, and I'll tell you the news about you know who."

"Whom," I said. She laughed, and I thought about taking back the little correction; instead, I asked if she liked German.

"My Mom signed the papers for the exchange student. The German girl is going to live with us next semester. Miss Schenkel says I'll be fluent by June. Hey, are you going to that coffeehouse with the nurse tonight?"

"Um," I said, remembering the nurse's invitation as I stared at Penny's rings and bracelets and for the first time saw that her nails were filed and painted a pretty peach color. They reminded me of Empress' red nails tapping on the armrest as Mom and I left her alone with Beth. It dawned on me that it had been rude to call an adult by her first name. *Stop,* I said to myself. The last thing I wanted to do was sympathize with Empress.

"Make up your mind already," Penny laughed, squinting at me like she wasn't sure if I was the same person she'd confided in about the all-important boyfriend. "Are you okay? You seem really out of it."

"I do?"

Penny nodded as she went on about the coffeehouse and the idea of getting together on a school night, which her parents would be against, and how she couldn't wait to get her license because she could drive to her cello lesson which is near Baskin Robbins—the new ice cream shop. "You play the cello?" She nodded and told me about her teacher's adorable dog. I listened to the sound of her voice, realizing that her banter, her very person had always stayed in the background, like she was my own personal foil, a wall on which to lean and consider the attributes of someone else. I'd relegated her to the imperfect tense—nothing definite or finished. Nothing worth, I'd decided, bringing into the discrete light of any given moment.

"So, are you coming to the coffeehouse?"

"I'll see," I said, and she laughed again, leaving me at Latin. "Next year take German," she said over her shoulder. "It's hard, but I love it."

I stared after Penny, wondering when she'd become so confident and how someone obsessed with a stupid oaf of a boy who didn't even go to our school could actually love German. I'd heard it was harder than Latin. I imagined telling her that I didn't want to ever again hear about her idiot boyfriend—if that's what he was. Then I pictured her running from me before twisting around and sticking her tongue out in revenge, realizing perhaps that all along I'd pretended to find him interesting and worse had thought her disposable.

The old Dad piped up in my brain, his seductive voice explaining about high types and all the people we had to avoid or use for our own purposes. I pictured a day when I hurried after him along Michigan Avenue, absorbing every word he uttered about the track. First, he described a jockey he said was as dumb as a doornail and then he went on about the sleazy track owner he hoped might give him a piece of the action. When I tripped and fell, bloodying my knee, he kept going and I missed most of the next story about a guy he knew in college—a high type with southern manners. When I realized he wasn't coming back I limped home, worrying sort of out of the blue that he'd look for another partner. Worrying even though without talking or interrupting—impulses I squashed rather than enrage him—I's been the perfect sidekick, agreeing with everything he said. Maybe the bright red blood, running down my shin, brought on the premonition that one day he'd dump me.

I shook my head, running my fingers against the lockers, staring at the clock hanging overhead, and swallowed, like this school was my home and I had to get to know it better. I wanted to go to the German room, peek my head in and wave to Penny like saying hello to a house guest you didn't know all that well. I could tell her that I might move to London. Maybe she'd have some good advice on whether to go or not.

Two boys shot paper wads into the wastebasket Mrs. Bell kept by her desk and one landed at my feet as I walked through the door to the Latin room. I grabbed the paper ball and squeezed, flattening it before tossing it to one of the guys, hoping he'd save it rather than dump it into the trash. Dad's constant refrain that some people were like trash rang hollow as I watched him catch the paper wad.

"Good throw for a girl," he said and tossed it back to me. As I grabbed it out of the air, my breathing stalled and like flying over a bump on a back road with Mom at the helm laughing at the clouds dancing overhead as she drank in the smell of manure, my stomach jumped and fell. I stared at my hand cupping the paper wad and for a moment worried I'd never seen my hand before.

"Congrats on moving up," a girl smiled as she scooted around me, the cuffs of her bell bottom pants dragging along the floor. Kids already in their seats studied the textbook that I suddenly couldn't wait to own for the rest of the year. As if he'd read my mind, the boy who'd thrown the paper wad, pointed to the thick book sitting on Mrs. Bell's desk. I tossed the wad back to him and checked out the map of Rome on the blackboard.

Mrs. Bell tapped on the book as she smiled at me. "Whoa," I said hoisting it to my chest, and she pointed to a seat near the window. I looked around the classroom, assessing the environment of Latin II: the rows of kids and what each person brought to class, the ratio of boys to girls, even the amount of light streaming through the wall of windows. *A new world,* I said inside my brain. Each person with a different story, but Latin the common factor among us since most Latin I students quit after the first year, a statistic I found comforting now that I was in Latin II with these kids.

I settled into my seat and stared outside at a few girls, obviously late, running through the woods that ran along one side of the school. Not one of them knew that I had a half-sister, I thought. We'd just learned about natural selection in Bio, and it seemed plausible that I'd been selected to have a half-sister and a pervert neighbor and a Dad who kept a secret. Maybe, I thought, I'd been chosen to be no one, empty like the girl Mom drew as an outline, not filled in and with no face except for the hollow eyes staring at her Dad hanging in the barn. My heart sped up because, as no one, I'd lose Latin. I'd be like Stephen with no driver's license—he must've dreamed of driving, I thought, and I ran my fingers over the textbook, longing to hug the book but worried that the boy behind me who cracked his knuckles so much I thought of yelling at him might laugh. Just then, outside the window, a tall skinny boy tripped on a tree root, and I wondered what he'd been selected for.

Mrs. Bell clapped her hands and began to recite sentences we were to memorize. As a class we repeated each sentence. No one seemed bored, and when we finished, the boy behind me asked if we could repeat each one. We discussed the construction and order of Latin sentences, and the same boy talked about the flexible word order in German, and Mrs. Bell became excited. She hurried to the board and wrote sentence after sentence in Latin and French where the placement of an adjective could completely change the sentence's meaning. I wrote all the examples in my notebook, scribbling fast. Then she passed out a poem by Horace from Ars Poetica. Each of us got a line to translate. I struggled at first, but soon mastered the translation. *If you wish people to weep, you must weep first.* When I finished writing the line on the board, tears dripped down my face, and I couldn't turn back to the class. I dropped the chalk and wiped my eyes as I crouched down and pretended to search for the chalk.

"Yes, Sally! Very good." Mrs. Bell read it to the class. I coughed, pretending to be suddenly overcome with a tickle in my throat, and hurried to the drinking fountain at the back of the room. As I gulped water and then splashed my face, I pictured Mom alone somewhere, scared to let go, scared to let her tears flow. As I breathed slowly, I thought it wasn't fair for me to cry so easily if she was stuck inside herself, bottled up. Before I got back to my seat, the bell rang, and I gathered up my books. "Double period tomorrow!" Mrs. Bell smiled as everyone filed out.

"Could I stop in after school?" I asked Mrs. Bell. "I'd like to go over the Cicero, if you had time. "

"Three fifteen?"

I nodded. "Vale!" We said together, and I fanned my face as I opened the door to the hallway.

Out in the corridor, I faced streams of kids clutching books, determined to get to the next class before the bell rang. Instead of dreading eye contact and the jostling, I faced the scene and wove between lanes of students packed in one of the wide, long hallways. Kids rushed passed me, hurrying to the next period. I caught the eye of a girl I knew from gym. We had been paired in the lifesaving classes, dragging each other across the pool in the cross-chest carry. She smiled. I felt like shouting 'hi' just to hear my voice for real. I even thought about letting her know that I wasn't going to ever be her or relegate her to nothing. She was one of the poor kids from Tower Gardens, a part of town Patty Scott said was full of lazy people, and I'd wondered what she'd meant but didn't ask her to explain, not wanting to insinuate that I wasn't willing to absorb her views and ideas. Now I wondered if all the people in Tower Gardens were lazy. Other people's ideas had filled my brain, obliterating my own before they even had a start. Perhaps if Mom hadn't returned to the Chicago Train station where she'd forgotten me, I'd have naturally become a wild child, savvy and street smart. "Are you my mother?" I'd asked a whole row of people like someone would say yes. One man had told me to stay put, and that way she'd find me. Like hugging a tree if you're lost in the woods, he'd said. But something inside me said to count the people on the crowded benches and memorize their faces. When she didn't appear amongst the long rows of faces and hairdos, a voice inside told me to go outside; she's probably waiting on the sidewalk angry that you didn't keep up. Just as I'd finally gotten the heavy door open, the conductor pulled on my hand and led me away to the lollipop man. Sitting alone in the conductor's office, licking the giant rainbow-colored lollipop got me thinking that I wanted to be outside running, talking to people. Not like Dad, tricking them into revealing something, but memorizing that which I saw: equations I'd make up of people on this side of the street added to those on the other side—sort of like Mom mixing paints to come up with the right hue.

"Hey, did you remember your leotard?" The girl from Tower Gardens stood by the drinking fountain calling to me as she wiped her mouth.

"Oh God, no."

"We're gonna start Interpretive Dance, and I didn't get one yet. She's gonna kill us!" We laughed at the same time, and I began to blink my eyes as she fluttered hers as if to draw attention to the thick layer of mascara she wore. Suddenly, she widened her eyes, and I widened mine too. Right away she took a step back, assessing me like she knew something was strange about my face as a mirror for hers. She walked backwards, and I blushed, stammering something about not knowing where to buy a leotard. Again, she looked me over, and without mimicking her I told her that I might actually have a leotard at home--maybe two.

"Do you want to borrow one? If I find them in my messy closet?" She nodded and giggled as I bumped into a short kid, carrying a briefcase. He reminded me of Stephen Fedkin, except that he and a tall boy joked about student council. I imagined Stephen running for office and then devastated when not a single person voted for him, even though he'd hung posters with his name in big letters everywhere. *Come with me,* Stephen's voice was in my ear, and then his face, inside the plastic bag, appeared before my eyes. *Get away from these people and your family,* he said, like he knew about Mom leaving me at the train station and now Beth and Dad. Mom didn't mean to, I wanted to let him know, but then I remembered that she'd left me in grocery stores and at the circus where the Ringmaster had announced to the crowd that he'd found a little girl who had lost her mother.

"I can't go with you. I'm really sorry," I whispered as I headed into a bathroom by the library. My stomach twisted for a moment, and I clutched my books, anchoring them to my body so I wouldn't float out the window that someone had cracked in order to smoke undetected in a stall.

You can't? His voice trailed off, and then he nodded and smirked as if he'd known all along that I was a fraud, a trickster. In an instant I thought of Dad, also a fake in his black suits and shiny shoes, loving Empress, sneaking out when he probably told Mom he had an interview or some important assignment. I vowed never to acknowledge him again. But then he appeared in my brain, lying in bed, shaking, moaning and begging for water. In this imagined scene, I ran to him with a cup of water and pressed my hand to his forehead. He calmed down before gulping the water. This scenario of me nursing him and making him comfortable lasted only a moment before my brain jumped to an image of my head in a plastic bag, suffocating with bulging eyes.

The girl who was smoking in the stall walked behind me. The trail of smoke made my stomach turn. I couldn't erase the image of my head in the bag as I swallowed hard to get rid of the nausea. When the girl finally left, I closed my eyes and imagined Stephen laughing, surrounded by friends as I suddenly appeared in heaven. *You actually did it?* He called to me from the group of kids I guessed had killed themselves too. *So you finally got here,* he said unimpressed, like he didn't need me anymore and was sick of begging me to be his friend.

I searched for Stephen's face in the mirror over the sink. I thought I could depend on Stephen to always love me and know me--somehow. Just the way I'd always thought of Beth as someone I could take or leave. I remembered begging myself to be nice to Beth as we watched *Rosemary's Baby*. "Beth, Beth," I said silently, picturing her like Stephen—tired of my indifference and the way I used her for back up, like she was worth no more than the saggy pink bag she had always brought to our house since that first day Empress dumped her off. *The sin of omission is no better than the sin of commission* Mr. Craft had said.

"I can't commit suicide," I said as Stephen's face and crooked glasses showed up above the sink. "I can't; I can't," I said, turning on the faucet to block my voice. "I have a sister, and I'm going to help," my voice trailed off as I stared into the mirror.

You can do it, a voice in my ear said in such an encouraging tone that my heart pounded and fire poured down my arms; I swallowed hard again and again so that I wouldn't throw up.

Good luck finding someone to be, Stephen said, and his sad eyes floated before mine.

How could you do it? I asked him, wishing for the first time that he'd never killed himself and that I'd helped him somehow. Then I left the bathroom, vowing to never use this bathroom again. Out of the corner of my eye, I saw Barbie Robert rushing with a load of books. Her face was flushed, and she looked worried. I was glad that I had to turn at the math wing before we came face to face. Then I thought I heard her call my name, and I turned quickly, but she was nowhere. *I could still help her with Latin,* I thought, imagining us in the library near her house—perhaps away from her fighting parents she'd be able to concentrate.

During Algebra I, I inserted my Latin worksheet in the algebra book and declined the verbs and managed to translate a paragraph of Cicero. Mr. Lott asked me to solve a problem on the board, and luckily it was so simple I got the right answer easily and could return to my Latin. By the last bell, I'd finished most of the translation and couldn't wait to show it to Mrs. Bell. I smiled at the wires wrapped around her teeth and at her nearly worn-off coat of red lipstick "I figure that by time you're a junior, I can make a good case for Latin IV."

We spent an hour translating one of Cicero's orations, and I couldn't help noticing how pretty Mrs. Bell's brown eyes were and how she glowed as I caught on to techniques for identifying clauses and word order. For a minute, I thought that she looked at me the way Mr. Craft had looked at me when I was younger—like I had special powers. I never cared about his charts and instructions for getting to a higher kingdom, but I understood Latin with or without Mrs. Bell. I felt that the dead language was part of me, and I almost thanked Mrs. Bell for pushing me into Latin II and away from Barbie Robert, but I didn't think she'd understand.

The halls were empty as I made my way to the front door. Mr. Novak passed, brushing against the lockers on the other side with his head partially lowered. "Hi Mr. Novak," I said across the wide expanse. He smiled and waved. Pinky stood in a wide stance under a clock with his arms folded. He squinted, searching, I feared, for an offender—someone like me who'd skipped school. I tried to compose my face, walk at a normal pace, and not breath hard.

Just before I passed him, he cleared his throat and yelled, "Mrs. Halbert—please check the library door!" Relieved, I scurried to the front door and then took off through the parking lot, shivering and smiling at the first hint of winter.

Clutching my new Latin II textbook and my notebook with the translation, I ran away from the school full throttle, jumping over curbs and tearing across streets without looking for cars. Starved, I turned down the street called M-A-C (Michigan Agriculture College) towards downtown and McDonald's. For once, Mrs. Broadback had remembered to pay me, and I had enough for a snack. Blue sky peaked through the overhang of oaks along M-A-C, and I thought of Mom squinting with her face turned upward. For the first time, I saw the blue shapes outlined in black and the green leaves adding to a design I was certain Mom would marvel at. Once I turned onto Grand River, I stopped to look at a mannequin in a red poncho in the window at Jacobson's. The red wool poncho reminded me of the blanket hanging off Beth's shoulders as she stood in the doorway of her suffocating living room. *She's your sister,* a voice inside insisted. I imagined Mom fitting the red poncho to Beth, and I felt like smacking Beth and yelling that Mom was not her Mom and she should go away with Dad and Empress. "I hate you," I screamed at Dad, picturing him eating a bowl of cereal in his pajamas, still unable to get to work or do anything. In another window, two mannequins wore pleated navy-blue skirts and loafers with knee socks. They could be Mrs. Broadback and me in London, I thought, an ocean and more separating us from Dad and Beth. Then I turned away, my stomach begging for food.

At McDonald's I ordered fries and a coke. I almost added *London* to the order. I laughed at my use of stream of consciousness that we picked out in a poem by Sylvia Plath. *Fries, coke, London,* I said silently. I could imagine that everyone, including the server, would be impressed that I'd been chosen to go to London, that I had to get a passport, and that I'd go to a different school. Finally, I'd walk into a new life—not Barbie Robert's and her weird dad, but Mrs. Broadback's world and London, a place I could only partly imagine. As I ate the French fries, I wondered why they tasted greasy and why I wished Mrs. Broadback had never asked me to go.

"You left your coke," the server pointed to my coke near the cash register. I thanked her and hoped the coke would erase the greasy taste, but it was too cold, and my teeth ached.

Nothing tasted right, and I dumped the carton and the coke in the trash outside.

I watched a woman pull out of her parking spot, and her hair and faint blush reminded me of Mrs. Broadback. My thoughts jumbled between liking Mrs. Broadback and realizing that I could like her and not want to be her or spend a whole year with her when I was beginning to fall in love with Latin and had responsibilities to people, especially Mom.

My stomach rumbled, and I went back into McDonald's, determined to get something down. I thought of Mom alone in our basement and choked as I ordered a chocolate shake. "School makes you hungry," the boy smiled as I dropped a quarter into his hand and cleared my throat.

I nodded, and when he brought me the shake, I considered ordering one for Mom, but I didn't know if she'd like vanilla or chocolate. Then as I ripped the cover off a straw, I pictured Danny, Mrs. Broadback, and even Mr. Broadback waving to me from a ship. Mrs. Broadback yelled that she'd forgotten to pay me, and I yelled back that I still had her red pants. Outside I wavered. Mrs. Broadback would be disappointed; I even thought she might cry if I told her that I didn't want to go and if I told her everything. I'd have to say that I didn't want to be her, but of course I'd never admit to Mrs. Broadback that I had wanted to be her or anyone else. I should give her a simple reason, I thought, suddenly wishing I hadn't thrown out the fries. The last thing Mrs. Broadback would want to hear was the jumble of competing reasons for staying in East Lansing. She'd be horrified to hear about Mr. Craft and Beth and Dad and Empress and how Mom and I were going to move.

When I threw open the back door, Mom looked up from the typewriter she'd moved to the kitchen table. I stopped, staring for a moment. "I'm helping Dad with an article. He's got to keep writing—creating," she said, adjusting the carriage. I dropped my Latin book and took a sip of the cold shake. When the phone rang, I stood for a moment before picking up the receiver. I listed possibilities: Mr. Craft begging for forgiveness, the nurse asking about tonight and the coffeehouse, Mr. Freds exasperated that I'd skipped school again. I swallowed hard, deciding that I'd tell him the truth: about Dad and Empress, or should I start back with Stephen's suicide? How much of the truth was necessary?

Suddenly I wanted help in vanquishing Stephen. I could hear Dad's voice warning me to forget about the truth and just get out of the mess of skipping school somehow. On the last ring I grabbed the receiver.

"You there?" Mrs. Broadback said, blowing smoke on her end while she talked so that she sounded tired and out of breath. "Look, I was going out, so I thought I'd run your skirt over—I doubt you had time to talk to your folks about London?" I saw the slacks she'd lent me on a pile laundry in the corner. I'd have to wash them, but as I watched Mom move my Latin book, I cleared my throat and blurted that I'd been moved to Latin II. "Is it still old Mrs. Bell teaching Latin? I had her and hated Latin," Mrs. Broadback laughed. "But I wasn't a student like you. Good for you, though. Good for you, Sally."

"I can't go to London, and I am so sorry, but I have Latin II now and she thinks I'll go all the way to Latin IV—not for a few years, of course." I was about to tell her that I might get involved with the teen center the nurse had mentioned, since that would sound like her sorority, but she cut me off. I realized that I talked too fast, but I didn't want to change my mind midstream.

"I knew it was a long shot—can you sit tonight?" She chuckled when I told her about the get-together tonight. "I guess you had to start socializing sometime." She blew smoke again and reminded me about babysitting next weekend.

"Thanks Mrs. Broadback."

"London?" Mom looked up at me the minute I hung up the phone.

"The Broadbacks are moving there—she needs a babysitter, to go live with them, but I have too much to do at school," I said. Mom looked at me without squinting, without seeing me as a future composition. "And here—at home," I added. She closed her eyes and then opened them, looking directly at me in a way that linked us without any filtering or fear that one of us would turn away.

"I'd love you to have that kind of adventure; I can't imagine what it would be like." She pushed her hair away from her face, and I noticed rings under her eyes, not like she'd been crying but like she hadn't slept. "Maybe you and I could go somewhere like that," she said. Then she went back to typing. I nodded and sat on the other side of the kitchen table, sipping the shake and declining new verbs I found in the next chapter of the Latin text.

"Should I take Dad anything?" I asked, watching her squint at the words she'd typed.

"Could you just ask him when this new President of MSU will start—the month?"

I ran upstairs, first checking my room for Beth. Both beds were made, and the window propped open for airing. I imagined Beth creeping through the window some night, crawling under the covers and perhaps suffocating herself while I slept.

"Let me take care of the baby," I whispered to an image of her brown eyes peeking above the covers. "We'll pretend it's a cousin." I dropped down to my bed and tried to imagine Beth's response. "Your nose and your eyes are like Dad's," I said to the image of Beth, choking and burying my face in my pillow as I imagined spit flying out of Dad's mouth as he screamed at her. But then I pictured him outraged at Mr. Craft, punching the air as he tried to hurt him for doing what he did to Beth. I wiped my face on the pillow and stared at Beth's empty bed.

I'm all you've got, Stephen's face showed up above Beth's bed. *Follow me, now,* he said. My skin prickled and my mouth went dry.

No! I yelled inside my head as my insides whirled and my heart went wild. *I have a sister now; never come here,* I said, focusing on the words, picturing them hanging in the air like something Mom might squint at and then draw.

"Dad," I whispered through the crack in their bedroom door. "Dad," I repeated, creeping to his side.

"What'd you say?" he cried out. Without his glasses, his eyes appeared to recede halfway back into his skull. His bushy eyebrows sprouted gray wire-like hairs, and his lips were mine, I realized—smooth and shaped like a bow Cupid held high while flying about. "Adams, September 1969," he said before I finished the question.

"Adams, September 1969," I repeated, and he nodded.

"You got it," he whispered. My heart calmed, and I smoothed my hair as I watched him breath in fits.

"Are you all right?"

"I'm getting there," he said and then rolled to his side. He'd lied to us and ditched me—his loyal sidekick—but now I wanted to stroke his hair and tell him he'd be all right.

"Adams is his name and he'll start in September 1969," I said, out of breath. Mom nodded, scrolling the paper through the typewriter. "Someone told me we look alike."

She looked up, staring at me like she was about to draw my portrait. Then she closed her eyes. "Who said that?" she asked. I hesitated, not wanting to hear about someone's bad motives. "You've got delicate features like Dad's side; I'm just a farmer. You're much prettier."

I backed up and watched her fingers fly over the keys. I wondered if most people didn't like themselves, down deep, or if Mom was strange because she had big goals like she could do anything, conquer the world, and yet she didn't see the beauty in herself the way she saw it in a tree or a cloud. She was everything and nothing.

I grabbed my Latin book. "Do you want to try some of this chocolate shake from the new place?" She nodded, and I handed her the big cup. "It's better with the straw," I said, and she took a big sip. For a moment she reminded me of the word *feral* we'd had on the vocab list. You could tame her, perhaps, but living in the wild would suit her so thoroughly. I imagined her organizing each day; foraging food and weaving hats and other things out of reeds and grasses. Her distrust of people and their motives stemmed as much from her father's suicide, I figured, as it did from a fear that the untainted world, challenging, willful, and exotic, was being ruined and usurped by unthinking conformists.

"That's good," she said as she released the straw and put the cup down with too much force so that the waxy paper bent and the cup itself began to collapse. "Shall we go there for dinner?" She smiled, straightening the cup and nodding like she'd try to appreciate something pre-packaged during this transition in our lives, during this moment of deciding how to go on.

"What about Dad?"

"We can bring him back a burger—isn't that what they're known for?"

"Maybe we could take Beth something, too," I said and headed to my room with my Latin book. Once inside, I opened the window, airing it of Stephen and what else I wasn't sure. I took Beth's pillow and propped myself up but had trouble writing the declensions neatly and charting out the complicated grammar patterns. I needed a desk and realized that if I somehow moved Beth's bed to the basement or the garage, I'd have space for one. Once the baby was born, I knew she'd never come back, or if she did, she'd need something more than the narrow bed and this closet like room. But a desk in my room would create a place for me and for my mind. The door Mom had turned into a low table in the basement could be a start. Maybe she'd let me have it.

I closed the Latin book and drew pictures of my new room in my notebook. Then I saw the scribbling on the wall by Beth's bed and drew my designs for a new room on the wall next to my bed. I added a lamp and drawers for my supplies. I was surprised how accurately I drew the dimensions of the room and how easily I rendered details like a rug and a wastebasket. I'd stared at Van Gogh's painting of his bedroom above the sink in the art room, and suddenly realized I'd copied it— except that I'd included a desk. Where Van Gogh had signed his name, I printed Sally Tallman in a flourish.

"Sally, someone is here," Mom called. I closed my book and ran downstairs. Mom smiled, pointing to Scott, who stood in the doorway like he wasn't sure to come all the way in the house.

"Do you want to go to the coffeehouse tonight? I talked to Penny, and she said you wanted to go." Scott spoke fast, looking at me, and then Mom.

"I want to go but could we go to McDonald's first? I have to get my parents and my sister some dinner."

He nodded and motioned to his car.

"Take this," Mom said, pulling bills from her purse.

"I didn't know you had a sister," he said.

"I do—now."

Once in the car, he talked about moving to Chicago and how much he wished he could stay until June so he could play baseball. "I'm pretty sure I'd make the team," he said, pulling into the McDonald's parking lot. "This is weird but if you ever wanted to visit Chicago, like to shop or something, we could maybe meet." I laughed, and he laughed, too only he sounded embarrassed.

"I just got asked to go to London. And I've never been anywhere." Then I told him that it would be cool to visit Chicago. He sighed, and then we got out of the car, and the doors slammed shut. I thought how Dad would cringe at the sound of the doors shutting and how much he hated Beth for slamming them shut. Now he might not care, I thought, and besides, I could hold the baby as she shut the door with a light touch.

In McDonald's, I bought two sack's full of burgers, fries, and an apple pie for Beth, because I remembered she loved apple pie. Back in the car, we breathed in the smell of grease and salt. "I'm starved," I said, sneaking a fry.

"Do you wanna just talk after we deliver the food?" His face reddened as he looked out the windshield.

"Kind of," I said. "Yeah that would be cool. About what?" I looked at him, and my head felt light as if I might faint. Looking right at someone I didn't know or hadn't tried to become was like Mom learning to like McDonald's. My eyes were stuck in place, staring too hard.

"About what?"

"What would we talk about?" I said, knowing the question was stupid but still stuck looking at him and hoping I'd know how to converse as me as a person I'd like.

"I guess anything," he said, pulling into our driveway.

About the Author

MARY PAULA HUNTER began her career as a choreographer/dancer creating works that fused movement and text. Eventually the writing won out. A transplant to New England, Hunter grew up in East Lansing, Michigan and holds a BA in English and an MFA in dance from the University of Michigan. She lives in Providence, RI with her husband, historian Richard A. Meckel.

Acknowledgements

I want to thank Bill T. Jones and the late, Arnie Zane for showing me that it was alright to dance and talk at the same time. I was never the same after they performed their audacious duets at Hamilton College when I taught dance there. I want to thank every audience member who supported me as I turned from abstract choreography to dance making that fused story and movement. I want to thank Laurie Stone in the now defunct VILLAGE VOICE who praised my writing as well as my choreography. She encouraged me without knowing it to begin on a journey as a writer, a teller of stories in their own right. And I want to thank David Lindsay-Abaire, the great playwright who at the old Dance Theatre Workshop produced my first full-length performance work in which my stories took center stage.

Generous teachers encouraged me and taught me how to shape the narrative: I am entirely grateful to Hester Kaplan, David Rutschman, Anna Solomon, and Erica Sklar. Thanks to those, too many to name, who read part or all of the manuscript.

Many thanks to the editorial staff at The Unsolicited Press.

Finally I could not have made this leap to becoming a writer without the support of my family: my children, Katherine and Peter Meckel and most importantly my husband, the historian, Richard Meckel who has always been my best and most caring editor. This book is dedicated to him.